M000036420

Praise for
KRISTINE KATHRYN RUSCH

Kristine Kathryn Rusch is one of the best writers in the field.

—*SFRevu*

Whether [Rusch] writes high fantasy, horror, sf, or contemporary fantasy, I've always been fascinated by her ability to tell a story with that enviable gift of invisible prose. She's one of those very few writers whose style takes me right into the story—the words and pages disappear as the characters and their story swallows me whole....Rusch has style.

—Charles de Lint
The Magazine of Fantasy & Science Fiction

The SF thriller is alive and well, and today's leading practitioner is Kristine Kathryn Rusch.

—*Analog*

Rusch's greatest strength...is her ability to close down a story and leave the reader feeling that the author could not possibly have wrung any more satisfaction out of the piece.

—John Mark Eberhart
The Kansas City Star

Praise for
DIVING INTO THE WRECK

Rusch delivers a page-turning space adventure while contemplating the ethics of scientists and governments working together on future tech.

—*Publisher's Weekly*

This is classic sci-fi, a well-told tale of dangerous exploration. The first-person narration makes the reader an eyewitness to the vast, silent realms of deep space, where even the smallest error will bring disaster. Compellingly human and technically absorbing, the suspense builds to fevered intensity, culminating in an explosive yet plausible conclusion.
—*RT Book Reviews Top Pick*

Rusch's handling of the mystery and adventure is stellar, and the whole tale proves quite entertaining.
—*Booklist Online*

Diving into the Wreck is highly recommended reading for anyone who enjoys space adventure stories, superb characterization, and tight plotting.
—*Grasping For The Wind.com*

The technicalities in Boss' story are beautifully played....She's real, flawed, and interesting.... Read the book. It is very good.
—*SFFWorld.com*

Diving into the Wreck is a rip-roaring good read. The universe it presents is original, and cries out for more adventures with Boss and her crew.
—*AstroGuyz.com*

Praise for
CITY OF RUINS

Rusch keeps the science accessible, the cultures intriguing, and the characters engaging. For anyone needing to add to their science fiction library, keep an eye out for this.
—Josh Vogt
Speculative Fiction Examiner.com

Praise for
BONEYARDS

Rusch's latest addition to her 'Diving' series features a strong, capable female heroine and a vividly imagined far-future universe. Blending fast-paced action with an exploration of the nature of friendship and the ethics of scientific discoveries, this tale should appeal to Rusch's readers and fans of space opera.

—*Library Journal*

Filled with well-defined characters who confront a variety of ethical and moral dilemmas, Rusch's third Diving Universe novel is classic space opera, with richly detailed worldbuilding and lots of drama.

—*RT Book Reviews*

Praise for
THE RETRIEVAL ARTIST SERIES

One of the top ten greatest science fiction detectives of all time.

—*io9*

[Miles Flint is] one of 14 great sci-fi and fantasy detectives who out-Sherlock'd Holmes. [Flint] is a candidate for the title of greatest fictional detective of all time.

—*Blastr*

What links [Miles Flint] to his most memorable literary ancestors is his hard-won ability to perceive the complex nature of morality and live with the burden of his own inevitable failure.

—*Locus*

SKIRMISHES

A DIVING UNIVERSE NOVEL

KRISTINE KATHRYN RUSCH

WMGPUBLISHING

Skirmishes

Copyright © 2013 Kristine Kathryn Rusch

All rights reserved

Published 2013 by WMG Publishing
www.wmgpublishing.com
Parts of this novel appeared in different form as the novellas *Strangers in the Room of Lost Souls* (WMG Publishing, 2013) and *Encounter On Starbase Kappa*, (*Asimov's SF Magazine*, 2013)
Cover and Layout copyright © 2013 by WMG Publishing
Cover design by Allyson Longueira/WMG Publishing
Cover art copyright © Philcold/Dreamstime
ISBN-13: 978-0-615-79524-9
ISBN-10: 0-615-79524-2

This book is licensed for your personal enjoyment only. All rights reserved. This is a work of fiction. All characters and events portrayed in this book are fictional, and any resemblance to real people or incidents is purely coincidental. This book, or parts thereof, may not be reproduced in any form without permission.

For Sheila Williams once again,
Because this series would not exist without her.

ACKNOWLEDGEMENTS

Thanks on this one go to my husband, Dean Wesley Smith, who always seems to find the best way out of a serious plot hole.

Thanks also to Allyson Longueira for shepherding this project into existence, to Colleen Kuehne for keeping me honest, and to Dayle Dermatis for making room in her hectic schedule for one more project.

And more thanks than I can express to Lee Allred, who helped me immensely with all of the military structure. Any and all errors are mine, of course, but I couldn't have even pretended to do this right without Lee's help. I also want to thank him for creating the writing term "disembodied organization," which will go along with "fake detail" in my future teaching terminology.

Thanks to the readers of the series who keep me honest. Special thanks to the readers of *Asimov's SF Magazine*, who've read this series from its humble beginnings.

SKIRMISHES

A DIVING UNIVERSE NOVEL

THE STANDOFF
NOW

1

CAPTAIN JONATHON "COOP" COOPER sank into the command chair on the *Ivoire*, and tapped the right-hand controls.

"Let me see that screen again," he said to Mavis Kravchenko, his first officer. She was a large woman whose size came from being raised in the real gravity of one of the Fleet's land-based sector bases.

Sometimes Coop thought she was as solid as the ground she was raised on.

Kravchenko worked two different consoles. She preferred to stand as her hands flew back and forth between them.

Right now, everyone on the bridge focused on Kravchenko, even though they pretended not to. Coop had a full crew running the *Ivoire*— or, at least, as full a crew as he could manage with half of his most experienced crew on the *Shadow*. His former second officer, Lynda Rooney, had taken her favorite people with her when he promoted her to command the *Shadow*, which was the only other functional Fleet ship in this sector.

Hell, the only other functional Fleet ship in this entire universe for all he knew.

He tried to keep thoughts like that out of his head. Even though he'd been here for more than five years now, the change in his circumstances still surprised him.

"You got the screen, Captain?" Kravchenko asked, using a tone that made him realize she'd asked him at least once before.

He tapped one more control. A holoimage of the sensor console rose in front of him. Kravchenko was running it in infrared rather than a normal visual spectrum. That didn't bother him. For this, infrared was probably better.

"I got it," he said, and peered at the information before him.

Images, trails, gigantic circles, all of which would mean nothing to the untrained eye. But Coop saw energy signatures, populated planets, and faraway stars. He layered heat signatures and energy readings onto the screen, then he opened a second holographic screen with the standard visual images of the same section of space.

On the visual, he could see the stars but not the energy or heat signatures. He also couldn't see what had caused those signatures.

On the layered infrared screen, he saw a dozen Enterran Empire vessels spreading out in one of their typical search patterns.

Cloaked ships. The Empire's cloaks were primitive, but effective. He had to actively search for them—and they certainly weren't visible to the naked eye.

He felt a familiar frustration. In the past, he could have easily handled a situation like this. His experience gave him a dozen different ways to deal with an aggressive space-faring culture like the Empire.

Except his experience and his training no longer applied. Now he had to be creative. Now he had to think like a smart man in a room full of children.

That wasn't fair, of course. The cultures here had a lot of smart people. They just lacked the knowledge he had and the technology he was used to.

Six years ago, he'd been a captain among many, part of a Fleet that went from sector to sector, never back where it had been. He had been one man in thousands, living a life spread across hundreds of ships, several star bases, and at least two sector bases at one time. He had superiors and subordinates, family here and on other ships, friendships that had spanned decades.

Now he had less than five hundred people who had gone through the same dislocation that he had. None of them were his superiors, all were his subordinates, and none were blood relatives. The only person with whom he had any personal history at all was his ex-wife Mae, who had become a friend.

He had a new life here in what had once been an unimaginable future, and by many counts, it was a good life. But sometimes the changes overwhelmed him.

Like right now. He needed at least twenty other Fleet ships, outfitted with the latest (Latest? The word made him smile to himself) sensor technology. He wanted to set up a full sensor blanket, so that nothing could cross the border from the Enterran Empire into the Nine Planets Alliance without him knowing.

But he only had two fully-equipped Fleet ships, and twenty more vessels, most of which he wouldn't even dignify with the word "ship." They were everything from the *Nobody's Business*, which was old, creaky, and designed for fewer than fifty passengers, to what passed for warships on Cros'll, the nearest of the Nine Planets to the border. Those ships were so badly designed that Coop was afraid one shot out of their weapons array might explode the ship and everything around it.

He felt like he was leading a squadron of two ships and a bunch of working ship models. Most of the ships around him wouldn't even have qualified as entries in the ship-building contest that the Fleet once ran every few years for its engineering students.

But Coop couldn't tell any of the so-called captains that. Just like he couldn't tell them how he had acquired his own training. Any sentence that began with "Five thousand years ago…." was guaranteed to cause the disbelief to begin.

What he needed at the moment was a sensor blanket, dozens of scout ships, and some intel from inside the Empire. But he had no intel that he could trust, a few scout ships that he couldn't spare, and no way to blanket anything with any kind of sensor, let alone block entrance into this region of space.

Kravchenko was doing her best. She had been actively searching for Empire ships. But she wasn't searching alone. He had most of the engineering crew monitoring the border. If he couldn't use ships to set up a sensor blanket, he would have his own people do it as best they could.

The rest of the bridge crew monitored their stations, apparently trying (and sometimes failing) not to glance at what they could see of Coop's screens.

"How long have the ships been there?" he asked Kravchenko.

She shrugged. "We didn't pick them up until an hour ago, sir."

An hour. He didn't believe that. He wondered if the ships wanted to be seen. After all, it was better for the Empire if the Nine Planets' ships crossed the border into Enterran space.

Then the Nine Planets would have invaded the Empire, not the other way around.

But his rag-tag army had instructions not to fire first or to cross that border *ever*. He had instructed all of the so-called captains to make sure they gave the Empire absolutely no reason to invade the Nine Planets.

If the Enterran Empire wanted to attack the Nine Planets Alliance and ruin more than a century of what could only charitably be called peace, then it could. And it would destroy untold amounts of property, as well as millions of lives.

The Empire probably wouldn't win against the Nine Planets—the Empire had never won against the Nine Planets—but the Empire would make life here miserable, which Coop wasn't willing to let happen.

He had promised Boss that he would guard the borders to the Nine Planets, and that was what he planned to do.

Boss. She was an interesting woman. She had been the first person he'd seen in this new time period, wearing what, he thought at the time, was an ancient and outdated space suit.

He later learned so much technology had been lost that his people seemed amazingly advanced to the civilizations now. Boss had helped him with the transition.

She had also wormed her quirky, eccentric way into his heart.

He wondered what she would think of his rag-tag army. She had suggested part of it; the rest Lynda Rooney had cobbled together with some local help.

But Boss wasn't here to see how it all worked. Boss was far away, in another sector, trying to find more ships.

Then Coop sighed as he caught himself in another lie, this time to himself. Boss wasn't just looking for more ships. She was digging into a boneyard of Fleet ships they'd discovered a few weeks ago, hoping to find out what happened to his people all those millennia ago.

"Do the ships see us?" he asked.

"I have no idea," Kravchenko said.

"I can monitor their chatter," Officer Kjersti Perkins said. She was his chief linguist, and had become one of the more invaluable members of his bridge crew. She could float from console to console, handling many of the problems that he didn't even see.

"If they won't notice, go ahead," he said.

"I have no idea what they'll notice and what they won't," Perkins said.

He smiled. She could be very literal at times. "Do your best," he said.

He wasn't sure whether or not he cared if the empire ships noticed. He had revealed his own ships days earlier. Initially, he had kept both the *Ivoire* and the other Fleet vessel, the *Shadow*, under a standard cloak. Standard for the Fleet, anyway. Even their simplest cloak was too sophisticated for the ships around him.

Before Coop's chief engineer had left with Boss, she had tried to build a simple Fleet cloak onto the *Business*. It hadn't worked. Fleet technology didn't blend easily with modern technology. Everything had to be adapted and modified, and no one had time for that.

Not after the attacks on the Empire's research facilities.

Coop frowned at those ship images. The Empire had every reason to attack the Nine Planets Alliance. All of the Empire's stealth-tech research facilities had been bombed or destroyed in the last two months.

Coop had destroyed the main facility himself, although he initially hadn't meant to. Boss had roped him into the attack, which she had believed would be a simple rescue mission.

Coop knew from the beginning there was no such thing as a simple rescue mission, particularly deep in enemy territory. He had initially refused to participate.

But Boss would have gone without him, and that might have been the end of her. He had decided at that moment that, after all of the losses he'd suffered, he couldn't suffer another. He had gone with her. What's more, he had actually planned the mission.

He had kept Boss alive, but at a cost. One of those costs had been riling the Empire. He had known it was coming, but Boss hadn't seen it. She wasn't military, and she wasn't used to dealing with a variety of governments. And much as she loved history, she wasn't good at seeing perspectives other than her own.

If Coop had been working for the Empire, he would have tracked down the ships and the attackers who had gone after the research facilities and destroyed them all. He suspected that the ships out there were doing exactly what he would have done in their place.

They had tracked someone or something here. Maybe they had intel that had brought them to the border between the Nine Planets Alliance and the Enterran Empire. He knew these ships hadn't tracked him across Empire space to the border, because the *Ivoire* and the *Shadow* hadn't crossed regular space to get back. They'd used their *anacapa* drives, a technology that the Empire didn't even have.

The *anacapa* allowed ships to move from one place to another in a matter of seconds. When the *anacapa* worked, it was an amazing device. When it malfunctioned, it killed or—in his case—displaced the ship in time. Five thousand years of displacement.

The Empire had no idea what an *anacapa* was. But it was conducting dangerous experiments with something it called "stealth tech," which was a primitive form of the *anacapa* drive. The Empire believed that stealth tech was a cloak, and nothing more.

And Coop would like to keep it that way.

"Get me the specs on those ships," he said to Officer Anita Tren.

She was tiny and barely saw over a console. But she could gather information faster than anyone else on his current bridge crew.

"I've already been working on it," Anita said. "We've got five warships out there, with five battle cruisers and five larger ships that can either move people and materiel or simply transport passengers. This is a show of force, Coop."

"I got that," he said. "But for whom? The Nine Planets? Or is something else happening at this end of the Empire that I don't know about?"

"We've been monitoring the information feeds in the Empire for a while," said Second Engineer Zaria Diaz. Coop liked having her on the bridge when Yash wasn't here. Diaz, who was as tiny as Anita Tren, had a talent for finding problems that no one even knew existed yet.

"And?" Coop asked.

"And nothing," Diaz said. "If they're here, they're here for us."

"Cloaked," Perkins said. She clearly didn't understand it.

"They're trying to sneak into the Nine Planets?" Anita asked.

"I don't think so," Coop said. "I think they want to appear before us and scare the crap out of us."

The bridge crew laughed. He appreciated that too. It had taken a lot to scare his people six years ago. Ever since they came into this strange future universe, they rarely scared at all.

They'd faced the worst, and survived it. He knew that some of them, even now, probably preferred death.

His thoughts rested for a moment on his former first officer, Dix Pompiono, and then he shook it off. Dix had given up. It was one thing to die in battle, another to die by your own hand.

Coop didn't respect the second choice.

Dix's choice.

"Shouldn't we warn them somehow?" Perkins asked.

"Warn them of what?" Coop asked.

"I don't know," she said. "That we can take them out if we want to. We have superior firepower."

One on one, Coop's ships outmatched theirs. Maybe even two or three to one. But two of his ships against fifteen of theirs, ten of them battleships in one way or another? He didn't want to go through that particular match-up.

"We're not doing anything unless they cross that border," Coop said.

And maybe not even then.

He only had pieces of a plan, not an entire plan. He hoped Boss would get back soon.

He hoped she would have answers.

He hoped she would bring back dozens of working ships.

THE DIVE
NOW

2

WE SKITTER OUT OF FOLDSPACE, and I look at the navigation screen on *Nobody's Business Two*. We have arrived exactly where Yash Zarlengo said we would.

Yash stands beside me, an athletic woman clearly raised in real gravity. Her thick muscles and strong bones make her seem larger than she really is. Or maybe it's her oversized personality, or the fact that—against all odds—I've come to trust her.

I rarely trust anyone. Even though I'm traveling with more than thirty people on the *Two*, I don't trust most of them. I expect them all to do something wrong. I barely know some of them.

But Yash both built and runs the *anacapa* drive in this ship. I might command the *Two*, but Yash makes sure we survive any trip we take into foldspace—a place that still makes all of us nervous.

We're not in foldspace now. Now we're way outside of our sector with no backup whatsoever. We're the only ship in a vast and mostly empty area of space. There's a starbase half a day from here, but it's not a friendly place.

Besides, the last time we were there, we attracted some scavengers who wanted to steal our *anacapa* drive. This time, we're hoping that those scavengers—indeed, anyone in this sector—aren't somehow monitoring our arrival.

Because we're sitting outside the Boneyard.

The Boneyard is the largest ship graveyard I have ever seen. And the sad part about it is that it looks like the majority of the ships inside come from the Fleet. None of us knows how those ships got here, and none of us knows why they've been left here.

That's what my team and I are supposed to find out.

I've got my divers. I've got Yash. And I've got soldiers to protect me, not just from the scavengers, but from anyone else who might be nearby.

I hate traveling with all these people. The *Two* is bigger than my original ship, *Nobody's Business*, and smaller than Dignity Vessels like the *Ivoire*. But I've never traveled in a ship nearing its maximum capacity of passengers, and I hope I never do so again.

I'm a loner, even though I'm running a major corporation now, and like most loners, I truly prefer to be alone.

That's why wreck diving suits me. Why it has always suited me. I was actually looking forward to this trip until the passenger list grew. Then I realized I was responsible for all of these people in one way or another, and they would be crowding the narrow corridors of the *Two*, and I've been annoyed ever since.

Well, not annoyed. Not really. Tense.

Worried.

I can't tell anyone how very worried I am.

I wipe my hands on the sides of my pants. My palms are actually sweating, which happens to me only when I'm extremely nervous. I like to blame my nerves on the fact that the entire cockpit is filled with people, but that's not the whole story.

Still, the crowd isn't helping. The cockpit is built for twelve, and we have fifteen in here, not counting me. Everyone who hasn't seen the Boneyard wants to see it right away, instead of waiting for the mission brief. We couldn't fit everyone who hadn't seen the Boneyard into the cockpit, even though Yash kept inviting more and more, until we're now squeezed.

She has no real idea how uncomfortable crowds make me. She knows I'm a loner, but she thinks that eccentric, something I turn on and off, like a smile. She doesn't realize that a lot of people disturb me on principle.

She never had the choice to be alone. She grew up in a society based on crowds. From what I can tell, the Fleet built space into their ships for people to have privacy, but those same people could choose from their childhoods on to be with others, and most did.

The very idea makes me shiver.

Just like standing in this cockpit makes me shiver. There are people behind me that I can't see, and that drives me crazy.

I could order everyone away, but I don't. This is a momentous occasion for a lot of the people here, and they really need to see what's before them.

My divers, on the other hand, aren't in the cockpit (except for Mikk, who is at the helm). My divers are used to me. They understand my needs and probably share them.

Besides, my divers know they'll be seeing the Boneyard soon enough.

They're in the briefing room, studying what little information we got on our previous trip, and waiting for me. We sort of lucked into the decision to keep the divers out of the cockpit. They chose not to come, and the others begged to join us.

Silly me, I didn't speak up when Yash said yes.

She does want them to see everything. And she really isn't paying attention to moods. Technically, I should do that. Just one of the many things I'm not suited for as captain of a large ship.

Not that I have the official title of captain, nor is this a large ship. It's my current diving vessel, and circumstances brought the crowd along with us.

Circumstances and the damn *anacapa* drive.

I keep thinking I'd've been calmer if I hadn't gone into foldspace—if all of us hadn't gone into foldspace. Foldspace makes everyone nervous—particularly the borrowed crew members from the *Ivoire*.

Foldspace is exactly what it sounds like—at least that's how everyone explains it to me. They compare foldspace to a fold in a blanket, which tells me they've all been briefed the same way as well. They even begin with the same phrase: *foldspace provides a shortcut in space.* Then they expand, using the same example.

Say you want to go from one part of a blanket to another. Rather than travel the entire length of the blanket, you fold it, and both parts touch.

That's how foldspace works. Plug in the coordinates from where you are and then add the ones from where you're going, activate the anacapa, and it'll fold space the way that we would fold a blanket.

Only now that I've been to foldspace a few times, I know the analogy isn't quite accurate. We don't immediately leap from one spot to another. We actually pause in foldspace. We stop there for a minute or two. Each time I've done this—which is more than I've wanted to—I've seen a different star map inside foldspace itself, leading me to believe that foldspace isn't so much a fold or a shortcut or points on a damn blanket as it is a different place altogether, one with its own stars—and maybe, its own people.

I have not discussed this with Yash. She's a fantastic engineer who understands more about the *anacapa* drive than anyone else I know. She's also very no-nonsense, and refuses to talk in hypotheticals unless she believes it will get us somewhere.

I've heard her discuss foldspace—mostly to dismiss the nerves that the *Ivoire* crew members still feel. The *Ivoire* got stuck in foldspace for two weeks, and then appeared in our universe, in what had been a familiar place to them.

Only they were five thousand years in their own future.

It's taken a lot of adjustment for the more than five hundred members of the *Ivoire*'s crew to realize they're stuck here, in a universe that only seems familiar. Some crew members have killed themselves. Others have left the service altogether.

The remaining ones divide into two rather loose groups: the ones who believe they can return to the Fleet and the past (which most of them still think of as the present) and the ones who have accepted that they now live in what they once considered an unimaginable future.

Yash is one of the realists. She believes that she's stuck here, in this time period, for the rest of her life. That doesn't stop her from seeking information about what happened to the Fleet, but it does make her much more willing to take risks here and now. She has also settled in. She looks at the rest of us as colleagues instead of people she will only know briefly.

It's been more than five years since the *Ivoire* arrived. I think Yash's perspective is the correct one. But who am I to say? I've dealt with the *Ivoire* crew, but I can't begin to understand the extreme dislocation that they've suffered.

Right now, Yash is as nervous as I am. Normally, she would sit at her newly built station as we traveled here from the Lost Souls Corporation deep in the Nine Planets Alliance. But she stood through the foldspace transition just like I did.

But I'm the only one who knows that her nerves came not from being in foldspace like almost everyone else's on board, but because she wasn't entirely sure where we'd end up when we emerged from it. And she wasn't worried that we were going to the past or some unknowable future. She was afraid we'd end up inside the Boneyard itself, maybe on top of, or inside of, a ship.

Even though I had recorded the coordinates the last time we were here—the *only* time we were here—she didn't believe that I had done so accurately. She spent a lot of time running diagnostics on the *Two's* entire system, making sure we were being accurate.

She's a worrier, although everyone says that part of her personality is new. There's a lot of new to deal with in my team. This is the first time I've mixed members of the *Ivoire* with members of my own diving team, and done so without Coop on board. In the past, Coop has always kept his own people in line, and I've taken care of mine.

We've run joint missions before, usually to great success. I've just never done so on a diving mission, which is nothing like anything the crew from the *Ivoire* has ever done.

"Let's open windows all over the ship," I say.

Yash looks at me sideways. I don't give commands in the proper language, at least for the military-trained *Ivoire* team members. Even now, even after knowing me for five years, they still are uncertain when I'm telling them to do something or simply making a suggestion.

I can rephrase, I suppose, but before I do, Yash nods. Joanna Rossetti, another of the *Ivoire's* best people, nods back. Rossetti is at the helm, partly because she can handle the *anacapa* augmentation on the *Two's* piloting system with no problem, but also because she is great in any surprise situation. She's had my back more than once, and I've been grateful for it.

She activates the controls that reveal the windows all over the ship.

The ones in the cockpit go from dark to clear, revealing the Boneyard in all its glory.

And glory is the word I mean. I love graveyards. I always have. Even land-based graveyards, which are, if I think about it, disgusting—bodies decaying in dirt, bugs, skin sloughing off bone. I'd rather have my body sent out into deep space, spinning forever in the starlight.

But that's too irreverent for me to say. I've never admitted it to anyone, not even Coop, who has become the closest thing to a confidant that I've had in decades.

I certainly won't tell him that I find the Boneyard beautiful. He looked at it only once—the day we discovered it—and found it terrifying.

All those ships from the Fleet, hundreds of them, maybe thousands, filling an area so large that it's bigger than some asteroid belts. It might even be the size of a small solar system. We have yet to measure it.

The old spacers who told me about it on the starbase Azzelia a few weeks ago said it was the size of a large moon, but what we have seen shows that they significantly underestimated its size, just like we did when we first saw it.

The Boneyard shows up as an emptiness on a star map, which freaks navigators out. It disturbed me the first time I saw it, and I'm still not sure how that's done. Because it should show up as a ship graveyard. It doesn't. It shows up as a blackness, a nothingness, in space itself.

I suspect some of that star map blackness is the energy field around the Boneyard. But some of that star map blackness is custom. On the old star maps, the Boneyard showed up as a black nothingness because no one could penetrate its borders, so it was a great unknown area. Back then, unknown often showed up on star maps as blankness—or blackness, given how the maps were designed.

That black emptiness, at least as it pertained to the Boneyard, got transferred to modern star maps.

When we went back to the Lost Souls Corporation after finding the Boneyard for the first time, we researched the Boneyard. Or we tried to. I have dozens of researchers of all types on staff. Those people know how to find any detail, if it's available.

Coop and Yash and members of the *Ivoire* did their best combing what Fleet records they had from way back when. They also set their best science team on the readings we picked up from the Boneyard itself.

We know this: the Boneyard, its force field, and its ships have been here for a long, long, *long*, time.

Maybe the full five thousand years that the *Ivoire* lost.

That's all we know for certain. We can only make educated—or maybe not so educated—guesses about the rest.

Coop's convinced the Fleet that he spent his life with, the Fleet he was born into, had fought a huge battle here. He hasn't said, but I know he believes that this battle was devastating, and the Fleet lost.

He thinks the ships are from that battle, and he believes that they constitute the bulk of the Fleet at the time—maybe even the entire Fleet. He worries that the Fleet got destroyed shortly after he left, and everyone he knew died in that hideous battle.

I know better than to remind him that everyone he knew then has died thousands of years ago. A careless member of my staff made a similar comment early on, and the cold, dismissive look Coop gave her hid the pain her remark had caused him.

If I had to guess, I'd say that Coop prefers the idea of the Fleet being destroyed in a battle that he can research and understand than the idea that the Fleet continued without him, heading into the vast unknown of space on missions he'll never know about.

Because he's usually an evidence guy. And the evidence we have so far points to something far different than one battle.

First of all, the size. The Fleet was large, but not so large that its final resting place would take more space than a small moon. Secondly, the only ships that we can see in the Boneyard are Fleet-made. If the Boneyard had been a former battlefield, there should be other ships inside it, ships from other cultures.

And then there's the type of ships. Yes, the Fleet was huge. But the ships here don't look like the images of the ships I've seen on the *Ivoire*. They're Fleet ships, but they don't seem to match the ships that Coop and his crew left behind.

Some look like the first Dignity Vessel that I found long before I met Coop. That ship had a completely different construction, with actual rivets holding parts together, something the Fleet of Coop's day hadn't used for centuries. I've mentioned that, and Coop says I remember it wrong. I don't mind the dismissiveness; he never saw that ship, so it's not real to him in some way.

But I've also told Yash, and she asked to see the specs. I've shown them to her. They made her very, very quiet. That disturbed me more than Coop's inability to listen.

The structure of some of the visible ships inside the Boneyard looks more like the structure of that first vessel than it does any of the Dignity Vessels from Coop's era. But we haven't been able to go inside to see for certain.

And I'm not going to come to any conclusions until I have gone into that Boneyard. Because I've learned, through countless dives of countless wrecks, that assumptions only get you in trouble. The more you assume, the more you search for whatever it is you've decided you're looking for.

That's one of the many reasons I'm relieved that Coop has stayed behind. He would approach this dive so very differently, and I'd be afraid that he'd infect my crew.

For this very reason, only my people will dive the Boneyard. We know very little about the Fleet—especially compared with the *Ivoire* crew. We won't make assumptions based on a shared past. We'll make our own set of assumptions, some of which will happen because of our ignorance of Fleet technology, but Yash will help with that, at least.

Although I do worry about having Yash on this mission. I need her because I can't operate the *anacapa* without her, but I don't want her talking to the dive team. In fact, when I briefed her on this trip, I made her swear that she wouldn't talk about the dive mission at all.

It was a dicey moment, because technically, I'm not her commander. Coop is. He still maintains his captain's rank, hoping to return the *Ivoire* to the Fleet one day. His crew—what remains of it—acts under that assumption as well.

Technically, he has loaned the *Ivoire* crew members to me for this mission—the engineering staff to protect the *Two* and my team, and the soldiers one level below.

Soldiers. If you had asked me years ago whether or not I'd allow soldiers on a diving mission, I would have laughed at you.

But Coop and I ventured into the Empire's territory a month ago and attacked them. We had a very good reason, but we knew that attack would have consequences. Those consequences include soldiers on every voyage Coop, I, or my team takes.

Those consequences have also given this mission even more importance. The more operable ships we find, the more we can use them to defend the Nine Planets.

But I'm getting ahead of myself. We have to get inside the Boneyard first, and that might not be easy.

The Boneyard has a force field around it, a field we had only begun to analyze on our first visit here before we got attacked. We're hoping that the field is a modified *anacapa* field, but we don't know for certain—and that's another thing that worries me.

I've had friends and relatives die because of malfunctioning *anacapas*. At the time, we thought it a strange energy form—we had no idea what it really was. The *Ivoire*'s crew has reassured me countless times that my crew is fine around a working *anacapa*, that it's only the malfunctioning ones which cause a problem.

Yash tells me that my team will be safe no matter what; she will make certain they're nowhere near malfunctioning *anacapa* drives.

I hope she's right. I've brought a few of my most trusted team members on this trip, but they don't have the genetic marker that enables them to survive inside a malfunctioning *anacapa* field. Every member of the team that will dive with me has the marker.

I'm not taking any chances.

Although, as I stare at the Boneyard unfolding before me, I realize that I've been lying to myself.

Of course I'm taking chances. I'm taking terrible chances. I'm taking the chance that we'll all get discovered here by the scavengers who attacked us the last time. I'm taking the chance that we can actually get into the Boneyard.

And I'm taking the chance that we can get out.

Maybe it's because I'm older now and more experienced, or maybe it's because I feel the weight of all these lives around me. But I'm much more aware of what can go wrong and what the costs are.

I'm also aware that the Boneyard will answer a lot of questions, and maybe, just maybe, it'll help us stop something I've wanted stopped for decades.

It might provide a way to stop the Empire from expanding, from taking over the entire sector, and yet another sector after that, and another sector after that.

Whatever we find inside this Boneyard might just save us all.

3

"I DIDN'T EXPECT IT TO BE AMAZING," someone says behind me.

I don't turn around. I step back and look away from the screens, most of which show the Boneyard as a gigantic unrelieved blackness, and look out the windows as best as I can. I have to look past several heads.

People turning to each other, people whispering, people cupping their hands over their mouths in awe.

They've seen it. They can leave now.

I think that, but I don't say it. Instead, I move just a little so I can look out the windows.

All I can see are bits and pieces of the Boneyard. It's bigger than I remember, more vibrant. The ships almost seem like they're in motion, which they probably are. Nothing stays completely still in space, but the movements are usually microscopic.

I'm not sure if my sense of movement is a trick of the mind or something to do with that force field.

Not that it matters.

The ships have my attention now.

They float, in various stages of ruin. Some seem just fine; others have gigantic holes where their bridges should be. Still others are missing wings or the tail section or the underbelly where, on most large Fleet ships, the family members live.

Some ships are just underbelly. Or just wings. Or the sides of a ship without any interior at all.

I itch to go inside any of those ships. *All* of those ships. I have missed diving. All of this corporate stuff—setting up the business, organizing a large workforce to modify Fleet technology to the modern age, working our patents and trademarks, doing our sales, and building our own small group of ships—takes time. I run an organization bigger than any I've ever belonged to, and I hate it.

Well, that's not entirely true. The hate part is true. The running part is less true. About a year ago, I passed the day-to-day operations to Ilona Blake, and she handles the personnel, the decisions, the conflicts. I still steer—I'm not going to let Lost Souls, despite its name, become a soulless organization. I'll do everything I can to prevent that.

That's something I care about.

But I'm passionate about diving. I just forget that sometimes. So much else happens—I start a business, I deal with people, I ignore regulations.

I've been deeply wrapped up in the *Ivoire* and Lost Souls.

But my heart belongs to diving—going into the unknown, learning about a ship, learning about a past. Exploring what remains.

Realizing that, no matter what happens to me on a day-to-day basis, it will be forgotten a year from now, and it won't matter to anyone else a century from now. No one will exactly be able to piece together all the bits of my life.

As a loner, that gives me comfort. As a lover of history, it gives me a sense that I'm part of something greater than myself. As a diver, it lets me feel closer to the unknowable past.

Outside of this ship, behind a force field we don't entirely understand, lie more ships to dive than I've dived in years. Maybe more than I've dived in my lifetime.

Part of me wants to stay here forever, go from ship to ship, learn about each one, and die decades from now with most of the Boneyard yet to be discovered.

But I am here on a mission. I dive for Coop and the survivors of the *Ivoire*. I want to let them know what happened to their Fleet, if I can.

And I want to get technology for Lost Souls. More ships, more equipment, more *knowledge*.

Those are the stated goals.

But for me, the unstated goal is the most important goal. I want to return to my roots. I've missed being alone in near-dark in a place I've never been before, trying to figure out where I am, what I'm doing, and how I will survive. I thrive on adrenaline, and diving has always given me that rather startling rush.

That adrenaline rush is actually something I need to be careful of. My old diving partners would remind me of that each time we went out. One of them would monitor me while she waited on the skip, so that I wouldn't use my oxygen more quickly than I needed to.

She's dead now. Many of my diving partners are dead. Or retired. Or they've vanished.

The original crew exists only in my head. But oh, how we would have loved this place. We would have dived it without a thought to war or the future or discovering someone's past. We would let the wrecks tell us their secrets without prejudging them at all.

I have never wreck dived for money—real dives, historical diving. I've taken tourists to old wrecks so I could afford my other trips. Trips that were mostly for me. I often did not report the historic wrecks I found. I let them remain, their history intact, taking from them only the information which they wanted to share with me.

All of that ended, of course, when I discovered my first Dignity Vessel—and that put me on the path that led to the *Ivoire*. To here.

To now.

"I'm still stunned at how big this place is," Yash says softly. She sounds unnerved. Maybe she is. We're about to get answers. They might not be the answers she wants, but we'll get some.

"Can we count how many ships are in there?" someone else asks.

Even though I've been introduced to these people more than once, I can't remember their names. Maybe I don't want to. Maybe part of my brain is happier if it is less crowded than this cockpit is.

"I'm sure we can," I say, "but it's not the best use of our time."

"Some of us have nothing to do at the moment, Boss," Mikk says from his position at the helm. He's learning how to work the new *Two* controls. He's one of my best people.

He has been with me for a long, long time. He's much more muscular than most divers, and always uses special suits. But those muscles have helped us when we've been on land-based missions, gravity-filled missions. He's helped me in more ways that I can say.

I trust him.

"Boss," he says, maybe sensing that only part of my attention is on him. "We can count."

I shrug. "I guess you could. But I'm not sure if it's worth our while. I'm not sure if we'll be accurate. It looks like there's a lot of parts in that Boneyard. And I don't want us using any equipment that will interfere with Yash's work."

Yash has the important job. She needs to figure out what that force field is made of and whether or not we can breach it. We can use the *anacapa* to go inside the Boneyard, but if the force field is active inside as well, then we might encounter a problem. Differing energy fields might interact and create problems like we once encountered with the malfunctioning *anacapas,* or the fields might repel each other.

Plus we don't know what the force field will do to our skip or to the *Two* herself. Or to our diving equipment.

And then there's the matter of the ships inside the force field. They might still have active *anacapa* drives as well.

Yash and I have gone through countless possibilities, and I know she's gone through even more than I have, because at a certain point, my brain just turned to mush.

I figure we need to know what we're facing, and then we deal with it.

It's Yash's job to get enough details so that we will know whether or not we can move forward.

"Well, Yash," I say. "Can we do this?"

"You can count all you want," she says to Mikk, or maybe she's speaking to me. She thinks I'm asking about figuring out how many ships are inside the Boneyard. I was referring to the Boneyard herself.

I let Yash continue.

She's looking at Mikk as she gives the rest of the instructions. "Just don't use sensors on that force field. Take images from the outside, then have the computers count or something. I think it would be better, though, if you can actually verify how big this damn Boneyard is."

She sounds distracted. She doesn't care what we all do, as long as we leave her alone to finish her job.

I'm not sure how far along she is on this job.

"How many people do you need to work on the force field?" I ask quietly.

She glances at me. "I'm going to do it alone to start. I've brought a good team. They'll back me up."

I nod. I know better than to ask her how long this will take. Her answer would sound like an answer I would give the crew: It'll take how long it takes.

Even though Coop wants answers yesterday, and even though we need more ships for our upcoming fight with the Empire, I'm trying to run this trip the way I would have run a dive in the old days: We'll be here until we're done.

I find that exciting. And liberating. And frightening.

Because I haven't lived like a diver in nearly a decade. I'm out of practice.

And I know I have to get my head on straight before I can lead a team inside that Boneyard. I have to think like a diver, not like a corporate executive or a woman who's worried about a war with a much larger power.

I have to think like the old Boss, and I haven't been her for a long, long time.

THE FIRST SKIRMISH
ABOUT FOUR YEARS EARLIER

4

Starbase Kappa slipped. Coop knew no other way to describe the feeling. The entire base had shifted just a little.

He put out a gloved hand and braced himself. He stood inside what once had been the control room, although on starbases, the Fleet called these rooms headquarters, probably because back in the dark, dark ages, long before Coop was born, the Fleet allowed strangers to stay in the bases.

Not any longer. Well, that was obvious. But in Coop's memory, the Fleet hadn't allowed strangers on starbases.

He turned toward Yash.

She stood near one of the control panels, a pile of tools scattered on a small built-in table to her side. She had managed to turn on the gravity the moment the team arrived, but she hadn't been able to get the atmosphere to work. The team needed environmental suits to explore the interior. Hers clung to her like a second skin. The visor half-hid her face.

"You feel that?" he asked.

"Yeah," she said, and she didn't sound happy.

They both understood why. That slipping feeling was unique: it generally happened on a ship when an *anacapa* drive kicked in. Only they weren't on a ship. They were on an old abandoned starbase, one that had caused problems in this sector for hundreds of years, if the stories Coop had heard could be believed.

The base had its own *anacapa*. All of the Fleet's bases had had one. If the base had been abandoned, the *anacapa* should have been shut down.

This one hadn't been. It was active and probably malfunctioning. That was one of the problems Coop's team was here to address.

He activated the comm in his environmental suit.

"Dix, did you do something to the *anacapa*?" he asked.

Coop's first officer, Dix Pompiono, had taken a small team into what had been the very center of the starbase to disable and remove the *anacapa*.

Coop didn't get an answer, which, a year ago, he would have thought odd. But for the past several months, ever since the *Ivoire* got separated from the Fleet, Dix's behavior had become increasingly erratic.

Initially, Coop had decided not to bring Dix on this mission. Then, in the last few weeks, Dix seemed like his old self. He'd even grown upbeat, something Coop hadn't thought he'd ever see again.

He'd been relieved, figuring his first officer had returned from whatever personal hell he'd assigned himself to.

Only now a prickly feeling on the back of Coop's neck made him wonder if Dix had deliberately misled him. Coop had had enough problems recently; he didn't need more. And Dix's emotional decline had been something Coop simply didn't want to accept.

"Dix?" Coop said again. Then he looked at Yash. "You want to try?"

"He hasn't answered for the last few minutes," she said, sounding annoyed and worried at the same time.

Coop bit back a harsh response. He needed his team to communicate with him, particularly here, on this empty base. But he didn't want to repeat the question. Not yet.

He was on edge. He'd been on that edge for months now, ever since the *Ivoire* got stuck. A man could live with extreme stress well in the beginning, but seven months in, it didn't just become tedious, it also became exhausting.

Plus, he was trying to focus on too many things at once. He had mentally declared his personal future off limits, but his past wasn't pretty either. He had thought this trip to Starbase Kappa would help with the *Ivoire*'s new reality, but now he wasn't so sure.

That slight slip happened again. Coop braced his other hand against the wall. He was standing near a control panel he'd had to pry open. The controls had deteriorated. This room had suffered at least a thousand years of neglect, maybe more.

He still had trouble wrapping his mind around the time shifts he and his crew had been subjected to. He knew that others—like Dix—had even more difficulty.

"Dix," Coop said again. "I need to hear from you *now*."

"Captain." The voice that came through the comm didn't belong to Dix. Instead, it belonged to Layla Lalliki, the *Ivoire's* chief science officer. She had gone with Dix into the *anacapa* control room, along with three *anacapa* specialists.

Coop didn't like hearing her instead of Dix. "I need Dix, Layla."

"Yeah, I know," she said. "And I need you here now, sir. Right now."

He finally understood what he was hearing in her voice. Controlled panic.

He glanced over at Yash. She had frozen in place.

"What's going on?" he asked Lalliki.

"Something you need to see, sir," Lalliki said. "I can't describe it. Please, sir."

Yash continued to stare at him, or at least he thought she did. The visors on the environmental suits were difficult for someone not wearing the suit to see through, unless the wearer activated an interior light. Usually, the opaqueness played to his crew's advantage.

Right now, though, he felt like ordering everyone to turn on that interior light. He wanted to see faces, nuances, emotions.

And that told him he was as nervous as his crew was.

"Do you need someone to stay in here with you?" he asked Yash.

She shook her head. "This can wait. I'm going with you."

And somehow, her matter-of-fact tone made his panic rise. He had to struggle to beat it back. She knew, like he knew, that he had made a mistake.

He shouldn't have brought Dix on this mission.

Maybe the *Ivoire* shouldn't have come on this mission at all.

5

SHE HAD TOLD HIM NOT TO COME, and he hadn't listened.

Her people called her Boss. She refused to tell him her real name. He was the captain of his own ship, a man who had only that as his identity now, and very little else. He wasn't going to call anyone Boss.

He had told her that, and it hadn't made any difference. She still hadn't shared her real name with him.

So he compromised.

The word "Boss" was in a different language—or rather, in the language his language had evolved into over thousands of years—and so he called her by that foreign word when he needed to use a name for her.

But mentally, he just called her "she."

She had been the first person he had seen when his ship arrived in this strange new future. She had been investigating his ship, stunned that it had suddenly appeared deep within a mountainside.

He'd been stunned too; the ship's coordinates told him the *anacapa* drive had brought the *Ivoire* to Sector Base V, but the space he was in didn't look like Sector Base V. Instead, it looked like an abandoned sector base from decades before.

Later, he learned that the *anacapa* had malfunctioned, bringing him and his crew five thousand years into their future. The language was different, once-familiar planets were different, everything was different except for the people. People remained the same, complicated, emotional

34

creatures who believed they knew everything and secretly feared they knew nothing.

This situation, as he sometimes called it, exacerbated that fear among his crew. And if someone had asked him before the trip into the future had happened how his crew would have handled it, he would have said, *Any crew in the Fleet would cope easily. We're always moving to new places. We have no stable homes, no set environment. We have no historic roots tied to planets or lifestyles. We would be fine.*

And he would have been wrong.

Because he hadn't realized that by coming five thousand years into the future, they had left their true home behind. The Fleet itself had become a legend with no names attached, just a mythical group of ships that came into an area, fixed it (or meddled, depending on the story), and then left. Many people now believed that the Fleet was a comforting children's story, that no group of ships like that had ever existed.

One of the first things Boss had said to him when she could talk freely to him—after he acquired enough of her language to talk with her—was how startled she was to see someone from the Fleet and how vindicated she felt. All of her life, she had argued that the Fleet was real, and now she had proof.

Not that she could show anyone.

This future that the *Ivoire* found itself in had a generations-long conflict between a large rapacious government and a group of rebels. But to be honest, almost every new situation the Fleet found itself in—and that was a lot of situations over the years of Coop's life—involved a large rapacious government and a group of rebels.

Once he had tried to tell Boss how common this was, but she wouldn't hear it. She claimed the Empire she battled was "evil" and the rebels "good."

She usually saw shades of gray when it came to the personal level, but on that universal scale, she was purely black and white. No empire could be as bad as the Enterran Empire (even though he had seen many that were far worse) and no rebels had tougher odds against them (even though he knew of many rebel movements that didn't make it through a year, let alone generations).

These rebels, whom she had more or less allied herself with, had joined forces into something they called the Nine Planets Alliance, which, Coop could have told Boss if she had been willing to listen, would someday be someone else's evil government, needing rebellion against.

But the Nine Planets Alliance had provided him a home, and for that he was grateful. That home was really Boss's. She had started a corporation that she called The Lost Souls, and she used it to rehabilitate Fleet ships and to study what she called stealth technology.

What she was studying was actually the *anacapa* technology of the Fleet. The *anacapa* technology did so much more than provide stealth capability. The fact that Boss was meddling with it—and would continue to meddle with it, without knowing what it was—was one of the reasons Coop had decided to speak with her in the first place.

Eventually, they had become allies. But she didn't run him or his crew. He took care of the *Ivoire*, and he made sure the distance between Boss's people and his remained clear. She could command the people in Lost Souls, but he commanded the *Ivoire* and everyone on her.

Boss understood that very, very well. She supported it.

So six months into his life in the future, when he finally decided on his first mission in this new place with his crew, he told Boss his plans to go to Starbase Kappa, which she called The Room of Lost Souls. She'd had an epiphany there, which was why she named her corporation after the place.

He didn't tell her to get her approval. He told her as a matter of courtesy.

He just didn't expect her reaction.

He hadn't expected it at all.

"No," Boss had said when he told her his plan. "You can't do this."

They were inside her office. The Lost Souls Corporation had bought a space station in the Nine Planets Alliance. The station housed two former Fleet ships for study, and parts of several others that had been discovered over the years.

Boss's office was large. It had three separate spaces—a huge entrance area with separate seating groups, a private area where Boss spent most of her time alone, and a conference room that was even larger than the main area.

Boss met with everyone in the entrance area. No one went into the private area. Boss was the ultimate loner, and she was still getting used to running a corporation. Sometimes Coop wondered how she had ever managed to command a ship—even a small ship. All that time with people had to wear her down.

She sat on the couch, frowning at him. She wasn't pretty—she was too thin for that—but she was athletic, with close-cropped hair and the graceful movements of someone comfortable in her own body.

He found her exceptionally attractive, and he tried to ignore it. If he were back in his own time, he might act on it—he rarely met someone his equal whom he was attracted to who wasn't also part of the Fleet—but here, he didn't know if he was just being needy and lonely, in search of a distraction and a bit of human contact.

Still, he touched her too much, casually in conversations, and usually she touched him back.

On this day, though, she didn't. Her eyes had become steely and her mouth was in a thin line. Her arms were crossed.

"You can't do this, Coop," she repeated.

He almost said, like a child, *I can do whatever I want.*

Instead, he said, "You told me that the Room of Lost Souls has been a danger to everyone who comes near it for its entire history. It clearly has a malfunctioning *anacapa* drive. My people can shut it down. Then we'll come back."

She shook her head. "You don't understand what could go wrong."

He felt a flare of anger. Of course he understood. He understood better than she did. She had no connection to the technology, and while he couldn't fix it himself, he knew more about the *anacapa* than she and her people ever would.

"I'm just telling you this as a courtesy," he said. "We'll do what we need to do."

"Coop." She leaned forward and touched his knee, as if she needed to get his attention. She *had* his full attention, so she didn't need to touch him.

And for the first time since he'd met her, her touch irritated him.

"You'll need our maps," she said.

"I know where the Room of Lost Souls is," he said. "It was our starbase, remember. It hasn't moved."

"You don't know that," she said. "It doesn't behave the way we expect it to."

"We can find it," he said.

He was shaking. The mission meant more to him than he wanted to say. He needed something to do. He had to feel useful, instead of like a charity case. *Look at that man. He used to be the captain in a legendary fleet. Now he doesn't understand anything. He just lives off the goodwill of others, and dreams of a home he'll never find.*

He shook the thought away.

"That's not what I'm worried about," she said. "The Room of Lost Souls is deep in Enterran space."

"I'm not at war with your empire," he snapped.

"I know." She was using a tone he'd never heard before. It was the tone that people used with a child or a sick person or someone incapable of understanding a certain concept. "But we don't want the Empire to know that Dignity Vessels actually work."

He hated that term, Dignity Vessel. She promised not to use it, but she lapsed all the time. The Fleet hadn't used the term Dignity Vessel in generations (well, thousands of years if he started counting from now). The term grated, showed her ignorance, and made him feel even more out of place.

"The Empire won't know. We're not flying in and flying out," Coop said. "We're using our *anacapa*. We'll arrive near Starbase Kappa and then we'll shut off the starbase's *anacapa* and return. We'll be gone a day at most."

"And if an Empire ship is there?" she asked.

"You said that the place is uninhabited," Coop said.

"I said that regular ships don't stop. They heed the warning. But the Empire has been running experiments in stealth tech, and knew years ago about the Room of Lost Souls. I'm sure they're still running experiments there."

Coop shook his head. "The technology at Starbase Kappa is ours. It has killed how many of your people?"

"I don't know," Boss said tightly. Her arms were crossed again, and she was leaning back on that couch.

"You've lost some people there," he said.

She took a deep breath. "My mother and one of my closest friends died in that Room. They didn't have the genetic marker that allows people to work inside your stealth technology."

"It's not—"

"I know," she said. "It's not stealth technology, and you don't fly a Dignity Vessel. Old habits die hard, Coop. And you know what I mean. You're picking nits so that we don't deal with what's really going on."

Now he crossed his arms. "What, in your opinion, is really going on?"

"You need something to do. You have a ship and no mission. It's not natural for you."

She saw him more clearly than anyone else ever had. Maybe that was why he was attracted to her.

Or maybe he just showed his emotions more these days, and anyone could have made that deduction.

"This is not a fruitless mission," he said with a bit more passion than he planned.

"No, it's not," she said. "Eventually, we'll have to deal with the *anacapa* on your starbase. But right now, everyone in the sector knows that the Room of Lost Souls is dangerous. It's an approach-at-your-own-risk site. Most ships don't land there. So there's nothing pressing about going."

"Yes, there is," he said.

She sighed. "Coop—"

"You're right. My ship is in need of a mission. But it's not just me. It's my crew. They're going crazy here. They're getting trapped in all of their losses and feeling as if they have no future. We need—I need—to remind them who they are and what they can do. I need them to become a *crew* again, Boss, not just some people who ended up five thousand years in the future."

She closed her eyes and tilted her head back. She was thinking about his point, clearly. Then she shook her head slightly, as if she had been arguing with herself, and finally she sighed.

She opened her eyes, brought her head down, and scowled at him.

"I don't like this mission. Can't we find something else for you to do?"

"We're not children," Coop said. "We don't need to be entertained."

"That's not my point," she said. "My point is—"

"That's exactly your point. I need my crew on a real mission, one any ship in the Fleet would take. The trip to Starbase Kappa is such a mission. We know that our tech is malfunctioning and killing people. We have to stop that. It's a real mission with a real objective, and it won't take a lot of time. It'll shore up some rusty skills and it'll get my team working together again. It benefits all of us."

"The Empire—"

"I don't care about your empire," he said. "If a ship shows up and threatens us, we'll destroy it. But if the starbase is as isolated as you say, that probably won't happen."

"The Empire can't know that stealth tech works," she said. "And I used the term deliberately. Because that's what they call your device."

"They won't know," Coop said. "How could they? Even if they see us appear, they won't know that the drive did it."

"And then they'll send the information to their headquarters and it won't matter if you destroy their ship. They will have seen a Dignity Vessel appear out of nowhere, and they'll see the so-called stealth tech in action."

"The ship will appear near a place of superstition, a place that some of your people believe is haunted. Surely the sighting will be discounted."

He sounded a bit desperate even to himself. He didn't want to, but he wasn't giving up this mission.

She ran a hand over her forehead. Then she sighed again. "Lord knows, I've taken a lot of risks in my time."

He knew, with that sentence, that he had convinced her. But he wasn't going to interrupt her.

"And you'll go whether I approve your mission or not."

"It's not your job to approve—"

"I know, Coop." She sounded tired. "I'm not the boss of you."

She echoed their arguments about her name. He smiled.

"No, you're not," he said gently. "But I would like your help on this. Your maps, your experience, anything you can tell me."

She nodded. The anger seemed to be gone, but she was clearly disappointed.

"Promise me that if the Empire shows up—"

"I'll make sure they never inform anyone about us or the starbase or the *anacapa* drive."

"Thank you," she said softly.

But he knew she didn't believe he could keep that promise—and he wasn't entirely sure he understood why.

6

Coop and Yash went down two levels to what had once been the heart of Starbase Kappa. A year ago, in his personal timeline, he'd come to this starbase with one of his closest friends and occasional lover, Victoria Sabin. They'd stayed in a fancy suite, had fantastic meals, and seen old friends.

Now he returned to a place abandoned and malfunctioning, filled with the ghosts of people who had died here recently because something had gone wrong with Starbase Kappa's *anacapa*.

At least, that was what he could tell from Boss's stories.

The Fleet always placed the *anacapa* controls in the most protected area, whether the *anacapa* was on a starbase or on a spaceship. According to the map that Boss had made four years ago, the *anacapa* section of the base was now near the edge of the base, levels below what Boss's people called The Room of Lost Souls.

The Room of Lost Souls was an actual room, on what looked, to the uninitiated, like the entry level of Starbase Kappa. If a ship docked, its crew would find the room relatively quickly. People had died there.

The *anacapa* was in a protected space that butted up against the floor of the Room of Lost Souls. What the actual room had been in the base's prime was one of many recreation areas that could be shut down or expanded if the operational facilities inside the starbase needed expansion.

The *anacapa* control room had been locked and guarded with some of the standard shutdown procedures that the Fleet used. Generally, when the Fleet decommissioned a starbase, it used the starbase's *anacapa* to move the base to a different sector of space. Then the Fleet engineers disassembled the starbase and used the parts that were still good or viable for a new starbase or a sector base.

The Fleet never wasted anything, which was one of the things that made Starbase Kappa so very odd.

It shouldn't have been here.

And it certainly shouldn't have been here after five thousand years.

The *anacapa* room had a double door system. The outer doors stood open only because Dix and his crew had left them that way for a rapid escape. The inner door remained closed because there was no way to prop it open. Regulations didn't allow it.

Some of the materials inside any *anacapa* area were different than the rest of the starbase. They were stronger, and provided protection against *anacapa* malfunctions.

Until this past year, Coop had had limited experience with *anacapa* malfunctions. Now they seemed to be the story of his life.

Although, the fact that the *anacapa* functioned at all after five thousand years had given him hope—a misplaced hope, or so Lalliki and Yash told him, but hope all the same. He knew that the *Ivoire's* arrival in this time and place had a lot to do with the vagaries of two different *anacapas*, malfunctioning in two different ways (or maybe several different ways), but part of him hoped that the malfunctions could be recreated in a lab.

His public policy was to act as if he would never leave this time period, but his personal hope was that someday he and his crew would find a way back to their time period, a way that would enable them to rejoin their friends and family and the familiarity of the Fleet.

Because right now, he felt like he was haunting his own life.

Dix's team had disabled the identification panels to enter the inner door. They had reported to Coop on that.

So he just had to push open the door and step inside.

He did, Yash on his heels.

The interior of the *anacapa* room was brightly lit and still filled with equipment, which surprised him, even though Dix had mentioned that when the team arrived.

Still, Coop did not expect to see viewing stations, a landing platform large enough for a warship in trouble, and all sorts of engineering equipment still intact.

He also didn't expect to see the *anacapa*, extending from its housing in the floor, and Dix reaching into the casing, his arms inside all the way to his shoulders.

Layla Lalliki turned toward Coop. She was tall and thin, and even though he could barely see her face through the environmental suit visor that protected her pasty skin, he got the sense that she felt out of her element.

Lalliki flapped her arms helplessly, a movement that no one comfortable in zero-g would ever use. But Coop understood it: she didn't outrank Dix, and what he was doing disturbed her. She wanted him to stop.

The three *anacapa* experts stood around Dix, clutching the repair tools. Coop didn't know these members of his crew very well, and he certainly didn't know them by what he could identify now, which was height and build. There was a short roundish one, another short thin one, and a taller one with shoulders so broad that Coop would guess that he was male.

Lalliki walked quickly toward Coop, but he signaled her to stop. He knew what was happening—or enough of it, anyway.

Dix knew a lot about a lot of things, but he was no *anacapa* expert. Still, he had spent most of the last six months studying the drive, trying to figure out what had gone wrong and what could be recreated.

He had come to Coop's cabin late one night and helped himself to some whiskey that Coop had been saving.

We don't understand these damn drives, Dix had said. *We can work them, we can repair them, but we're playing with things we only partially get.*

I'm sure the specialists would disagree with you, Coop had said, deciding not to mention the whiskey. Instead, he had poured a glass for himself.

If they disagreed, they would know what foldspace is, Dix said, then sighed. *I think we're screwed, Coop. We need some kind of access to our own past, something still functioning. We shut down Sector Base V, and it was a mistake. We can't make that mistake again.*

Coop had forgotten that conversation until now. It had been months ago, and he and Dix had had countless conversations after that. Many of them had been about Dix's family, his love for the Fleet, and the woman he had left behind on the *Geneva*. Dix had been in love, the kind of love Coop had never experienced, and losing her was tearing him apart in ways Coop didn't completely understand.

Coop walked over to the *anacapa* drive. He could hear it thrumming softly. The *anacapa* seemed unobtrusive invisible to those who worked with it regularly, but it wasn't. It made tiny noises and caused small motions like that slip he'd felt earlier.

Coop never learned exactly how to work on an *anacapa*—it wasn't required for leadership—but he did know enough about it to recognize that the drive was still intact. Dix had just gone into the center of it to adjust it, somehow.

And Coop had an idea as to how.

Dix didn't look up as Coop approached. Dix's environmental-suited arms were deep inside the drive, his hands—probably still gloved—tinkering with the interiors. The light from the *anacapa* illuminated Dix's face, adding shadows where there generally were none, and making him look thinner than he usually did.

Or maybe that wasn't the light at all. Maybe Dix had grown even more gaunt than usual. Maybe he had been wasting away, and Coop hadn't even noticed.

"Dix," Coop said. "What are you doing?"

"I'm getting us back," Dix said.

"The mission is to shut the drive down, remove it, and take it back to Lost Souls," Coop said.

"It's a stupid mission," Dix said, and at that moment, Coop knew his friend had gone over an edge. His first officer would never talk with him that way. Dix had expressed that kind of opinion in his darkest moods months ago, but had returned to the exceedingly competent man Coop had known.

Everyone around them shifted as if they expected Coop to lose his temper. He wouldn't lose his temper—not here—unless it was appropriate. And right now, nothing was appropriate except getting Dix away from the *anacapa*.

"I *told* you," Dix said. "I *told* you *repeatedly* that we needed a functioning *anacapa* that was as old as the one on Sector Base V to get us back. This is it, Coop. You *know* that."

"We fixed our *anacapa* too," Lalliki said before Coop could stop her. "It's not in the same condition that it was in six months ago. Even if we found a way to link the two devices—"

Coop held up a hand, silencing her.

"I had forgotten, Dix," Coop said softly. "You should have reminded me before we left on this mission."

He crouched so that he was closer to Dix and so that he could see Dix's hands inside the device. He was working on the controls, but Coop didn't know which ones. Most of the *anacapa* access happened on a control panel, not inside the device itself.

"You wouldn't have listened if I had said anything. You would have left me behind," Dix said.

Coop would have, too. He would have had to leave Dix behind because the very idea of tampering with an *anacapa* without training meant that Dix was unstable.

"You want to get back," Coop said, careful not to frame that as a question. "We all do."

Dix raised his head. His eyes had deep shadows beneath them.

"You all believe it's impossible," Dix said. "You wouldn't even try. We're stuck here, Coop. *Stuck*. And Starbase Kappa is our last chance."

Coop swallowed hard, trying not to show the nerves that had suddenly infected his stomach. Sometimes ideas on the far side of crazy were the right ones. Sometimes those ideas were the difference between succeeding at something and complete failure.

But he also knew he wanted to get back as badly as Dix did. So did the entire team. Their training, though, their training included acceptance of things they couldn't change. They weren't supposed to reach for a scenario that had a 5% success rate.

Although, if Coop thought about it, this one scenario—hooking up the old Starbase Kappa *anacapa* to the *Ivoire's* (repaired) *anacapa*—probably had a less than one percent success rate.

"You're right," Coop said, hoping he didn't sound patronizing. "Dammit, Dix, I hadn't thought of any of this and I should have."

Dix's eyes narrowed. Had Coop overplayed his hand? Dix knew him extremely well, better than almost everyone else on the crew except Yash. Dix and Coop had served together for more than 15 years.

"Yes, you should have, and you didn't, and now I'm working. Let me finish," Dix snapped at him, and Coop realized that the Dix he expected, the Dix who would have seen through his playacting was submerged in a mixture of hope, confusion, and some kind of mental break.

"One second, Dix," Coop said.

"I *knew* you'd try to stop me," Dix said. "Get the hell away or I'll break the damn drive."

Which would be better for everyone at the moment, but Coop didn't say that. He didn't want Dix to know what he was thinking.

"I'm not trying to stop you," Coop said in his calmest voice. "I'm trying to help you."

Dix made a dismissive sound and turned his attention to the drive again.

Coop could have phrased that better. A lot better, in fact.

"What I'm saying here is that you're not an *anacapa* expert," Coop started, "and we have four people who know the drive better than anyone else on the *Ivoire*. Let's get them involved—"

"Why?" Dix said, raising his head so quickly that it looked like it hurt. "So they can screw this up? They didn't come up with this idea. They say it's impossible. They say the conditions are *wrong* for the *anacapas* to mix. I say how can you know without trying? They say we'll get stuck somewhere worse, maybe foldspace again, maybe a hostile alternate universe, maybe our past instead of our future. I say what can it hurt? They say we're pretty well set-up here in this future, with the help of that woman you're screwing and the little band of so-called scientists around her. I say—"

"I've heard the arguments," Coop said, trying to ignore the insubordination, recognizing it for the crazy that it was. "And I'm telling you, my old friend, that I believe you. They're part of my crew. They'll have to do what I tell them. If I tell them to follow my instructions, they'll have to."

Dix shifted just a little. His arms had to hurt from being in that position for so long.

"You tell them to instruct me what to do and I'll do it," he said.

He clearly wasn't going to let go of those controls. Dammit.

"The *anacapa* is delicate," Coop said. "I think they'll need hands on—"

"See, that's where you think you're so clever, Captain Cooper," Dix said, the sarcasm dripping from his voice. "And you're not. You're not clever at all. You want me to let go of the interior of the drive so your people can put me into the brig, and you can go ahead with this crazy mission that will destroy the drive and our chances to get the hell out of here. You want to stay because you've fallen for that woman, and you don't care who it hurts."

Coop winced, and hoped Dix didn't see it. Yes, Coop had developed a relationship with Boss, but it hadn't become sexual—yet. He had a hunch it would. He wasn't ready. And he certainly wouldn't give up his whole life and everything he knew for her, no matter what.

But Dix didn't believe that. Dix, who needed to get home to the woman he had left behind. Dix, who probably loved her in exactly the way he accused Coop of loving Boss.

"Dix," Coop said as calmly as he could. "I'm afraid that you're the one who is going to screw up the drive so badly that we won't be able to get back."

Dix snorted with disbelieving laughter. "I'm sure you *don't* believe that, Coop. You know better."

"No," Coop said firmly. "*You* know better. You know that we're not certified to work on *anacapas*, but we are the ones the others trust. We're the ones who give the orders. So, listen to me: I agree with you. We need to combine the *anacapas* and see if we can get back to our universe, our people, our Fleet. But you and I aren't the ones who can work on the drives. We're the ones who tell others what to do, *even if they don't agree with us*. Remember?"

Dix froze. Coop could actually see him thinking.

Coop's heart rate started to increase. Dix was contemplating what he said. Maybe Coop had managed to reach the last part of Dix that was thinking clearly.

"Captain?" The voice didn't belong to anyone in the *anacapa* room. It belonged to Anita Tren, whom he had left in charge of the transport they had brought to the starbase from the *Ivoire*.

Everyone moved, which meant everyone heard the voice. Even Dix. Anita had not used a private channel.

Another dammit. Coop didn't want Dix to be distracted, to have time to think. (Or, to be more accurate, to revert to the worst of the crazy.)

"We have a problem, sir," Anita said without waiting for Coop to respond. "Are you there?"

Dix shook his head, and leaned even closer to the *anacapa*, hunching away from Coop as if he expected Coop to strike him.

"I'm here, Anita," Coop said. "What is it?"

"Sir," Anita said. "Twenty soldiers have arrived. I think they're from the Enterran Empire."

Coop frowned. Whatever he had expected, it wasn't this. "Twenty? They're in ships?"

"No, sir. They're on the starbase. Apparently they docked on the far side from us, several levels down. We weren't looking for them because we didn't think anyone came to this base. I'm sorry, sir."

"They're on the base?" Coop couldn't quite wrap his brain around it.

"Yes, sir. They look hesitant, sir, but they're armed."

Armed. Coop didn't repeat that one. Armed. He hadn't expected it. Should he have expected it? He hadn't expected Dix either.

Clearly, Dix wasn't the only one whose thinking had been clouded of late.

"Dix," Coop said. "I want you to step back from the *anacapa*. Let the experts do the work you're trying to do."

"No," Dix said. "They won't listen."

"Dix, I don't have time—"

"Yeah, I know," Dix said. "And neither do I. You have a military mission, Captain. I have a humanitarian one. Let me finish what I'm doing."

Whatever chance Coop had had of convincing Dix to step back was gone. Coop stood.

He could stun his old friend, but weapons' fire in this closed space wasn't the best idea. And the environmental suit, with its three layers of protection, limited their options.

"Keep an eye on him," Coop said to Yash. And then he added her on a private channel, "See if you can figure out a way to stop him."

"I'll do my best, sir," Yash said through that same channel. "Be careful."

Coop nodded an acknowledgement. He couldn't promise her that he would be careful, however, because he didn't know what careful was any more.

7

It felt weird, going through the familiar corridors of Starbase Kappa, only without the stores, the restaurants, the spectacular and different hotels. The starbase didn't even have echoes of those old businesses. Nothing familiar remained except the shape of the hallways, and of course, the stairs.

Coop had a map of the old starbase in his head and the partial one Boss had made on the bottom of his visor, but even then, moving to the lower levels was slow going. He was actually afraid he might get lost.

He didn't have time for that. Not with twenty soldiers from the Enterran Empire on a lower level.

Right now, they believed they had the element of surprise. He only had so much time before they realized they didn't.

He had told ten members of his team to join him, but only one other officer. That officer, Joanna Rossetti, sidled up to him the moment she arrived.

"Let me handle this, Coop," she said, as she should have. Fleet procedure did not allow a captain to go first into a hostile situation.

However, who would punish him now for disobeying regulations? The Fleet? It wasn't nearby, and besides, the Fleet he knew hadn't existed for five thousand years.

His crew could call for a court-martial and maybe even use procedures to remove him, and then what? He would still be stuck in this time period, and so would they. Someone else would captain the *Ivoire*, but what would that someone do, especially after some kind of crew rebellion?

"I got it, Jo," Coop said.

Rossetti shook her head. She pushed past him as if she could protect him, which always made him smile. She was small, built for space—the small ceilings, the nooks and crannies. She functioned best in zero-g, unlike some of his team.

But in a fight, he was better. He had come up through the ranks at a time when the Fleet fought several battles, not just in space, but hand-to-hand.

He didn't expect that here, but he had another complication: he had made a promise to Boss. He had said that he wouldn't let her evil Empire find out about his ship.

He might not follow Fleet guidelines throughout this encounter, and that would be on him, not on a fantastic officer like Rossetti.

She had brought five soldiers with her, the same five that had helped with the first ground battle the crew of the *Ivoire* had fought in this strange new time period. Four others joined as they kept going down levels. They were all armed heavily, and their environmental suits had real body armor.

He glanced at Rossetti. She was covered in protective gear as well. He was the only one who wore a standard environmental suit.

Of course, if the people they were going to meet wanted to start something, they would go after Coop anyway. The difference between the environmental suit he wore now and his armored suit was that the armored suit would protect him well against weapons he had seen in this time period. His environmental suit would only survive a few heavy-duty (and well-aimed) shots from laser weapons before becoming compromised.

"Anita," he said into his comm link, "you have anything more on these soldiers?"

Anita was watching from the transport. The condition of Starbase Kappa's equipment didn't allow anyone to monitor from here.

"They're not that disciplined," Anita said. "They start to leave the area they arrived in, then they stop and talk about something. Two at least have planted themselves near a door, weapons raised, shaking their heads every time someone beckons them."

Boss had said there were a lot of superstitions about this place. Could the stories be so horrible that trained soldiers were unwilling to come into it?

If so, that might work to Coop's advantage.

For a moment, he toyed with letting the outside soldiers set the agenda, and see if they would come after his people at all.

Then he decided against it. He needed to find out who they were, what they wanted, and why they were on this base with weapons. If Boss questioned him later, he would say he was making certain they weren't from the Empire.

But deep down, he knew the truth.

Deep down, he was spoiling for a fight, and he hoped to hell that this group would give it to him.

8

OVER ROSSETTI'S OBJECTIONS, Coop strode first into the landing area where the soldiers still milled. He almost said, *Welcome to Starbase Kappa*, but he refrained. Instead he stood, with his arms crossed, near the door into the main part of the base and let his own team catch up to him.

If the uniforms were any indication, Anita was wrong: there weren't twenty soldiers here. There were fifteen soldiers and five civilians. And Coop recognized the ornate blue uniforms because Boss had shown him examples.

He was facing members of the Enterran Empire, just like Anita had thought.

Coop waited until they noticed him, which took a full two minutes. They had clearly been arguing amongst themselves, but he couldn't hear any of it because it was on their private comm links.

He turned on the speaker on his suit. That temptation to welcome them to Starbase Kappa rose again, but he still didn't say anything. He would let them begin this encounter.

When they noticed Coop and his team, four of the five civilians started in surprise. The soldiers grabbed their weapons tighter, locking them in place, standing at attention. So there was discipline after all—and that was a good thing.

It meant that the breakdown of discipline when the Empire's group arrived showed extreme fear.

Boss had been right: this place did terrify the entire sector.

The only civilian who hadn't been surprised stepped forward. He was taller than the other civilians, and wore a bulky environmental suit with actual oxygen containers, a square helmet that was made of some kind of clear material, and thin gloves like the ones Boss had worn when Coop first met her. Her environmental suit had been more sophisticated than this guy's, but not of any higher quality.

"You got the secret room open!" the civilian said through the speaker on his helmet. He sounded both excited and enthusiastic.

He took another step toward Coop, but one of the soldiers grabbed his arm.

The civilian tried to shake the soldier off and failed. Still, Coop could see how eager the civilian was. The civilian's clear helmet allowed Coop to see his face. The civilian had curly black hair, dark eyes, and avid features. He was thin, but not athletic or space thin. And he had deep lines around his nose and mouth, almost as if his face were forcing him into a permanent frown no matter what he did.

"How in God's name did you get that room open?" the civilian asked, doing his best to ignore the soldier who held him back.

A female soldier stepped in front of the civilian. She was younger, with a taunt expression on her narrow features. Her eyes were hooded and her mouth a thin line. Her hair was so short that Coop could barely see it through her helmet.

She turned slightly toward the civilian. Coop recognized the movement. She was chastising the civilian through a private channel.

Then she looked back at Coop. "You're trespassing."

The civilian reached for her, as if he were disagreeing, but she stepped ever so slightly out of his grasp.

"Oh." Coop deliberately sounded surprised. He glanced around himself as if seeing this level for the first time. "We thought this place had been abandoned."

He knew he spoke with an accent, and his sentence structure was probably a bit too perfect. Just by speaking, he identified himself as someone outside this sector.

He hoped they wouldn't care.

"The Room of Lost Souls is property of the Enterran Empire," the woman said. "Didn't you see the postings?"

He hadn't seen any postings. He wondered if he had missed them because the *Ivoire* had come here using the *anacapa* drive instead of flying through Empire space.

"The maps we have state that this place had been deserted for generations. The maps also state that we should avoid it." Coop smiled, even though he knew they couldn't see his smile. Sometimes people could hear a smile in his voice. He was gambling on that. "That admonition intrigued me."

"And you are?" the woman asked.

Coop wasn't about to answer that question. Even if he had felt inclined to answer it, he wouldn't have known how.

So he took a tack from one of the Fleet's new-encounter playbooks. He answered a question with something that sounded friendly but was really a question. "I take it you're from the Enterran Empire."

"Yes," she said.

"I need to talk to him," the civilian said to the woman. He almost sounded panicked. "He got the secret room open."

Coop studied them for a moment. He had thought Boss's concerns about the Empire might have been a bit paranoid until this very moment.

The civilian's eagerness to get to the area where the *anacapa* still functioned, disturbed Coop greatly.

"Technically, I didn't get the room open," Coop said. Technically, his team opened the room before he arrived on the starbase, but he didn't add that. "Give us a little time. I had no idea this place belonged to someone. I'll get my people out of here."

At the moment, he needed to be the cooperative stranger. He wanted these people to think him no threat at all, just a man who had stumbled into the wrong place for the wrong reason.

Maybe they would confide in him—or if they didn't *confide* exactly, they might at least let information slip. Then he could decide how to proceed.

"I'd rather you show me how to get into that room," the civilian said.

The woman shot him an annoyed glance. "We need to check out your people," she said to Coop.

"Why?" he asked. "We all know this base is empty."

"Your people seem to have no trouble in this base," she said as if she found that suspicious. Of course she would.

She knew about the genetic marker.

She knew that anyone without a marker died in places like Starbase Kappa. And the death wasn't pretty.

Apparently, the Empire team that faced him now found the fact that his crew could easily work in this environment suspicious.

Hell, he'd find it suspicious too if he were in their position, especially if what Boss said were true: that the Empire was trying to control what it called stealth tech.

"Plus," the woman added, "we didn't see you entering this part of space."

He felt a little cold. They believed he had stealth tech—a cloak they couldn't penetrate. He wondered if they believed him part of Boss's group, or if they worried that another group existed.

"I'm not sure why you would have expected to see me," Coop said, in that same casual, comfortable, off-hand way he'd been speaking. He wanted this woman to relax around him, and so far, she hadn't.

She hadn't even changed her posture. She still blocked the civilian man who kept raising a hand, almost like a child trying to get the attention of an adult.

"Our postings don't lie," she said, as if it were a test. It probably was.

"We've already established that I didn't see the postings," Coop said.

She tilted her head, as if reluctantly granting him this point.

"We've posted most of this region, informing ships to turn away. We also state that anyone who gets through will be considered trespassers and might get shot on sight."

"Apparently, your postings aren't as numerous as you thought," Coop said. "And it sounds like they make idle threats, since we never saw a ship of yours on our trip here."

Once again, he hadn't lied. But he also knew why he hadn't seen any of those ships. He hadn't come the way that this woman expected, and he needed her to tell him how many ships there were, how far away they were, and what they knew—if anything—about the *Ivoire*.

"You might not have seen us," she said, "but we should have seen you. We had an information shield in place."

It took him a moment to understand the terminology.

"Does she mean they had enough ships to put up a sensor blanket?" Rossetti asked on their private link.

"I think so," Coop said, glad that his visor didn't allow the woman to see him talking to Rossetti. "Have Anita contact the *Ivoire*. We need to know how many ships are in the immediate area, and whether or not their sensors have pinged ours. We need to know if they've found the *Ivoire* or not."

"Got it," Rossetti said.

Coop tilted his head, as if he had been thinking. He hadn't moved enough for the woman to realize he'd been conversing with his own people.

"An information shield," he said. "You believe that we would have passed through one on our way here?"

"I know you would have," she said. "There's no other way here. You would have had to go through our sensors."

"And you don't think there are gaps in your sensors," he said, not really asking a question, but stating it and making it sound as if she were naïve to expect a gap-free shield.

"There aren't," she said firmly.

"And yet we're here," he said.

"You could've cloaked," the civilian said, as if he couldn't contain himself. "Stealth tech—"

"No cloak is good enough to mask against our sensors," the woman said, more to the civilian than to Coop.

"And yet," Coop said, pausing for emphasis as he repeated himself, "we're here."

The woman glared at him. She straightened her shoulders. "You came in a small ship, one that cannot have traveled through deep space."

Coop felt a surge of relief. She didn't know about the *Ivoire*. That didn't mean her ships hadn't found it, but so far, no one had communicated that information to her.

"So," he said, with just a touch of amusement, "now you know the capabilities of my ship. Have you flown one like it?"

"I know, based on the size and the power configuration, that it couldn't have traveled here on its own. That's a short-range vessel. If I had to guess, I would say it's a troop transport."

She was good. She clearly hadn't seen a Fleet transport vessel before, but she had figured it out. None of the transports or the life pods or the smaller fighters had *anacapa* drives. They were simply too dicey to use without a full engineering staff.

"Until you people showed up," Coop said, "I had no reason to bring a troop here."

"So what are you doing here?" the civilian asked.

That was a harder question to answer. Coop tried to keep it simple. "We're exploring. None of us had been here before."

"And somehow you got into the secret room," the civilian said.

"It didn't look secret," Coop said. "In fact, I'm not even sure what you're referring to as the secret room. We've found some doors that were harder to open than others, but we didn't find any hidden spaces at all."

Again, true.

The civilian tried to step forward, but the soldier who held him pulled him back. "The secret room is the door inside—"

"What's the point of your exploration?" the woman said quickly, as if she didn't want the civilian to finish his statement.

Coop shrugged. "The point of our exploration is what's always the point of exploration. Information, mostly. But I have to admit, there's just a bit of an adrenalin high going into a new place, particularly one that's been deserted for this long."

"Did you expect to find something here?" the woman asked—and the question felt pointed.

"Of course not," Coop said. "This place has been abandoned for a long time. Abandoned places get scavenged. I figured there would be little here, except of exploratory or informational value."

"You keep repeating the word information. What are you trying to find out?"

"Aren't you interested in where this place came from?" Coop asked. "Your guides and warnings seem to give it mythic powers. We wanted to see that."

"Captain," Anita spoke through his private link. "So far as we can tell, no one has discovered the *Ivoire*. There are a dozen ships quite some distance away, but their sensors are trained outward, not inward. They seem to believe nothing can get past them."

Coop almost nodded. He'd expected that. It was the kind of mistake an overconfident military made.

"Anita," he said. "I want you to listen carefully. On my order, I want the *Ivoire* to activate its *anacapa* and vanish for a least six hours. Then, at the same time, I want you to activate the transport's cloak."

"Their equipment is sophisticated enough to break through our cloak," she said.

The woman across from him said, "I don't believe you."

For a moment, Coop wasn't sure what the woman was referring to. He would have to parse it out when he was done with Anita. So he shrugged again.

He said to Anita, "I know they can see through our cloak. I want them to. Because, if they are monitoring the *Ivoire*, and it disappears when the transport disappears, they'll think the mechanism is the same. They're not close enough to the *Ivoire* for their equipment to show any difference."

"Got it," Anita said.

Beside him, Rossetti chuckled. "I like the way you think, Captain."

He permitted himself one small smile before answering the woman in front of him. She had said she didn't believe he was interested in a place of myth. He made sure he was using his easy-going voice again.

"You don't believe that we were interested in a place called on all maps The Room of Lost Souls? Who could avoid such a place?"

"Anyone with an instinct for self-preservation," the woman said. As she spoke, the soldiers behind her shifted. Her words seemed to mean more to them than to Coop.

"You keep threatening that something bad will happen," Coop said. "Are you going to kill us for visiting here?"

"No," the civilian said. He turned toward the woman. "For God's sake, Commander, we *need* to talk to these people. There are at least thirty of them and they all have the marker."

The woman stepped toward the civilian. "You are here on my sufferance. One more word, and I'll send your people back to the ship."

"Actually," the civilian said to her, "you're here because of me, and you have no right to order me around."

Such animosity. Apparently the lack of discipline wasn't the only problem this group of soldiers had.

"Fun as this all is," Coop said, "it has nothing to do with me or my people. We had no idea we were trespassing, so we'll leave. Just give us thirty minutes and we'll be out of your way."

He hoped thirty minutes was enough time to get Dix out of that room. In fact, he hoped Yash had already gotten him out of there, even though no one had notified Coop that she had been successful.

Then the starbase slipped again. Coop held back a curse. Two of the empire's soldiers scurried through the door they'd entered from. The others shifted nervously.

"What the hell?" the civilian said as he extended his arms for balance. "That's new. You're doing something, aren't you?"

"Now, Anita," Coop said to Anita on the private channel. "Have the *Ivoire* and the transport disappear *right now*."

She acknowledged him.

Then he looked at the woman and the civilian before him and said through his speaker, "What am I doing? I'm talking to you. This place has been moving like that ever since we arrived. We thought it was normal."

"It's not normal," the civilian said. This time, he successfully shook off the soldier holding him. "Commander, they're clearly doing something in that room. Something important. You know this place has been changing size. I'll wager that what we're feeling is something they did. Maybe they've been manipulating the Room all along."

The woman's head moved back slightly. Anyone else would have thought that the civilian's words bothered her, but Coop knew better. She had just gotten word that the transport had vanished.

"I think we're done talking," she said to Coop. "You'll all come with us now."

"Weapons," Coop said on the private channel to his soldiers. They responded quickly, pointing their laser rifles at the entire group before him.

Her people responded with their weapons out. Coop knew that his people would make it out of a shootout. Hers wouldn't.

"I don't think we're going anywhere," Coop said to the woman. "I've told you our plans. I was very clear. We need thirty minutes to leave this place."

"Your transport is cloaked," she said.

"Standard procedure," he said. "We do that as we power up and prepare to leave. That way no one tracks us because they don't know our origin point. Don't you people do the same thing?"

He hoped it sounded plausible. To him, it sounded like the bold-faced lie it was.

"I don't like what's happening here," the woman said. "You're coming with us and we will remove the rest of your people from here."

Coop let the contempt he felt into his voice. "I don't think so. We've offered to cooperate. You should take us up on that."

Her eyebrows went up, and she tilted her head just a little. "Is that a threat?"

He shrugged. He wanted her to see that. "You can take it however you want. I think of it as friendly advice. Two of your soldiers have already left the area. It's clear that your crew lacks discipline. I watched you for a long time before you even noticed me, and my people have been watching you longer than I have. You can't get most of your crew out of this entry. Apparently they're afraid of this Room of Lost Souls, as you call it, and that fear trumps whatever discipline you have."

Her expression didn't change, but she moved her head just a little, enough so that he caught it. The civilian behind her looked at all of the soldiers around him as though they had betrayed him. Only the four other civilians looked calm.

Had they been inside this starbase before? Was that why they weren't afraid?

"Now," Coop said as reasonably as he could. "You could let us leave of our own accord, or you could try to force us to go with you. I don't recommend the second."

Even though it would probably please Boss. It would be an excuse to get rid of these people, to make certain that any knowledge of the *ana-capa* ceased to exist.

"Let me go with them," the civilian said. "I want to see how they got into that room. It'll be cooperation, and I can make sure they leave."

Coop felt a moment of irritation. He wanted to leave here with no loss of life, and he had almost been there. They hadn't seen the *Ivoire*, and they didn't know where the *anacapa* drive actually was. If this civilian came with them, then the shooting would start.

But he didn't dare say anything, because if he voted either way, he would influence their decisions.

"Leave the room open," the woman said.

"Which room?" Coop asked, continuing to play his game with her. He theoretically didn't know, so he wouldn't be able to leave the proper door ajar.

"All of them," she said.

"Fine," he said.

"No!" the civilian said at the same time.

Coop's irritation grew. This idiot wanted to die.

"I have to know how they got in," the civilian said. "If that door closes and we get trapped...."

He let the thought hang, but he didn't need to. From the woman's expression, she understood. And, from the half-second look of dislike that flashed across her face, she probably didn't care if the civilian got trapped in one of those rooms.

For the first time, Coop wondered how many people she had lost to this starbase. He would wager it was quite a few.

"He can tell you how he opened it," the woman said to the civilian.

"No," the civilian said. "It's clearly not easy. If it were, we would have opened it already. We've been trying to open that door for *years*."

Coop sighed silently.

"The price of knowledge," Rossetti said softly through their private link.

"Let's hope she says no," Coop said to Rossetti.

"Fine," the woman said, even though she clearly thought this a bad idea. "Rigley, Lerner, go with Vilhauser."

Two of the soldiers moved beside the civilian, who had to be Vilhauser. One of the other civilians turned toward the woman in charge, apparently asking on a private channel if they should go too. She shook her head as she said no, almost as if she couldn't believe they were questioning her.

Coop smiled again. Civilians. He had often felt a similar annoyance with Boss's people.

"If your people try anything," the woman said to Coop. "We will blow up your ship."

"It's cloaked," he said, with fake confidence, hoping that she did indeed mean the transport and not the *Ivoire*.

"And our sensors see right through that cloak. Would you like me to tell you where it is at the moment?"

The transport probably hadn't moved. He hadn't given the order for it to leave the starbase yet.

"No need," he said. "I believe you."

He also believed she thought she had superior firepower. She acted like someone who knew she had the upper hand.

He would let her continue to believe that. He had a more pressing problem.

Did he take her people hostage and fly them back to Lost Souls? Or did he kill them when his ship left?

He didn't like either option, but he couldn't see another that he liked better.

And that bothered him more than he wanted to admit.

9

HAD COOP BEEN THE COMMANDER in charge of the Enterran Empire's mission here, he would have had his soldiers escort the interlopers off the starbase. The fact that the woman didn't do that spoke less to her command capabilities than to her uncertainty as to whether or not her people would survive a trip deep into the so-called Room of Lost Souls.

Even though she probably knew that these two soldiers would survive a trip deeper into the base, the soldiers didn't. He could see it in their rigid posture, the set looks on their faces.

They were good men, young, and probably on an early posting. One of his mentors had called soldiers like this fodder, and Coop didn't disagree. The difference was that a good captain knew that wars, battles, and situations like this one needed fodder. Any captain who took the loss of such people personally wouldn't last.

That was why he had called that captain a mentor. Coop had learned a valuable lesson from him. It was another reason that Coop didn't get to know the junior members of his very large crew well. If he became attached, he didn't make good decisions.

The woman clearly agreed. She'd sent her people in without a smidgeon of remorse. She had a job to do, and she was doing it as best she could.

The civilian, on the other hand, was so excited that Coop thought he might burn through his oxygen. The civilian literally bounced up the stairs, moving with a rhythm that would normally have suggested that the gravity in his boots was failing. But Yash had turned on the base's gravity, so what the civilian's boots did or didn't do didn't matter. Still, he was moving quicker than he should—than anyone should with such limited oxygen reserves.

Had the civilian been one of Coop's, Coop would have cautioned him. But honestly, if the guy died going up these stairs, one problem would be solved.

The empire soldiers moved slower, almost as if they didn't want to protect this guy. They were doing a poor job of it. They soon found themselves in the middle of Coop's group, rather than at the front or the back of it. They clearly couldn't see anything, which he thought just fine. He didn't care what they could or couldn't see; he needed his people to keep an eye on them.

"So," Rossetti asked him on the private channel as they made their way up the stairs. "Are we evacuating?"

"I don't see any reason to stay," Coop said, then realized that wasn't an official answer. He was feeling less and less official as this so-called mission went on. He should have felt more efficient. He had originally designed this mission to return to Captain Jonathon Cooper, and instead, he was getting farther away from that man.

Then he glanced at Rossetti. She flanked him, and gave him a look too. Funny how it bothered him that she couldn't see him, but it didn't bother him when others couldn't see his expression.

"Yes," he said in his captain's voice. "We're evacuating."

He knew the others in his crew heard this, but he added something for Anita, just to be clear, "Anita, I want you to handle this. We need all non-essential personnel off this base as quickly as possible."

"I'm not sure what's essential," she said.

"Leave the team that's with me, and everyone else can go," Coop said. "Yash, did you hear that? Get Dix out of there."

"Not possible, Captain," Yash said.

Coop's stomach clenched. What had Dix done?

"Take him out physically if you have to," Coop said.

"We'll be taking the *anacapa* too, then," she said. "He won't let it go."

"We can't leave it," Coop said, hoping that Dix was listening in.

"Coop!" Dix had been listening. He sounded drunk, even though Coop knew he wasn't. "We can recreate the scenario now. Get those Enterran people to hit this thing with one of their weapons as we activate it. That should work."

"It won't work, Dix," Coop said, feeling tired. "A combination of two *anacapas* and a shot from a weapon that no longer exists sent us here. There's no guarantee that any of that will work on the way back."

"I think it will," Dix said.

"You're evacuating the starbase, Dix," Coop said. "Whether you want to or not."

"Fine," Dix said. "Just make sure someone hits this weapon at the right time."

Coop put his gloved hand against the wall for a brief moment, and then closed his eyes.

"You all right, Captain?" Rossetti asked.

No, he wasn't all right. He had made the wrong choice to come here, it had had the wrong effect on him, and now he was going to have to do things he didn't want to do.

"I'm just fine," he lied, and climbed the rest of the way up the stairs.

10

THE FIRST THING COOP SAW as he stepped onto the *anacapa* control level were the doors his team had propped open. The civilian saw them too. He ran forward, arms extended, as if he had found a holy shrine.

He would have disappeared through the first set of doors if Coop hadn't hurried to keep up with him.

"Oh, my God," the civilian said. "Oh, my God."

His exclamations got louder as he stopped in front of the second door. The *anacapa* control room spread before him.

Coop tried to see it through the civilian's eyes, and realized he couldn't. To Coop, this broad expanse of room, with its warship landing area and its intact equipment, was the most familiar part of Starbase Kappa. It looked like part of a starbase in flux, not like a place that had been abandoned for five millennia.

But to this civilian, the *anacapa* control room had to seem completely strange. The civilian had only known Starbase Kappa as the ghostly Room of Lost Souls, empty rooms, with nothing more than a still-active piece of equipment that mysteriously killed people.

Now the civilian saw the working heart of the starbase, technology beyond his imaginings, and it had to be overwhelming.

He went around and around in circles, head up, then down, like a child spinning for joy. Although he wasn't spinning for joy so much as trying to take it all in.

"What *is* this place?" the civilian asked. "There's *equipment* in here."

The two soldiers who were supposed to guard him hung back. The room clearly scared them. But they didn't say anything. They just watched, overwhelmed and on alert.

Coop ignored them, and focused on his people. The team he had taken to the landing area had followed him up here, and joined Yash, Lalliki, and six others who still hadn't evacuated. Those eight formed a half-circle around Dix, who was still arm-deep into the *anacapa* drive.

He grinned when he saw Coop.

"We can *do* this," Dix said on the private channel. "I know we can."

Coop wasn't sure how to answer him.

"I think the only way we can remove Dix is to hurt him," Yash said on a different channel, "and I'm not sure exactly how to do that. I'm afraid there will be an effect with the *anacapa*."

"What *is* this place?" the civilian asked again. He had stopped moving and faced Coop. Clearly, the civilian wanted answers.

"Layla," Coop said on the private channel, "would you show our visitor the equipment. Don't explain it. Pretend like we just found it too. I also want them to think that Dix is trapped in that drive."

"I'm not trapped," Dix said. "I'm just not going to let go."

"I know that," Coop said.

Lalliki approached the civilian and touched him on the shoulder. He glanced at her gratefully. Clearly this civilian expected full cooperation from her. It was as if the man had never experienced a hostile situation.

Maybe he hadn't.

But Coop's people had. His soldiers spread out along the wall, preparing for anything.

Coop went over to Dix and crouched in front of him, like he had done before. The interior light from the *anacapa* was still on, and Coop could see Dix's face. He looked exhausted and exhilarated at the same time.

"These people are from the Empire that Boss doesn't like, Dix," Coop said softly. "They're not going to cooperate with us."

"Not willingly," Dix said, "but I know how to make this work."

Coop sighed. He was tired of the disjointed thrum of the *anacapa*, tired of the people around him, tired of the failed attempt at regaining that sense of himself that he'd had before entering this sector seven months and five thousand years ago.

He was also tired of crazy.

Dix's eyes were too bright. "We'll give the *anacapa* to these Empire people. They won't know how to shut it off. We get the *Ivoire* here, we rig the transport to hit the *Ivoire's anacapa* with just the right shot, and then we're home."

Coop opened his mouth to tell Dix all the reasons this wouldn't work, and paused.

It would get Dix away from the *anacapa*, and that was step one.

"Great idea, Dix," Coop said.

"Captain," Rossetti said, "the *Ivoire*—"

"Let the *Ivoire* know what we need," Coop said to Rossetti, with emphasis. He hoped she understood what he was talking about. Because Dix had either not heard or forgotten the order to take the *Ivoire* out of the system. "We're going to follow First Officer Pompliono's plan."

Rossetti froze for just a moment, then moved her head as if she were shaking off a comment. Then she said in a voice Coop had never heard before, "Yes sir."

"Get that *anacapa* out of the casing," Coop said to Dix. "Yash, help him with that."

"Captain?" Yash said. He could hear the unasked question in her voice. *Should I wrestle it away from him?*

"One step at a time, Yash," Coop said, hoping that Dix wouldn't understand.

Then Coop stood. He said through his headphone speaker, "Um, Mister Vilhauser, is it?"

The civilian stopped the moment Coop spoke his name. He came toward Coop, still too eager. Coop resisted the urge to look at the man's oxygen tank.

"It's *Doctor* Vilhauser," the civilian said, but without rancor. He was correcting a colleague.

Coop smiled, keeping up the fiction, hoping the fake smile would sound real in his voice. "We have no interest in this equipment here. If you want your people to take care of it, we can help you with that. It seems that the equipment my first officer is dealing with is still operational. He can shut it off and give it to you."

The civilian looked stunned. He glanced at the soldiers who had accompanied him, and then back at Coop.

"You would do that?'

Coop gave what he now thought of as his signature shrug. "We have no use for this stuff."

"Coop," Dix said on the private channel. "I'm not going to shut this off."

"He knows that," Rossetti said so Coop didn't have to. "He's gambling this idiot won't know the difference."

"How do you know how these things work?" the civilian asked.

"It seems pretty straightforward," Coop said. "We've shut others off all over the sector."

"There are *others*?" The civilian was practically drooling.

"Not anymore. We have some, we destroyed some. You seem so interested that we figured we can just give this to you." Coop felt very calm about lying to this man. He wasn't sure why. "Consider it a goodwill gesture."

"Vilhauser," one of the soldiers said, "You need to check this with Operations Commander Trekov."

"No, I don't," Vilhauser said. "This is a scientific mission under my direction. You people aren't in charge. And this is a boon to the Empire."

Then he whirled, apparently realizing he had spoken through the public channels, not the private.

"And, uh, we—ah—we're grateful," he said to Coop. The civilian nodded at the *anacapa*. "Can we just carry that?"

"Yeah," Dix said. "Let me give it to you."

He stood, cradling the drive. It had to feel bulky and heavy. Coop had never held an active drive. It probably vibrated, too. He wasn't quite sure how Dix managed to keep his arms around it.

"Better yet," Yash said, "let's put it in here."

She emptied her equipment case. It didn't protect against the effects of the *anacapa*—it wasn't designed for that—but it looked official.

On the private channel, Dix said, "Engineer Zarlengo, let's do it my way."

"The case locks, Dix," Yash said on the same channel. "They won't be able to mess with the lock, even if they want to."

Then she glanced at Coop, as if expecting him to resolve this.

But he didn't have to. Dix set the *anacapa* in the case. Yash shut it, locked it, and then picked it up. It took both hands.

She extended the case to the civilian. "Be careful," she said. "These things can be tricky."

He took the case. "We know," he said in that much too eager voice.

Then he cradled the case to his chest and walked toward the main door, still a bit bouncy.

"Let's go," he said to the two soldiers who were supposed to guard him.

"But the commander—"

"She'll understand." He looked over his shoulder at Coop, the civilian clearly trying hard not to grin. "You'll evacuate like you said, right?"

"We gave you our word that we were leaving," Coop said.

"You still haven't shown me how to work the door," the civilian said.

"We'll leave it open," Coop said. "And unlocked."

This time, the civilian nodded. He seemed to have forgotten his desire to learn how the door worked now that he had the *anacapa* in his grasp.

It had been a long time since Coop had seen someone both this greedy and gullible. Coop had never been able to use both to his advantage before.

"Thank you," the civilian said, and bounced his way out of the room.

"Now," Dix said on the private channel, "all we need is the *Ivoire* and we're ready."

Coop glanced at him. Dix had believed all of this too.

"The first step is to get to the transport," Coop said on the same channel.

"Don't we want to go to the *Ivoire*?" Dix asked. He really wasn't thinking clearly. How long had he been this off?

"We don't want them to see it, Dix," Coop said gently. "They'll become even more suspicious than they are."

"Oh yeah." Dix's voice had a creepy tone that Coop hadn't heard before. "Then let's get the hell out of here."

Coop couldn't agree more. He signaled his team to leave the room and head for the transport.

"Close the door after us," he said to Yash. "And make sure shutdown protocols are in place."

She nodded.

"Won't they notice?" Dix asked, sounding worried.

"Believe me, Dix," Coop said, "they're not going to notice a damn thing."

11

THEY GOT DIX onto the transport first. Coop didn't have to tell Lal-liki to keep an eye on Dix; she already was.

Coop's entire team moved fast. They went through the airlock, closed the exterior doors, waited the requisite few minutes, then hurried inside the transport, each moving to their usual station.

Coop went to the cockpit. It was crammed with unnecessary personnel. But Anita was here, and, after a moment, Yash joined them. Windows on three sides were clear, and the screens were up, showing the entire station and the Empire's ship.

It was larger than Coop thought it would be, about half the size of the *Ivoire*. Unlike the *Ivoire,* the ship was long rather than wide.

"They're having a hell of an argument," Anita said. "I've tapped into their comm. You want to hear it?"

Coop looked at the images on the screen. Three people stood on the lower landing area to the Room of Lost Souls. One was crouched.

"No, I don't need to hear," Coop said. "They're not letting him onto their ship, right?"

"That's right," Anita said. "They're afraid he's too close now. They're telling him that the stealth tech is creating a field near their ship and he has to leave it behind. He's telling them he can shut it off, and he's trying to open Yash's case."

"Let them worry about that, then," Coop said. "We need to get out of here."

"You're going to leave them with the *anacapa*?" Anita asked.

"No," Coop said. "You're going to give me the controls."

She moved aside, and as she did, the door to the cockpit slid open.

"Where's the *Ivoire*?" Dix said. "You promised the *Ivoire* would be here."

"The *Ivoire* won't be back for—what is it, Anita? Four hours?" Coop settled into the pilot's chair.

"About that," Anita said.

"You promised!" Dix said. "We need the *Ivoire*."

"Get him out of here," Coop said. He bent over the controls.

Dix yelled in the background, mostly shouting Coop's name, shouting that he'd promised, that someone should stop Coop because Coop had lied to all of them.

Coop hit the controls, taking the transport slowly away from the starbase. He slapped his palm on the comm, activating it. "I want everyone to strap in. This won't be fun."

Dix was still yelling, but Coop wouldn't turn around.

"I can't get him out of here, Captain," someone said. Coop didn't recognize the voice without looking.

"Then strap him in here," Coop said.

"Nooooo!" Dix said, and something banged behind Coop. "You can't do this."

Actually, *no one else* could do this. Oh, Coop supposed almost anyone in the team could follow his orders, but he didn't want them to. It wasn't right. He'd gotten them into this mess. He was going to get them out.

He set the target, and he set the speed. Then he waited until the transport was at the edge of the weapons range.

"They stopped arguing," Anita said. "They've powered up their ship. I think they're coming after us, Captain."

"I don't think so." Coop felt calm. In fact, he hadn't felt this calm in months. "I think they're getting their ship away from the *anacapa* drive."

And that was smart, especially if most people on board that ship did not have the genetic marker. They were worried that the so-called stealth tech emanating from that container would kill everyone without a marker.

"I thought you wanted to target all of them," Anita said, and he smiled just a little. His staff knew him. He hadn't said anything about targeting anyone.

"Coop, you can't!" Dix said. "You can't!"

The transport reached the very edge of the range. Coop slammed both hands onto the controls. One palm hit the speed setting while the other sent every weapon the transport had at the landing deck of Starbase Kappa.

"Coop, nooooo!" Dix screamed.

The transport went from a cruising speed to its maximum in less than a second. Everyone got knocked back, even Coop. He had plugged in coordinates near the *Ivoire's* last position.

At that moment, the weapons' fire hit the landing deck. It exploded. Starbase Kappa pinwheeled away, mostly intact, but bits scattered. Coop wasn't close enough to see, but he knew what it was: pieces of the starbase, pieces of Yash's case, pieces of the civilian and his two guards.

The wave from the *anacapa* wasn't visible, but it hit them all the same, loud and screeching and heart-pounding. Coop had been hit with a destroyed *anacapa* wave in an unprotected environment in the past before and it had felt awful. The scientists didn't know why, and until this moment, he hadn't cared.

He gripped the seat.

He couldn't see the wave move outward from the explosion, but he knew it had, and he knew that the Empire ship wasn't out of range. It bobbled, then rolled, and then floated, as all of its systems died.

The Fleet's transport ships had been built to survive an outside *anacapa* explosion. No ship in Boss's universe had been built that way. The wave would continue outward and would probably hit all of the Empire ships guarding this part of space. It wouldn't take out any other ships, since the Empire ships were keeping interlopers out of here.

Coop stared at the Enterran ship for a moment. Its commander had had the right idea; she had just been too late. He felt for her. She had been in the wrong place at the wrong moment. He had known that the second he saw her, and he had known he couldn't warn her.

He found a stable orbit near a moon not far from the site where the *Ivoire* would return. He kept the cloak on.

His crew said nothing. Even Dix had grown silent.

Coop ran a hand through his hair and turned around.

Dix looked like he had died along with the *anacapa* drive. His eyes were sunken, his lips bleeding where he'd clearly bitten them.

"Do you know what you've done?" he asked, his voice hoarse.

"Yes," Coop said. He sounded firm and confident, and like the captain he had once been.

The cockpit crew stared at him with the same expression Dix had. Apparently they had all held on to a bit of hope. Maybe they had thought that the insane scheme that Dix had come up with would reverse the circumstances of their journey into the future, and send them back to the proper place in the past.

Even Coop had felt that hope, not as a real thing, but as a pressure.

He had destroyed the pressure.

But unlike the crew, he wasn't feeling sad. He was feeling alive, for the first time since he got here.

He hadn't resurrected Captain Jonathon Cooper of the Fleet. That man was gone. But he had found a new man, Coop Cooper, who captained the *Ivoire*.

He had done what he set out to do. He had destroyed the malfunctioning *anacapa*. No one would die in this area of space ever again because of his people.

And he had kept his promise to Boss. The Empire didn't know about the *Ivoire* or his working *anacapa* drive.

His first mission in this new place had been a success after all. Just not the kind of success he had expected it to be.

Dix's lower lip was trembling. His eyes were filled with tears. He was shaking his head.

"We're never going to go home again, Coop. Never. The circumstances will never, ever be right again."

They hadn't been right this time either. Coop had argued that and argued that. So had his engineers and scientists. But apparently no one had believed them.

"I know," Coop said. "This is our home now. This place. Our training taught us how to move forward. It's time we do that."

"I can't," Dix said.

"You will," Coop said.

They needed time to mourn their lost lives. But first, they had to accept that their past lives were lost. He had helped them with that this day. That was the greatest success of the mission, the fact that it had exploded the false hope along with the damaged *anacapa*.

It had helped him. And now that he was back on firm footing, footing he understood, he would be able to help them too.

The *Ivoire* had been missing its leader. He was back now, and he would make the best choices he could.

The first thing he was going to do was return to the Nine Planets. Now the fight against the Empire was his as well as theirs. His actions against the Empire would be seen as an attack. He would take the blame for that, just like he would take the blame for destroying his crew's hope.

He had broad shoulders.

And it was time he finally used them.

THE STANDOFF
NOW

12

COOP PACED ON THE BRIDGE. He had his hands clasped behind him, and he walked. Fortunately, the *Ivoire's* bridge had a lot of room. He would peer at the consoles his bridge crew worked, absorbing the work little bit by little bit.

It didn't help him.

Boss and her team hadn't yet sent word of what they were doing.

Even though Coop had talked to her about the importance of quick action, he worried she hadn't heard him. She talked with him about the necessity of doing the correct dive, of making certain her people made it through everything, of the caution diving required.

He remembered how she had explored the sector base nearly six years ago, back when he had met her, and he knew she was doing the same thing in the Boneyard. A few hours in, most of a day out, acquiring information through a slow drip.

He wanted her to act quicker.

He wanted her to show up here, now, with a dozen working Fleet ships.

Not that it would be possible for her to do that. Even if she found a dozen working Fleet ships, he didn't have the crews to work them. His crew had trained hundreds of people at Lost Souls in the mechanics of the *Ivoire* and the *Shadow*, but understanding how things worked and actually making them work were two different things.

And then there was the question of a lifetime of military training. Almost no one outside the *Ivoire's* crew had it at Lost Souls, and he didn't know how to impart it.

He knew that he was having a rescue fantasy. He'd had it before—suddenly the Fleet would find the *Ivoire* and bring them back to their time—and he knew it for the impossibility it was.

Every few minutes, he would stop at his command chair and look at the sensor screen he had up.

The Enterran Empire ships remained along the border. Five warships, five battle cruisers, and five support ships that could probably double as battle ships, if need be. The ships also remained cloaked, but he had a hunch they knew that *he* knew they were there.

He had a hunch they were waiting for him to do something. Back off? Attack them? Confront them?

He had no idea.

He also had no idea what to do about them. He had no battle plan, no future plan, no way of knowing what was best.

Just his rescue fantasy, which was absolutely worthless.

"Captain," said Second Engineer Zaria Diaz, "I have something. I have no idea if it means anything."

Something was better than nothing, but he didn't say that. He walked over to her station, hands still clasped behind him. He towered over her, but it didn't seem to bother her.

Of course, most people towered over her, so she was probably used to that.

"What do you have?" he asked, wishing, hoping, praying it was something he could use.

"We have a voice print match."

Whatever he had expected, it hadn't been that.

"A what?" he asked.

"We've encountered one of these commanders before," Diaz said.

"*We* have?" Coop asked.

She nodded.

He was trying to remember talking with any commanders when they had destroyed the ships near the research facility. He hadn't. His people had had contact with others on the facility, but he couldn't imagine his team having time to take voice prints.

"Where?" he asked.

"Starbase Kappa," she said. "Remember that? You spoke to a woman there. She seemed to be in charge."

He straightened. The soldier with short hair. Young, thin mouth. She'd tried to prevent her stupid scientist from messing up the first contact, but he had pushed.

In fact, that stupid scientist had gotten a lot of people killed.

Or so Coop thought. He hadn't seen anything about it—he'd even had some of his people check, years later of course. The Empire didn't report a lost ship or a lot of deaths, but that didn't mean anything. Often big governments tried to keep their losses quiet.

He had also seen nothing about the so-called Room of Lost Souls. He probably should have asked Boss's friend Turtle about it. Turtle seemed to know all sorts of things she shouldn't have known, like how to find Boss in an emergency. That made him leery of Turtle, but it also made her useful.

"You're certain this is the woman?" he asked Diaz.

"We have her voice from before," Diaz said. "We have a lot of her voice then, and a lot now. I've checked and double-checked."

"Do we know who she is?" Coop asked.

"I'm guessing," Diaz said, "but from the content of her conversation, I think she might be in charge of this whole mission."

Coop frowned at the array of ships before him. Still cloaked, still waiting.

If indeed that woman was in charge of this mission, then she had more information than he was comfortable with. He had kept his promise to Boss; no one had seen the *Ivoire*. But that woman had known that Coop's people were able to get around on Starbase Kappa, that they attacked for no reason, and that they used a weapon the woman didn't understand.

Coop had deliberately killed her scientist, probably destroyed or seriously damaged Starbase Kappa, and harmed several ships.

He was, in fact, amazed she had survived. "What kind of information do we have about Starbase Kappa after we left?"

"I'll look," Diaz said.

"I want you to continue monitoring everything here," Coop said. "Get someone else to look. And have that person double-check the voice prints. Also, see if we have a name for this woman, and if so, figure out just who she is. Not just her position now, but how she got here, what her past actually is."

"Are we looking for something special, Captain?" Diaz asked.

He frowned at those ships, displayed on his screen. He wasn't sure how to answer her. He had a feeling, a worry.

"I want to know if she tracked us here."

"That's not possible, sir," Diaz said.

He wasn't quite sure what Diaz was thinking of. An exact tracking wouldn't be possible. But putting together clues might be.

"Get me that history," he said.

He needed to know if she was here to attack the Nine Planets or if she was here to confiscate his ship.

An hour ago, he would have thought she was the first wave of an invasion force against the Nine Planets.

Now, he wasn't so sure.

THE FIRST SKIRMISH

ABOUT FOUR YEARS EARLIER

13

OPERATIONS COMMANDER ELISSA TREKOV saw the weapons' fire first. It came from what to her eyes looked like a blank spot on the screens in front of her. Fortunately, the *Discovery's* sensors saw through the cloak that created that blank spot to the transport vessel that had left just moments ago.

She bent over the controls on the bridge of the *Discovery,* not because she was flying the large science ship, but because she was arguing with the three people she had just left on the Room of Lost Souls. She still wore her environmental suit, even though she had removed the bubble helmet. It rested on the seat behind her.

She hadn't had time to remove the suit because that damn Vilhauser, on the station, wasn't listening to her.

But if she hadn't been bent over, essentially hogging two stations while the bridge crew tried to work around her, she wouldn't have seen the weapons' fire from the transport vessel. Those flashes of light had given her just a few precious seconds to make a decision.

She hoped it was enough time.

Thank God she had ordered the *Discovery* to detach from the lower landing area on the Room of Lost Souls. She had planned to leave Vilhauser behind, along with two very good soldiers, because the idiot scientist wasn't listening to her, and his actions threatened her crew.

Now there was a second threat—the weapons' fire, cool and white across the dark starscape.

The betraying bastard who commanded that transport vessel had waited until his ship was as close to the edge of his firing range as possible. Those shots would take only seconds to arrive, but those seconds were enough.

"Calthorpe, activate the stardrive!" she said, as her gloved hand slapped the emergency beacon. They were going to need help, and she wanted to make sure they got it—even before she got the *Discovery* out of here.

Her first fucking solo command, and she wasn't sure the ship would survive it. She could've handled one threat, but not two. There was Vilhauser and the damn device, and now that betraying bastard on the transport had decided to get involved.

She had no idea what would happen if the transport's weapons' fire missed the *Discovery* and hit the Room of Lost Souls.

And she didn't want to find out.

The bridge crew hung back more than she would like, but half of that was her fault. An operations commander usually didn't take over the controls of a ship. Technically, she wasn't in command of this ship. Sub-Commander Calthorpe was.

And she had just relegated him to navigation.

To his credit, he didn't complain.

Not that he could, when his ranking officer was effectively taking over his command. He hadn't complained when she opted to go the Room of Lost Souls, either. He hadn't even cautioned her, although he had given her a look that had chilled her.

Not because he was angry at her, but because he didn't approve.

So many people didn't approve of the way she commanded anything.

And now, she was going to get in trouble for everything she had done—unless she got the *Discovery* out of here.

The weapons' fire slammed into the lower level of the Room of Lost Souls, slicing off the landing area. Bright white light nearly blinded Elissa, and she would have ordered the crew to dim the screen but they were already ahead of her.

The *Discovery*'s stardrive kicked in, and she let out a small breath. Not only would they get away from the debris field, but they would get away from the transport before the betraying bastard realized that his shots had missed their target.

Then something hit her ship, rocking it and knocking out all the lights. She went from leaning on the console to falling away from it and slamming into the ceiling.

Sudden zero-g. She activated the gravity in her boots—or tried to. Nothing happened.

Things hit her—people, pieces of equipment. She had set down the suit's helmet and now it had to be among the things floating around in the darkness.

She could breathe, but her chest—her entire body, really—felt odd, as if it had been electrified. Her heart shivered—literally shivered—before returning to its usual rhythm.

Around her, she heard gasps and cries and echoey bangs as people hit things. She reached up and grabbed on to something on the wall/ceiling/floor nearest her. The first thing she had to do was orient herself.

As she held on, she realized that the ship—this very large ship—was rolling over and over and over again, like an out-of-control children's toy. She had been floating free, moving with her own momentum; the stuff around her was moving at a different pace, and the ship was moving too.

Only its movements were even less predictable because it had just activated the stardrive, and then the whatever hit them and pushed them in yet another direction. Because Elissa was effectively blind to the exterior of her ship, she had no idea if something big in the debris field was going to hit her or not.

Something big like the Room of Lost Souls itself.

Son of a bitch. That betraying bastard hadn't missed. He had deliberately targeted Vilhauser, and the resulting explosion had caused this ripple.

The thought hit the forefront of her brain, a grasp for understanding and nothing more. And that was all she needed.

She couldn't focus on what had happened. She needed to focus on what was about to happen.

She had to save this ship and everyone on it.

"Grab something stable!" she yelled. "Grab something stable right now!"

She had to get the crew thinking, because she doubted there was enough time to do much else.

Right now, the ship had oxygen and the temperature was reasonable. The gravity was gone, and so far as she could tell, everything—all of the equipment—had been shut down.

The backups on her suit weren't working, not that she had access to all of them. Some of them were in the stupid helmet, which of course, she couldn't see.

There was ambient light, however, because the crew had turned the windows to clear. Something was glowing from outside the ship, providing some light inside the bridge.

It had just taken time for her eyes to adjust.

She could see shapes, and little else. Unidentifiable material of all sizes floated around her.

People were easier to see—long bodies, limbs flailing, reaching for something to grab on to.

Thank God bridge crews had mandatory loss-of-gravity training exercises. The crew knew how to handle this.

Although, when she ran the exercises, she had never shut the lights and power off at the same time. And, dammit, neither had her instructors, which meant that no one else's instructors had done so either.

She hoped to hell that emergency beacon she'd sent had reached the fighters and transports she'd sent for earlier. Even though she had asked them to remain out of range, they might have seen the explosion. With luck, someone would be here soon.

She let out a small breath, her throat sore even though she hadn't been yelling. Everything about her body, not just her heart, felt off. Whatever had affected the systems had had an impact on her as well.

Which meant that it had done the same to her crew.

She hoped that whatever it was had a localized effect, because if it didn't, it would move outward as a wave. Which meant it would hit everything in its path—the fighters, the transports, everything.

But not the squadron, right? It was too far away.

She was guessing. But the guessing gave her some comfort. Because if the whatever had moved out as a wave, it would dissipate, and its effects wouldn't be as severe farther away from the actual explosion itself.

Besides, the distress beacon could be received all over the sector. Even away from her squadron.

She hoped.

Because her ship needed rescue quickly.

It needed rescue now.

14

ELISSA'S OWN MOMENTUM HAD STOPPED. Now she was moving with the ship itself. She could feel it turn. It also groaned, and that sound worried her more than anything. Something was bending, shifting, twisting, and that wasn't good.

She wondered if there had been a hull breach on any of the levels. If so, then the atmosphere would dissipate in the bridge a lot more quickly. The problem was, she didn't have a way of examining the hull, not with everything shut down.

She held on to something jutting out of the wall/ceiling/floor. She couldn't quite tell, but she knew that she was probably nowhere near the consoles, since this jutting thing was unprotected. She had felt the wall/ceiling/floor around it, and realized the jut was intentional. Which meant that she was clinging to something a human wasn't meant to get near in a traditional workday on the bridge.

"Everyone found something to hang on to?" she asked.

No one answered her. She still saw limbs flailing in that twilight, and then someone floated by.

She couldn't be the only person still alive, could she? She was the only one in an environmental suit, but her helmet had floated past her twice, and the human head was a vulnerable thing. If the whatever that had hit after the explosion had killed people without environmental suits, then it should have killed her, too.

She had to assume her crew—her well-trained crew—was in shock.

"Speak to me, people," she said, her voice calmer than she felt. Her heart still seemed off. It trembled, even though it was beating, and her stomach was—well, the only word she could use was itchy. Even her skin felt crawly, like she had walked into a super-charged room.

That thought made her shivers grow worse. Only the new shivers were real ones—shivers from an emotional reaction, not from something happening to her.

"I…I'm okay." The female voice sounded uncertain, and Elissa couldn't identify it.

It wasn't like her crew to be shaken up, even by a disaster of this magnitude. She didn't like it.

"Let's try this," Elissa said. "I want names, then condition."

After that, she would worry about location, assignments, and getting this ship working again. One thing at a time.

It would calm all of them—including her.

"Lieutenant Homer Ryder, ma'am." Ryder's voice sounded strong, but it echoed in the quiet. "I'm bruised and banged up, I might have a broken ankle, but I think I'm all right. I've had worse, ma'am."

Elissa let out a small breath. She had expected injuries. She just hoped they wouldn't be too severe.

"Lieutenant Nisha Lee." Lee didn't sound as strong. Her voice had a rasp to it. "I hit my head, ma'am, but I don't think I have a concussion. I'm a little dizzy, but I expect that to pass. I also dislocated my shoulder, but I managed to fix it."

Elissa winced. She knew how painful shoving a shoulder back in the socket could be. She had no idea how someone achieved that in zero-g, but apparently Lee had.

"Officer Phoebe Gatson." There was the faint voice that had spoken a few moments ago, the voice that Elissa hadn't been able to place. "I got a few cuts, but I stopped the bleeding. I don't think anything major is wrong, but I tell you, my body feels like it's been through some kind of super-charged environment."

That feeling that Elissa had. Apparently Gatson shared it.

"Me too," Lee said.

"Yeah," Ryder added. "Whatever hit us had some kind of physical component." Then he caught his breath as if he realized what he'd said. "I mean, it affected our bodies, not—"

"I know what you mean, Lieutenant," Elissa said, "and I'm feeling the same way. And like you, I'm convinced it came from that thing that hit us."

"I feel dizzy too, ma'am. Officer Alistair Binek," he added that last as if he wasn't sure she would recognize his voice. She did. "And I'm pretty sure I cracked a rib. Nothing serious. I can breathe just fine."

"I think I broke a few ribs," said a new female voice. "Provisional Lois Baxter, ma'am. I'm breathing all right, and I don't think my lungs are damaged. I suspect I'll feel this more when the gravity comes back."

Baxter was the only Provi on the bridge crew, and one of Elissa's best crew members, even though—or maybe because—she had worked her way up through the ranks.

"With luck, Provi," Elissa said, "we'll have the gravity on soon, and someone medical will be able to ease the pain."

"It's not a problem right now, ma'am," Baxter said.

Her crew was doing its best to convince her that they were fine. But she heard something in the voices, something that told her they were not fine, any more than she was.

"Officer Malachi Locke, ma'am. I'm pretty sure my right arm is broken, maybe in more than one place. But I'm functional, especially while the gravity is off." Locke sounded almost cheerful, so Elissa knew it was a front.

She was about to respond when one more voice spoke up, sounding shaky.

"Officer Sepp Trombino, ma'am. I had a bloody nose but I don't think it's broken. I've had a broken nose. I know what it feels like, and this isn't it. My body has that same uncomfortable feeling everyone else has described, but I'm good to go, ma'am."

She smiled. Trombino was one of her more gung-ho officers, but he often complained his way through things. She didn't mind right now. They all had reason to complain.

She went over the responses in her head. Seven responses. She should have had eight.

"What about Calthorpe?" Elissa made sure her voice remained steady as she asked about the only person who hadn't checked in.

She waited, watching the shadowy things float past her. Unidentifiable, even by shape. She couldn't tell, but it seemed like the flare from outside the ship was fading as well.

"Anyone? Is Calthorpe near you? Did he hit his head? Is he unconscious?"

"Someone keeps bumping me," Ryder said from across the bridge. His voice echoed just a bit.

Now that she had asked everyone to identify themselves, she could recognize voices, even when they sounded just a bit off. She was beginning to think that whatever happened had affected her hearing as well.

Or maybe it had had the same impact on her brain as it had had on her heart.

That made her shiver yet again.

"Some*one*?" she asked.

"Yes, ma'am," Ryder said, his voice even. She didn't hear uncertainty in him or even distress. And she should have heard distress, since he believed he had broken his ankle. "First, some fabric brushed my face, and then a little while later, I felt skin."

That turned her stomach, and it shouldn't have. She was usually made of stronger stuff than that.

"Anyone think that it might've been you bumping into Lieutenant Ryder?" she asked. "Anyone?"

"We all banged around a lot, ma'am," Binek said. "I know I hit a lot of stuff at first. Might've been people, ma'am."

A chorus of voices added their agreement.

"Since that initial explosion, has anyone brushed up against a fellow crew member?" Elissa asked, realizing that everyone's brains were working too slowly. She had never encountered this before. It put the entire ship at even more of a disadvantage.

No one answered her with an affirmative. No one answered that question at all.

She took a deep breath and let it out. Was it her imagination, or was the air noticeably cooler than it had been a few minutes before?

"All right," she said. "We're going to have to assume that Calthorpe is unconscious. If he floats past anyone, please find a way to ground him."

She was still shivering. Shock? She hoped not. She didn't need it, not right now. She needed to be clear. They all needed to be clear.

"Now," she said, "we need to get near the console. We need to turn lights and atmosphere back on. Then we need to assess the damage."

Something banged far away, as if it came from outside and was echoing through the ship. She could feel a vibration through her hand.

It couldn't be one of the fighters. She would have seen its lights through the portal, right? Besides, it was too soon for one to get here.

Or maybe her sense of time was off.

She made herself take a deep breath.

If the Room had exploded, then there was a lot of junk out there. Even if it hadn't, there would still be some parts—not to mention bits of Vilhauser and her two excellent soldiers—floating near the ship.

Plus, that device, that malfunctioning device that had caused her to separate from the Room in the first place, might not have come apart in the explosion. She had no idea what that device was, and she had no idea what it could do.

Everything was supposition at this point.

Everything.

Including their odds for survival.

15

THE CREW WAS USED TO WORKING IN ZERO-G, but they were used to working in zero-g while lights were on. They hadn't had drills for working in near-darkness since she had been on board, and maybe some of them never had.

One of Elissa's officer training instructors had run the class through darkness drills. Elissa had found them disconcerting. Several talented officer recruits actually washed out because of those drills. Those recruits had hated working in those conditions, and one of them even demanded that the instructor guarantee they would never encounter such a thing.

He had laughed. *Clearly,* he said, *you've never been in battle.*

Elissa had been in battle many times, and she'd even commanded disabled ships, but nothing like this.

She had to squint to locate what she believed to be the ship's consoles. The light coming through the windows was fading, and soon they would only have starlight to work from, and not much of that.

She had learned a zero-g trick as a child. She closed her eyes and mentally erased any effect of gravity. That wiped out the so-called rule that the console had to be on the floor, the windows on the wall, and nothing on the ceiling.

She got rid of concepts like floor and ceiling altogether.

Her ability to mentally erase gravity had made her stand out when the officer training had moved from zero-g with a ship whose attitude controls were working to a ship whose attitude controls had malfunctioned.

She used those skills now, while the rest of her crew probably struggled with attempting to mentally map the actual layout of the slowly rotating ship.

She let go of the jutting thing and floated toward what she believed were the consoles. She grabbed a rounded edge and pulled herself in. Yep, these were the consoles. They had always had a slight vibration as power thrummed through them.

They had no vibration now.

She used one hand to hold herself above the consoles, and then she counted the edges from her spot.

The console wasn't one big piece of equipment, but several pieces, and if she knew where she was among those pieces, then she knew what faced her on those dark boards.

Lieutenant Nisha Lee joined her. Elissa knew it was Lee, not because of her small size—several of the bridge crew were small—but because of the faint jasmine perfume she always wore. The scent was mixed with sweat now, and probably a hint of anxiety, but Lee said nothing.

She was using both arms, so that dislocated shoulder truly had gone back into its socket.

Two other crew members floated down from various positions and found a place beside Elissa. She cared less about who they were than what they could do.

She was in front of navigation.

"Lieutenant," she said to Lee, "I believe you have the environmental systems."

"I know, ma'am." Lee held her position with one hand and moved the other on the console. She sounded distracted, but Elissa wasn't sure if that was because she was ignoring the radiating pain in her shoulder or because she had other problems.

Elissa could orient the ship with this part of the console. She moved her fingers up, searching for the raised controls. They should have popped up the moment the lights went out.

But they hadn't. The console felt flat and useless under her hands.

"Commander," said Trombino. He was the person who ended up beside her on the left. "Nothing raised up here. This console still is on standard control."

"This one too," Lee said.

"And this one," said Gatson. She was one console over from Trombino. "I'm already under—if that's the word—trying to manually activate. Nothing wants to work, ma'am."

Nothing wants to work. Of course not. They weren't going to catch a break.

"Do what you can," Elissa said. "The same with the rest of you. I'll move to the door controls."

A small backup control unit was built into the wall beside the door. To the untrained observer, the backup control didn't do much. But everyone on the bridge knew that the cover plate could be removed, and with a passcode typed into a keypad, an override system could be activated. The keypad was manual, meaning that it operated on a spring rather than a computer.

Only ten members of the crew had that passcode. Two of those people had to be on the bridge at all times. It was an order that most ship commanders ignored, and indeed, had the explosion happened while Elissa was coming back from the Room, only Calthorpe would have had that code.

Elissa moved to the door. Beyond it, she heard more groaning from the ship herself. She didn't like it. Nothing on the other side of that door should've been subjected to the kind of stress that caused that noise.

She made herself focus. Her fingers found the ridge in the wall beside the door. She dug her nails under the edge, then pulled. The control panel opened easily.

Just for the heck of it, she tried to turn on the lights from here. She pressed the familiar depression on the panel, and—nothing happened. She let out a small sigh, as silently as she could. She wasn't frustrated, not really, but she was growing worried.

She removed the panel, holding it in one hand as she typed on the keypad with the other. The controls eased out of their holder, and her shaky heart sped up. She recognized the feeling for what it was: a surge of adrenaline mixed with hope.

Her fingers slid along the raised control panel. The pattern was familiar. Every commander had been taught to do this one blind. Someone figured that a commander might have to do this behind her back or sideways or upside down, often without seeing what she was doing.

Sometimes the in-the-field experience *did* make it to training.

She activated the panel, worried slightly that the internal lights on the panel itself didn't come on, then decided to ignore that. She didn't care as long as she managed to get the systems working inside the bridge again.

She hit the switches, then looked over her shoulder.

The twilight seemed dimmer—she had been right; that flare was fading—but she could see her crew, staring at her.

"Well?" she asked, and her voice had bit more edge than she wanted it to.

She saw Lee swivel slightly, focus on the console in front of her, and move her arms just a little.

"The controls didn't raise," she said.

That would have been a first step. So would the lights coming back on.

Neither happened.

No response meant that this panel, too, was damaged.

Someone sighed on the other side of the bridge. The sound echoed in the silence.

Elissa couldn't think of anything to say. She didn't know how to reassure her crew.

"How do you think they're doing in the rear of the ship?" Trombino asked. He sounded desperate.

Or maybe she just heard desperation. She understood it. She was trying to fend it off herself.

"I think whatever happened hit all of us," she said. "Even if there were power elsewhere in the ship, we'd have to wait until they restore it here before we dare venture out of the bridge."

She didn't tell them about the groaning, but she suspected they'd all heard it. And if they thought about it, they knew what it meant.

"Can we open up a console and see if we can repair it inside?" Binek asked.

"It won't matter," she said. "Something disabled all of our systems."

"How can you know that?" Binek asked, and she wasn't guessing here. He *did* sound desperate.

Elissa lowered her head, then realized she had a piece of information none of the rest of them did.

"The gravity in my boots doesn't work," she said. "I would wager if I put on the helmet for the environmental suit that the oxygen isn't working. I'm convinced all systems are down."

"How is that possible?" Trombino asked.

"Did those strangers have some kind of weird weapon?" Ryder asked.

Apparently, she had one other piece of information that her crew didn't have.

"The weapons' fire from the strange transport ship didn't hit us," Elissa said. "It hit the device that Vilhauser wanted off the Room."

"You're kidding me," Binek said. "That thing he was so excited about? It killed him?"

"Yeah," Elissa said softly. And there was a good possibility that it would kill all of the rest of them too.

16

No matter what they did, they couldn't access the proper controls on the console. The bridge remained in darkness. At one point, Ryder managed to grab Calthorpe and strap him into a chair. Ryder said Calthorpe was unconscious, but something in Ryder's tone made Elissa think that maybe Ryder wasn't telling the crew everything.

She decided not to ask. She couldn't do anything about Calthorpe, even if he were badly hurt, so it was better to try to get the ship back under control.

If she could get the ship under control.

The flare had faded to nothing, but her eyes had adjusted to the dimness. She still couldn't see clearly, but she could make out shapes. And some of those shapes were the crew, doing their very best.

They had two major problems: the ships that were closest to them, the fighters and the transports, hadn't arrived. Which meant that they were probably disabled as well, although, she had to hope, not as disabled as her ship was.

That meant rescue might take a while. The commanders in her squadron would have to make the right decisions: how to protect the area, maintain the information shield, rescue the crew members in the fighters, and come get the *Discovery*. Theoretically, the *Discovery* should have been their first priority, but the commanders served with the officers on the transports and fighters. Sometimes personal loyalty trumped orders.

The second problem her crew had was more immediate: it was getting colder. The air might last hours, but if the temperature dropped significantly, the crew wouldn't last hours.

Elissa had managed to snag her environmental suit helmet, and as she suspected, nothing about it worked. It just provided an extra layer of clothing. A super-strong layer, but a layer nonetheless.

Still, she had one and her crew didn't.

They were her priority.

"Okay," she said. "We're going to do two things. Binek, I want you to check the nearest life pod. See if its systems got fried. If the systems are fine, we will finally have a solution."

She doubted that the systems were fine, but she didn't say anything. Stranger things had happened.

"Secondly," she said, "we need to open the equipment locker and remove the environmental suits."

The equipment locker was part of the bridge. She wouldn't have to manually open that door to the corridor. And the word "locker" was a misnomer; it was actually a small room off the bridge. The locker had a door with a manual override. The door opened with a simple pull if the power to the ship went down.

Someone had been thinking on that design, at least.

"You think some of the suits will work?" Trombino asked. Again, he sounded a bit too eager, as if he were clutching onto anything.

"I am not in the guessing business, Officer," she said, her tone flat. A man prone to great highs would also fall to a great low if things did not turn out as he expected. She didn't want to raise his hopes. "We're taking this one step at a time."

"Yes, ma'am," he said. She could see his form, outlined against the portal, moving to the far side of the bridge. Apparently, he would be the first to the equipment locker. That was fine.

She followed.

Someone else—she couldn't tell who—pulled the door open. It groaned, much like the sounds she had heard from outside the bridge.

The interior of the locker was dark, the kind of blackness that hid your hand half an inch from your face.

"Ma'am." Binek spoke from behind her. "I checked the pod closest to me. None of its systems work. I didn't go in all the way, because it's even colder than in here. But I'll go deeper if you want me to."

"No need, Binek, thank you." She wished they could catch a break. She had never been afraid of dying in space, but now that she was faced with that reality, she vaguely wondered why she hadn't been afraid of it. It was a bad way to die.

"I'm just going to pull the suits out so that we can see sizes," Trombino said. "That work, Commander?"

"Yes," she said.

He extended a hand holding a suit, and someone smaller—Gatson?—grabbed it. He continued to take and extend suits until no one picked up the final one.

"Should we put Calthorpe into his suit, Ma'am?" Trombino asked, his tone carefully neutral.

Ryder answered before Elissa could even gather a thought.

"No," Ryder said.

With that one flat word, they all knew: Calthorpe was dead.

The bridge was silent for a long moment, until a groan echoed in the compartment. The groan came from outside, probably from the way the ship was twisting.

"You have a suit, right, Commander?" Trombino asked.

"Yes," she said.

"You know," he said, "this locker's big. We could get in it before the cold really sets in. Our combined body warmth—"

"Might get us an extra ten minutes," Gatson said. "I'm not sure I want to be in that kind of darkness for an extra ten minutes."

"An extra ten minutes is the difference between living and dying sometimes," Elissa said. "If we need it, we'll go in there."

"No one'll find us in time," Lee said. "No one would think to look."

"Unless we marked it somehow," Binek said.

"There are the reflectors on the last suit," Trombino said. "I'll pull them off, see what I can create."

Elissa didn't argue. They needed to keep moving, needed to keep busy. Despite what she had said to Gatson, Elissa agreed with her: An extra ten minutes probably wouldn't make much of a difference.

But she had to plan for everything.

"While he's doing that," Elissa said, "let's see if there's something we missed."

"Ma'am," Binek said softly. Somehow he had come up beside her. "I could try to go to the rear of the ship, see if anything is working there."

She shook her head before remembering that he couldn't see her. "We don't have an airlock between the door here and the corridor. We run the risk of venting all of our atmosphere."

She didn't say anything about the groaning outside the door. She hoped she wouldn't have to explain further.

"I just think we need to explore all of our options, ma'am."

"Me, too," she said just as softly. "The problem is that we have so very few of them."

17

It only took Trombino ten minutes to make a sign out of the reflectors on the remaining environmental suit. He placed them on the door to the suit locker. The strips spelled *In Here*.

Elissa then sent her crew inside. They didn't want to go, but she made them. The longer they kept warm, the better chance they had.

Her cheeks ached with cold and her nose was numb. As she closed the locker's door, she promised her bridge crew that she would join them shortly.

She just never specified that she would join them in the locker. She had a hunch none of them would make it, and she would join them in death.

Or rather, they would join her, since she would die first.

But she was going to do everything she could to prevent that.

She had no idea what had been in that wave that had hit them after the explosion, but she knew it had something to do with that malfunctioning stealth tech.

And she also knew that she lacked the scientific knowledge to figure out how stealth tech worked. Everyone who knew that was either on the other side of that creaking door or had died in the initial explosion.

So she could do only minimal things.

Her crew had tried to do the normal restarts. She was going to try some abnormal ones.

Nothing had power, but she didn't see any fried equipment either. Whatever had gone through hadn't burned out the controls. It had just disabled them.

And if she could figure out a way to jumpstart them again, she might buy some more time.

But focusing on everything had gotten her nowhere. Now she was just going to focus on the environmental systems.

Her crew needed warmth.

Somehow she was going to provide it.

She crawled under the console that contained the environmental controls. It had taken force, but she had managed to open the interior. She couldn't see clearly, so she was going by feel.

But her gloves were getting in the way. She could feel the shapes of things, but not what they actually were.

She had to take the gloves off.

She hesitated for just a moment. The gloves protected her skin. Eventually, though, that wouldn't matter.

Or maybe not so eventually. She took a deep breath of icy air, and then pulled her gloves off. She reached into the guts of the console and found the controls. She touched them, and her fingertips burned.

She brought her hands back, shocked, and it took a moment for her brain to process what she felt.

Ice. She had felt ice. Ice at very, very cold temperatures burned the skin.

She glanced at the locker door, wondered how her people were doing. They were probably warmer than she was.

Wait, no probably about it. They were.

And they knew by now that she wasn't going to join them any time soon.

She took another deep breath, feeling the chill move all the way down her lungs, and reached back inside the panel. By will alone, she would make this all work. And the first thing she was going to will was that the burning sensation wouldn't bother her.

Then she was going to find a way to turn on the environmental systems, if it was the last thing she ever did.

18

SHE WAS WARM, SO THEREFORE, SHE WAS DEAD.

But she was comfortable, and she had this idea that death wasn't comfortable at all.

Elissa opened her eyes—no scraping eyelids, no freezing eyeballs. It took a moment to focus, and then a moment longer to process what she was seeing.

A ceiling. With lights. A brown ceiling, with soft lights.

The air was warm.

And she was on a bed. Without restraints.

Which meant there was gravity.

She raised a hand—or tried to—but an alarm went off, and something brought her arm down gently.

A woman with hair almost as short as Elissa's walked into the room, followed by Flag Commander Janik. The woman didn't surprise her; Flag Commander Janik did.

His skin was gray and his tight black curls had some white, which caught the light. She hadn't seen him look so tense before, almost as if the stress had aged him prematurely.

"Welcome back, Commander," he said. The sound of his voice was almost painful.

She blinked, grateful that the simple movement was so very easy. "You rescued us."

Her voice did scrape, not because of ice in her throat, but because she was thirsty.

"*I* didn't," he said with a bit of a smile. "The *Stillwater* did. She came directly to you, and managed to get the survivors out."

The woman beside Janik grabbed water, and helped Elissa sit up so she could drink some of it. She had never felt so weak in her life.

The *Stillwater* had been one of the anchor ships in the information shield. There was no sensible way for the *Stillwater* to have reached her first.

She processed that and another word, "survivors."

"There were transports that were closer than the *Stillwater*," she said, her voice a little less raspy. "And fighters."

"Yes," Janik said. "They got hit with the same thing you did."

Thing. He didn't know what happened. No one had told him. Had anyone been alive to tell him?

"You said survivors," she said. "How many?"

He glanced at the woman, who nodded and looked rueful at the same time.

"Just your bridge crew," he said gently. "And not even all of them. Calthorpe didn't make it."

"I knew that," she said, trying to process. God, her brain was working slow.

"I want to update you on your condition," the woman said to Elissa. Then she looked over at Janik. "Flag Commander, you can talk with Commander Trekov later."

"Wait," Elissa said, and would have lifted a hand, if something didn't keep pulling her arm down. "Just my bridge crew? They were the only ones on the *Discovery* who made it. No one else?"

"No one else," Janik said softly.

"What about the transports? The fighters?"

"Eight people survived, Commander," Janik said. "Including you."

Her heart rate increased and it made her feel wobbly. Something was still wrong with it. Something was wrong with her.

"How many died?" Elissa asked him.

He tilted his head. "Later, Commander. When you're better."

"*No*," she said. "Now."

"Six hundred," he said. "We think. We lost a lot of information."

"Lost information?"

The woman had her hand on Janik's arm, pulling him back. "Let her rest."

"I'll tell you later, Commander," he said, obviously complying with the woman.

But Elissa didn't want him to wait. She needed to know.

"You couldn't repair the ships?" she said. "They were destroyed, from that wave. But the information should be there."

"It's not," Janik said. "We can't get them back up, no matter what we try. They *look* fine. That's the irritating part. So everything from your mission is gone. Everything."

Including six hundred lives. Her breath caught. She couldn't go there yet. She couldn't process any of this. She didn't dare.

So she looked at the woman. "And me? Why can't I lift my arm?"

"We're repairing your hands," she said almost cheerfully. "You can't feel it, but they're in a solution that is good for new skin. We kept you in a coma while we did something similar for your face. The new skin there is not as delicate now."

New skin. On her face. New skin, and new other things? She couldn't tell. But she felt strange enough to know that more had happened to her physically.

"I nearly died," she said, and it wasn't a question.

"There was a debate as to whether or not you *were* dead," Janik said. "But the medical staff on the *Stillwater*, they revived you. They had to. You're a hero, Commander."

"A hero?" For killing six hundred people? She didn't ask that part, but she had a hunch Janik heard it in her tone.

"You saved your bridge crew against the longest odds I've ever seen," he said. "By rights, none of you should have made it. You saved them. They all agree on that."

"So they're okay. They're not here?"

"They're better than you are," the doctor said, clearly answering both questions. "And now you're going to rest. Everything else can wait."

That last was pointed at Janik. He nodded. "I'll be back, Commander. We can debrief later. We want you well first."

She closed her eyes. Debrief. A hero. Six hundred dead.

How ridiculous.

And such an opportunity. She could lie about everything. Not even her bridge crew knew what happened.

The thought felt alien, a product of the ambition she could barely remember. She had wanted her own command. She got it.

And six hundred people died.

She would tell Janik why. She would tell them about the troubles with the command structure of the Special Research Posting, the way she couldn't handle Vilhauser, the mistakes she made on the Room of Lost Souls. She would tell Janik it was her fault that their scientific mission failed and good people died.

She would tell him.

And then she would enlist his help in finding the betraying bastard—whoever he was.

Whatever he was.

Even if she no longer had a command, she would find him.

And she would make him pay.

THE DIVE
NOW

19

IT TAKES YASH TWO DAYS to figure out the force field. She can modify our *anacapa* to enter it, or so she tells me. She has also discovered where at least part of the force field comes from.

Apparently the force field originates from what we believe to be the center of the Boneyard. Then the field gets reinforced by some kind of nodules or amplifiers around the edges of the Boneyard.

Yash stresses that this is all theory, and she would like to go inside to confirm.

She's not going in, at least not on the first few trips. She's our expert on the *anacapa*, and if something happens, I need her to get us out of there.

We're standing inside the *Two's* conference room, staring at the holographic image that Yash has created of the Boneyard floating at the edge of the long table. She and I point, our fingers going through the images as we try to figure everything out.

The three other people in the conference room sit on the comfortable chairs and watch.

Orlando Rea, Elaine Seager, and Nyssa Quinte have dived with me for years. I initially hired them, not for their diving abilities, but because they have the genetic marker that enables them to work inside a malfunctioning *anacapa* field.

Initially, I didn't know that they had a marker. I just knew that the Empire had tricked them into going into a malfunctioning field on the

Room of Lost Souls, and they had survived. They, and three others, had realized what the Empire had done, and had left almost immediately, refusing to work for anyone connected to the Empire.

They signed on with me over five years ago to take on the Empire and destroy it for so carelessly risking their lives.

I risk their lives too, but I do it with their permission.

They were terrible divers in the beginning; they're among my best now.

And they know me. They know I will consult with them before we do anything dangerous.

So they're listening intently as Yash and I discuss our next move.

"We could take the *Two* here," Yash says, putting her finger into a wide, empty spot near the edge of the Boneyard. "You can dive from there."

I shake my head. "What if there's a ship there that doesn't show up on our sensors? We'll appear in its space, get damaged, and become a permanent part of the Boneyard."

We've had variations on this discussion for days. Yash takes my comments almost as a personal insult. She believes we'll be just fine. She trusts her readings.

I don't. I've gone into too many dark situations, too many places filled with unknowns, to accept that this journey will be an easy one.

Yash says she's been to dark places too, places filled with unknowns. I know she has, usually with the full force of the Fleet behind her. She sometimes forgets how very alone we are out here, that Coop and the *Ivoire* won't swoop in to rescue us, and if our comm system malfunctions, we won't be able to ask anyone else—known or unknown—to help us either.

Yash gives me a look that I have come to recognize as complete contempt. She won't say anything—she's too well trained for that—but there are times when she thinks I'm either too cautious or not cautious enough.

She prefers Coop as a captain, and when he's not around, she believes that she knows best. She would clearly take the *Two* into the Boneyard.

I refuse.

"I want to take the skip," I say. "We'll run this first trip like a dive."

"I'm not familiar with what that means, exactly," she says.

"I know," I say.

I never dive-trained her. I don't want an amateur diver coming with me on any dive, not any more. I've taken too many tourists. In other words, I've done my time with beginners, and I'm not going to train any more beginners unless I absolutely have to.

She waits, so that I have to explain what I mean.

"The four of us take the skip," I say indicating the others in the room. Elaine gives me a small smile; she's heard me give a similar speech before. Once nervous and out of her depth, she has come into her own. Some of it is her age—she's not much younger than I am—and some of it is her experience with me. She knows I'll win this argument.

Orlando has leaned back in his chair and crossed his arms over his small frame. He's the only one built like a wreck-diver—thin and wiry. I used to think him bookish (and he was), but those traits have made him one of my most reliable assistants.

Nyssa is also thin, but she's not as good a diver as Orlando. She's become my best dive medic. She has a calm that can't be faked, an ability to go in and deal with whatever's gone wrong as if what she's facing is a normal occurrence instead of something only dive medics see.

Yash looks at the three as if she's never seen them before. I can read her thoughts as clearly as if she's spoken them: No one at that table knows how to repair an *anacapa* drive—and the skip's drive is new and relatively untested.

"You have no idea what you'll be facing," she says.

I suppress a smile. She's not stating the obvious because she thinks we don't understand. She's stating it so she doesn't make a less professional observation.

"I know," I say.

"There's no one from the Fleet on this dive team," she adds.

"I know that as well," I say.

"Coop wants someone from the Fleet on every dive team," she says.

There it is. Coop told me that repeatedly before we left, and I repeatedly reminded him that I'm in control of dives, not him.

"Coop's not here," I say.

"I wouldn't have signed on if I thought you were going to disobey him," Yash says.

"And I wouldn't have let you sign on if I thought you would forget who is in charge of this mission and who has been in charge from the very beginning."

Yash tilts her head back in surprise. I'm not sure if she's surprised at my tone or at her own mistake.

"I don't agree with you on this," she says with a little less edge. This is the voice she usually uses to talk with Coop. "You could get trapped in there. You could die."

She says that with one eye to the others as if she expects them to be surprised by this. They're not. They've heard that speech from me dozens of times. All of my divers have. That's one of my personal rules: I tell the divers the dangers they're going to face, and they get to choose the level of their participation.

People who have dived with me a lot have heard the "this could kill you" speech more times than they can remember.

"Better us than the entire *Two*," I say.

Her lips thin. She turns to the others at the table. "No offense," she says to them, then turns to me, "but I was talking to you."

I smile. I've heard her give this speech before, primarily to Coop when we were trying to find the Fleet's old Sector Bases. He truly shouldn't have been doing what he needed to do—he's the captain of a large ship that still functions as a traditional vessel.

I run a large corporation, but if I die tomorrow, no one will miss me. Business will go on as usual. I have set it up that way.

"I know the risks I'm taking," I say.

"I don't think you do," she says.

This is beginning to irritate me. "It doesn't matter what you think. I'm the most experienced diver I know. Not even Mikk has more experience than I do."

Of course, all of the other divers who were more experienced than me are now dead, but I don't add that.

"We need experience here. I'm going to run this dive, and I'm doing it my way. If you like, I can take you out of the cockpit and you will have no more responsibilities unless something happens with the *anacapa*."

Her eyes narrow. "You need me."

"I need your expertise," I say. "I have that. You've figured out the force field. I'm sure someone else can take it from here—not as well as you—but they can. And they can consult with you if we need something else."

She shakes her head once as if she can't believe I proposed such stupidity. I can't quite believe I said it either. I'm bluffing for the first time in a long time. We do need her, and we need her more than almost anyone else on board the *Two*, except maybe—just maybe—me.

"You may not be able to communicate with us from inside the Boneyard," she says.

"I know," I say.

She glances at the others, and I catch a bit of desperation in her that I haven't seen before. Or maybe, that I haven't *recognized* before.

"It's some kind of modified *anacapa* field," she says. "Time may operate differently in there."

Part of me wishes she hasn't said that out loud. I understood it from the moment she told me how the force field operates. But I'm also glad she said it, because now the dive team knows.

They know the true risk.

Time might go faster for us, so we'll look outside the Boneyard, see the *Two*, then watch it disappear in a matter of seconds, even though the ship might have waited for weeks. We might come out in the future, just like the *Ivoire* did.

Or we might never come out, forced to remain in that Boneyard until our food runs out. Then we die.

Those are just two of the risks we're taking. The skip might get torn apart by the *anacapa* forces, or there might be a defensive weapon inside the Boneyard that will attack us the moment we breach the force field. The ships themselves might hold dangers we haven't even suspected.

I look at Orlando, Nyssa, and Elaine. "You know you don't have to go," I say.

Orlando chuckles, as if he has expected this. Elaine's smile grows.

"And miss the adventure?" Nyssa asks. "Are you kidding me?"

Yash frowns at them. She thinks them too flip. But I know that what I'm hearing is more than bravado.

Diving becomes a part of you. For some of us, the greater the risk, the more enjoyable the dive—particularly if we survive it with no casualties and no serious problems.

That's where I'll have my issues. I've lived with regrets—too many mistakes on my part, too many serious problems. Too many deaths—and those regrets can color my command.

I don't want the regrets to have any place here.

As with all of my dives, I accept that I might die here.

I'll do everything I can to make sure that no one else does.

20

THE ANACAPA DRIVE IN THE COCKPIT of the skip hides in a black box near the command console. There's no other place for something that large.

The problem is that the skip is small, compared to the *Two*. Compared to most ships, really. I still think of the skip as big, but that's only because it has two rooms, separated by a galley kitchen. My first skip had only the cockpit area and another smaller area for cooking—although on that skip, cooking wasn't recommended.

I have to be careful not to trip over the *anacapa*. I'm not used to it being there, and even though Yash marked it with a lot of yellow warning stickers, I still fail to see it at times. I've bruised my shins on it more than I care to think about.

I'm flying the skip. That's the other reason I'm going on this first mission; I want to be the first pilot to use this skip's *anacapa* drive while we're away from the Lost Souls. If something goes wrong, it's all on me.

I know that something can go wrong with the *anacapa*, and not just because the *Ivoire* had trouble with theirs. The technical staff on the *Ivoire* balked for years at putting an *anacapa* drive into anything smaller than a Dignity Vessel.

The extra Fleet ships that are small and travel inside the *Ivoire* don't have an *anacapa*. That includes two-man fighters and troop transports. There are a few leisure ships as well, small things for the officers to use, and they have no *anacapa* either.

When I first requested an *anacapa* for the *Two,* Coop stonewalled me. Then he listened. And finally, months later, he had me talk with his engineering staff, who looked shocked at the very idea.

They all believe that the *anacapa*, even a small one like the one in the skip, is too powerful for most ships.

I suspect they're right. But we've tested this *anacapa* several times, and it seems to work well. Just like the *anacapa* in the *Two* works well.

Still, Yash joins me on the skip to watch me input the coordinates for the blank space inside the Boneyard. She wants to make sure everything works correctly.

She hangs around an extra minute or two, until I pointedly thank her. She still wants me to invite her on this mission, and I will not do so, no matter how hard she tries to get me to change my mind.

Orlando boards already partially suited up. We have new diving suits, courtesy of the *Ivoire's* technicians and the training they've given the engineers at the Lost Souls. Because of the things we've learned, we've modified a lot of our equipment—from environmental suits to weapons to our food-prep stations.

We've changed and patented more things in the last five years than I ever could have imagined. But we've stayed away from anything that even touches on *anacapa* technology. We don't want some brilliant engineer inside the Empire to stumble on an oddity in our design and then use it to create something powerful, like an Empire-based *anacapa* drive.

Orlando straps into his seat, the rest of his special diving suit waiting beside the airlock. He assumes he's going with me into whatever darkness we decide to explore.

I'm not sure I'm leaving the skip on the first dive. I'm the only good pilot we have on this short trip. All of my other pilots, the really good ones who are not Fleet-based, do not have the marker. I'm not going to risk them, not yet.

So I'll probably stay behind with Nyssa, but I haven't said anything. We don't make diving assignments until we reach our first location.

Nyssa brings a lot of medical equipment as well as her suit. She's prepared for all eventualities, which I greatly appreciate. I have seen more strange medical emergencies on dives than I have on anything else, including the one military mission Coop and I went on together.

I shudder thinking of that. People died on that mission.

"You okay, Boss?" Elaine asks me. She hasn't suited up. She doesn't do so unless she knows she's going to dive. She's one of the divers who has learned she's most comfortable wearing nothing but her suit, but she doesn't like wearing her suit in a normal environment.

That's the only part of her which shows how late her training started. The rest of us can wear our suits all the time.

But we all have problems. Even though I'm the best diver in the group, I'm prone to the gids—breathing too much, using up too much oxygen. I get excited or nervous or just too focused to pay attention to my breathing and my oxygen usage.

I need someone on the skip to monitor that for me, particularly on any dive I take after a long layoff. After a few days of diving, my gids go away. But I'm a dangerous diver in the beginning.

Elaine doesn't get the gids. If anything, she's too cautious. But that caution makes her someone you always want at your side, no matter what you're doing. She'll think the problem through and then take appropriate action.

I find it amazing whenever I consider the fact that she's only been diving a little over five years.

Some people take to it right away, some—like Elaine—learn it solidly and slowly, and most everyone else can't manage much more than a tourist dive.

"I want everyone strapped in before we go," I say.

I ostentatiously strap myself into the pilot's chair to prove my point. Normally, we don't strap in when we use the *anacapa*. It almost takes longer to attach the strap than it does to go through foldspace to our destination.

But I have no idea what's going to happen, and I'd rather have us locked in than floating unconscious around a damaged cockpit. I know of a lot of people who would have survived an accident if they'd only been strapped to their seats.

No one complains. They all strap down. Nyssa gives me a curious look, as if she doesn't entirely understand it, but she says nothing.

I go through the safety checks twice, then I separate the skip from the *Two*. I can almost feel Yash in the *Two*'s cockpit, staring at the skip and wishing she were on board.

Or maybe she's staring at it, praying that we're not as foolish as she thinks we are.

I move the skip far from the *Two*, but away from the Boneyard. Apparently I don't entirely trust Yash either, or maybe, more accurately, the *anacapa* that she built. I'm worried that it'll malfunction in the wrong place, and take others with it.

That's why I didn't use the skip's *anacapa* drive inside the *Two*. An *anacapa* can be activated anywhere. It doesn't have backwash or sonic squeals or other problems that regular ship drives do. The *anacapa* makes a little sound, slides a few places, and then—suddenly—we're in foldspace.

But if we come back at the wrong coordinates, or if the *Two* has moved even slightly from its original position because of drift or inattentiveness, we could appear half inside the *Two* and half outside, breaking us apart or doing the same thing to the *Two*.

I'm not willing to risk it.

When we get a safe distance from the *Two*, I turn in my seat and look at my crew. Elaine clings to her strap as if it offends her. Orlando leans back in his chair, ready to be taken on an adventure. Nyssa's gaze meets mine, and she nods just once, silent permission to get this mission underway.

"Here we go," I say, and activate the *anacapa*.

The skip slips slightly, that funny, tiny bump that says the *anacapa* has been activated. Normally, the slip feels almost like the group has tripped on a rug together, or the attitude controls have gone out on the ship just for a second before the pilot rights it.

This time, that slight slip feels bigger, more of a tilt. I attribute that to my imagination. I've been heavily focused on the *anacapa*, and worried about it, so of course I'm going to feel this particular slip much more than I normally would.

Or so I tell myself.

The sensors on the skip darken. The screens on the control panel go black for just a moment, and then they're back, registering yet another star map that I don't recognize. I hit "capture" so that the skip's console records everything, not just the telemetry it receives, and then I brace myself for that move out of foldspace.

Which comes almost immediately. Another slip, a bump, a shake—and blackness. This time, all of our equipment goes dark.

My stomach turns. I'm holding my breath. Dammit, I actually thought that this would work. Then I wonder if that's what everyone thinks when they're about to die.

The ship settles, but I see nothing.

I turn toward my divers. Nyssa's eyes are wide. Orlando is sitting up, trying to keep a calm expression on his face. Elaine looks terrified.

Then the *anacapa* slips again, and we're back in foldspace. The sensors come back online, the screens activate, and I see that same star map—at least I think it's the same star map—before we slip again.

The skip bobbles. My heart is pounding.

The equipment is still running, the screens showing me the Boneyard. From the outside.

With the *Two* beside us.

This time, I don't trust the equipment. I know what happened to the *Ivoire*. I know that we don't understand exactly what we're playing with.

I know things can (have?) gone wrong.

I clear the skip's windows and look outside the vessel with my own two eyes.

Yes, the Boneyard is ahead of us, the *Two* to our right, just like it was when we left, moments ago. At least I hope it was moments. We were in foldspace twice.

I have no idea how long we were gone—as measured by the *Two*, anyway.

"What just happened?" Elaine asks.

I let out a small breath. We're back, anyway. We didn't die. That's something, at least.

But we didn't get into the Boneyard either.

"Boss?" She sounds panicked now. "What happened?"

I shake my head. "I wish to hell I knew."

21

HERE'S WHAT WE KNOW: we know that our first attempt at getting into the Boneyard didn't work. We also know that there was one unbelievably scary moment in that trip where everything went black.

We know that is the moment when we should have arrived in the Boneyard.

The rest is all theory.

Yash and I have hashed out this theory in constant meetings. We've experimented with the skip, taking it out together, just me and her, some distance away from the Boneyard, and then activating the *anacapa*. The *anacapa* works fine away from the Boneyard.

On our journeys in the skip, we've gone into foldspace and then come out of foldspace at the new coordinates—which are never in the Boneyard or near the Boneyard.

Yash believes the Boneyard repelled us somehow. I think our *anacapa* malfunctioned. But the real key here is that neither of us knows what happened at all.

We're guessing.

The readings we got didn't help either. Nothing is helping.

Yash seems ready to pull out her hair.

Me, I'm not willing to go through that again. I think I'm pretty adventurous, but upon reflection, I realized I'm adventurous only with certain things.

Like wreck diving. I'll take all kinds of chances when I go into a wreck—sometimes alone—in darkness and emptiness. I *like* those chances.

But the thought of being stuck nowhere in a small skip with three other people, none of whom really know how to work the device that will get us home, well, that has me spooked beyond belief.

I think of it now, after we've gone through the experience, and I wonder if we even should have tried it.

Which brings me to this moment:

Yash and I in the *Two*'s conference room, again.

We've picked the conference room because we can pace. We can shout at each other if we have to. And we have all of the equipment in there along with some privacy settings so that we can double-check our assumptions—those assumptions that are double-checkable, of course.

Yash looks haggard. Her hair falls around her face, and her eyes are sunken. I might have to order her to eat, if I can figure out a way to do it.

This is the first indication that I've had as to how very important this mission is to her. Apparently, she has some secret hopes as well. She wants to know what's in that Boneyard more than anybody.

She flops into one of the chairs. "The Boneyard's force field is defeating me," she says.

Yeah, it is. But I don't say that out loud. I've said it before, and it's led to some shouting matches. We're not going to shout any more, or at least, I'm not. We're going to figure this thing out, if we can.

"Maybe we should go back to the beginning," I say. "What we do know."

"We know that we can't get in there any more than those scavenger friends of yours can." She always calls them that, because I believe that the initial scavengers followed me from Azzelia after telling me about the Boneyard. I believe they thought I was an easy mark, and I'd be trapped there, and then they could pluck my ship.

They were wrong.

So far, they haven't shown up here. Thank heavens.

I am about to say something about the scavengers, about the way we're constantly monitoring for them, when something else she says stops me.

"'We know that we can't get in there,'" I say, quoting her. "*Do* we know that? I mean, do we really know that?"

"Yes," she says. "It repels us, it throws us out. We went somewhere dark and scary."

So much anger and sarcasm in her voice. I don't say anything because I understand it. Yash went somewhere dark and scary for two full weeks, then escaped it to find herself here.

She has a right to anger and sarcasm on that topic. I had tried hard not to complain about what happened when we tried to get the skip into the Boneyard, but apparently I had failed at that.

"Yeah," I say. "It threw us out, *when we used the* anacapa *drive.*"

She tilts her head back and looks at the ceiling. Then she lets out a small breath.

"Son of a *bitch*," she says. "Son of a fucking bitch."

She gets up, circles the chair, and goes to the head of the table. There she taps on the holocontrols. I just watch her work. She's looking at a virtual screen about eye-height because that's what she prefers.

I've learned not to look over her shoulder or ask questions as she does.

"We got stuck," she says.

"You guys did," I say. "We didn't. I don't think the same thing happened to the skip as happened to the *Ivoire*."

"I'm not talking about the ships," she says. "Or even the *anacapa* drive itself. I'm talking about you and me."

She taps the holocontrols again and the screen vanishes. She places her hands beside the controls and leans forward, as if she's about to address a crowd. Instead, she turns that intense gaze on me.

"We had a plan," she says. "We were coming here, working fast, taking the skip in, and then taking our time."

"Yeah," I say, not sure where she's going. I assume that's still the plan.

"We figured we were using the *anacapa* for *all* travel. All of it. That's where we're stuck."

I had been inching toward that statement. She's hit it almost immediately and has probably moved even faster in her own head.

"Can we go in without an *anacapa* drive?" I ask.

She swings her head toward me, her gaze becoming even more intense, if that's possible. "You mean without it on," she says.

"Yeah," I say.

"The other skip doesn't have one at all, does it?" she asks.

I want to say, *I don't know how it could if you didn't install it*, but I'm still trying to play good captain here. "No, it doesn't."

"That force field is just a modified *anacapa* field—"

"You *think* it is, you said." I'm getting nervous now. "You said you didn't know."

"I know enough," she says. "If you do what I say with the regular skip, you just might get in there."

Just and *might* were not comfort words. *Just* and *might* made me a lot more nervous than I realized.

"And what happens if we can't get in?" I ask.

"Nothing," she says. "This isn't one of those force fields that destroys ships. It just...repels...them..."

She says that last so slowly that I know she's had yet another realization. She stands all the way up.

"That damn thing," she says, more to herself than to me. "They've figured out a way to repel an *anacapa* drive that they don't recognize."

"What?" I ask.

She shakes her head, curses distractedly, and then sits down. She taps something on the table screen before her, and curses again.

"Want to share?" I ask.

She still doesn't answer. I'm going to hover if she doesn't tell me what's going on.

Then she looks up, her expression remote. She's not in this room; she's elsewhere, thinking about something I'll probably never understand.

After a moment, her eyes focus—on me.

"Boss," she says, and I nearly jump. Like Coop, she does her best not to use the name everyone else uses for me. "You don't understand. The Fleet has long believed it needs to have a device that wards off *anacapa* drives."

"Wards off?" I ask, trying to ignore the way she still talks about the Fleet in the present tense.

"For as long as I've been an engineer, the Fleet has worried about what would happen if someone steals one of our ships with a drive. I mean, we've lost hundreds, maybe thousands of ships over the centuries, but we always recovered the *anacapa* on the ships whose location we know. We've had ships stolen, but not the larger vessels. Just the fighters and the transports—"

"The ships without an *anacapa*," I say, beginning to get this now.

"Exactly," she says. "But we've always worried that those ships we left behind would come back and bite us in a way we can't quite foresee. And they might even be able to catch up to us, find us anywhere, because of the way that the *anacapa*s can link up."

Two *anacapa* drives linked up to pull the *Ivoire* into the future, using what had been designed as a rescue technology. The sector base received the distress signal from the *Ivoire* and answered it, pulling the *Ivoire* to the base. Only it was the base five thousand years in the future that had received the signal, not the one in Yash's timeline.

Intially, Coop had sent a near-constant distress signal from the *Ivoire*, trying to pick up other nearby signals. But after shutting down the *anacapa* on Vaycehn and the one on the Room of Lost Souls, he never even received a ping—no contact at all.

I hadn't even learned he'd done that for years. And then it took months after that for him to tell me how deeply disappointed he was that he hadn't even gotten a faint signal in response.

I have never thought about the implications of this part of the technology. If someone else has captured a Dignity Vessel, then theoretically they could use the same technology to end up in the very heart of wherever the Fleet is now.

No wonder they were trying to build a defense against it. No wonder they hadn't; it was mostly theory. In practice, they hadn't needed it.

"You're saying they finally invented it," I say.

"That's exactly what I'm saying." She curses again, then pirouettes. I've never seen Yash do anything so youthful and girlish before. "You know what this means?"

"You've found evidence of the Fleet," I say.

"Not just evidence," she says. "Evidence they survived. Evidence they've moved forward. Evidence of their damned trajectory."

The trajectory has been an issue almost from the beginning. Theoretically, the Fleet moved in a planned direction. Theoretically, Coop could have diagrammed where the Fleet would be—kinda sorta. The Fleet never stayed a set period of time. Sometimes it remained in one location for a hundred years. Sometimes it remained only a week. So he can't really map where it would be, not without finding stops along the way.

This Boneyard is, in other words, a stop. An important stop, not just because of the ships stored here, but because of the way they're stored.

My mind races, trying to deal with the possibilities. The Fleet made it to here. It was able to set up these ships with some kind of protection.

But it also felt it needed something that repelled *anacapa* drives. Was that a precautionary protection—a just-in-case something new gets invented in the future—or was it in response to a real threat?

And what of the ships?

"Could this force field be designed to hold *anacapas* in place?" I ask. "So that the ships won't accidentally drift out of the area?"

Yash shakes her head slightly, not because she's disagreeing with me, but because she's obviously forgotten I'm here, and my question reminded her of my presence.

"It could," she says after she processes my question. "Yes."

"Then we wouldn't be able to fly in without one, either, right?" I ask. "I mean, no one else can. We'll need an *anacapa* to get in."

"The right kind of *anacapa*," she says. "One the system recognizes. That's the only kind that'll go inside the Boneyard."

I let out a breath. We're screwed, unless we take the *Ivoire* inside. I'm not sure I want to do that. I'm not sure I want to go back and tell Coop the *Ivoire* is the only way in.

"However," Yash says slowly, "I wonder…"

"What?" I ask.

"I think we can get in without an *anacapa*."

"You just said we couldn't," I say.

"There are other ways to get through that force field," she says. "If I can open it—"

"We can take a ship without an *anacapa* inside?"

She nods.

"I have no idea why you're so confident about this," I say.

She grins. "Because I needed a rest a few years ago—I guess, a few thousand years ago—and I did a post-doc on the *Brazza* just to keep my hand in."

"A what?"

"I got an advanced degree in something that's not my specialty," she says.

"And that something was?"

"Shields," she says.

I'm still having trouble. "Ship shields? But they're—"

"All kinds of shields," she says, and her grin widens. "Including force fields."

"Like this one," I say, wondering why she hasn't told me this before.

"Oh, no," she says. "Not like this one. This one wasn't even a glimmer in my professor's eye. This one was so beyond theory that we didn't discuss it."

"Then why are you sure you can solve this?"

"Because this force field has at least two purposes: to handle ships with *anacapa* drives, and ships without."

"Yes," I say, feeling dumber than I have in years. "And…?"

"And, Boss!" She slaps a hand on the table. "And! That's the difference. Underneath it, if you strip the *anacapa* stuff away, you have a force field. A regular, normal Fleet force field."

"And you can beat that," I say, hoping that's her point.

She nods formally, grinning like a fiend.

"And I can beat that," she says.

THE SECOND SKIRMISH
ONE MONTH AGO

22

COOP SAT ON THE BRIDGE, his full bridge crew around him. Boss had a seat to his left side, out of his range of vision. He had asked her to remain quiet, and hoped she would listen. She worried him as much as this mission did.

The only reason he had agreed to it was because Boss would mount a mission with or without him. She had no tactical skills. She didn't know how to command the Fleet ships that she had. She would bring herself, Lost Souls, the ships, and everything they'd done to the attention of the Empire.

She would get people killed. Maybe even herself.

He let out a small sigh. If he were honest with himself, that was the only reason he was doing this. He couldn't bear to lose Boss. He wasn't sure if that was because he loved her more than he had loved anyone else, or because he had experienced so much loss that her death would be the last straw.

No matter what it was, he couldn't face it—not now, not even when she was doing something stupid for someone she loved.

They were mounting a rescue mission for a woman that Coop didn't even like. Rosealma Quintana, known as Squishy, had defied all of Boss's orders and had probably provoked a war with the Empire.

Squishy and her team had destroyed several imperial research facilities. She had gotten caught on her way back to Lost Souls. Since Squishy ran the so-called stealth-tech program at Lost Souls that was, in reality, a program that morphed into ways to modify the *anacapa* drive, she was a valuable asset.

The fact that she had gotten caught would give the Empire information that they didn't deserve to have. She'd been in their custody for days before Boss even heard about it. Squishy had probably already given up too many secrets.

Coop had never encountered a culture that had trained its soldiers to survive certain interrogation techniques. Squishy wasn't a soldier. She was a scientist. And no matter how strong her resolution to hang on to her knowledge would be, she wouldn't manage it. No one could.

Given how much time she'd been in the Empire's custody before Boss got the news of Squishy's capture, Coop was inclined to write Squishy off. It was the kind of command decision he had had to make throughout his career, and it was cruel. But sometimes, it was all that a captain could do.

Although, a couple of times, he had broken the rules, once for the woman he'd divorced but still cared for.

Boss didn't understand, not entirely. And she was convinced Squishy hadn't talked to the Empire yet. Nothing Coop said could dissuade her.

So Boss was going to go, with or without him.

He preferred it to be with him.

He knew he could get her out of there. He also knew the only way to do it was to reveal the *Ivoire* to the Empire in a way that would get this ship noticed, and it would probably start a war.

Boss denied that. She believed if Coop did his part, the Empire wouldn't figure out what his ship was.

Boss didn't understand how empires reacted to attacks on their important research facilities—not in a deep way, anyhow. She knew they would want retaliation. She just didn't know how badly.

All of that made him leery. Curiously, it made him leery about Boss herself.

He expected her to try to take over this mission. He expected her to demand that she be in charge.

But she hadn't—at least, not yet. They had agreed on a mission plan, and she vowed she'd stick to it.

He would believe it when he saw it.

"Lynda's ready," Anita said to him. Anita hadn't questioned this mission—at least verbally. But when he went over the mission with his entire bridge crew—and without Boss—Anita raised her eyebrows, just once, as if silently asking, *Really? Do we want to be part of this?*

Since she hadn't asked the question out loud, he hadn't had to answer it out loud.

He glanced around the bridge. Everyone was watching him, waiting for the command to leave the Lost Souls and head into foldspace. Anita had just given him the last piece. Lynda Rooney was ready too.

Lynda now commanded the ship Boss had named the *Shadow*. It was a former Fleet ship, rebuilt at Lost Souls. Boss's people had found it mostly intact, but it still had needed massive repairs. Boss would have taken the *Shadow* with one of her own people in charge if Coop hadn't stepped in.

He commanded the mission, but Lynda commanded the *Shadow*. Both ships were flying with minimal staff. Each had one hundred Fleet veterans in operations, and fifty trainees from Lost Souls. That was the true definition of skeleton crew, made worse by the fact that he had added thirty assault teams to each ship.

People who would normally be on the *Ivoire* in a support capacity were now using old, rusty military skills to make sure Boss didn't do anything stupid.

Coop glanced at her. He couldn't help it. She looked so demure in her chair, her close-cropped hair framing her small face, her hands clasped in her lap. She looked like a woman most people wouldn't even notice.

Until her gaze met his. Then he saw the strength in it. He saw *her*, clearly, and his stomach clenched.

Even with the assault teams and his precautions, she could die on this stupid rescue mission.

She was insisting on going into the facility herself. She believed she could get her friend out with minimal casualties.

He couldn't dissuade her from that. And he didn't dare go with her this time, because he needed to provide external support.

Boss nodded, the movement small, as if she heard the question he hadn't asked—or hadn't asked out loud, anyway.

Yes, they were going. Yes, she would follow the plan. Yes, they were taking a risk.

"Lynda's ready," Coop said to Anita, "and we're ready. Double-check the coordinates on the other side with her. Once she confirms, we're heading into foldspace."

If everything went well, it would only take them a moment to cross the Empire and invade its most secure region.

That alone was an act of war.

His second against a government he had no real argument with.

And this time, the Empire would notice.

23

THE JUMP TO FOLDSPACE LASTED ONLY A MOMENT. It registered on the sensors long enough for Coop to glance at the readings, and then the *Ivoire* arrived in Empire space.

The Empire's research station sprawled before them, going on for miles and miles. The thing was as big as Boss's friend Turtle had claimed.

Turtle bothered him. She knew things she shouldn't have. She had probably gotten the information in ways that Coop wouldn't have liked either. She had brought the news of Squishy's capture to Lost Souls, and even though Boss had trusted the information because of some long-ago established code between the three women, Coop hadn't trusted it.

He hated the fact that the only maps they had of this research facility came from Turtle.

But the facility was top-secret, and Turtle's coordinates had gotten the *Ivoire* here.

The *Shadow* arrived a moment later, which also relieved him. That ship moved into position.

The research station—so secret he couldn't even find its name—had layers and levels and sections that suggested the thing had been added to over the years.

He had seen the maps and the holographic recreations, but they still hadn't prepared him for just how large this thing was.

He glanced over his shoulder. Boss had paled. Apparently, she finally realized the magnitude of what they were about to do.

"Last chance," he said to her, hoping she'd abort.

She took a deep breath. Everyone watched her. She nodded, even though he doubted she knew she had done that.

For the first time that he'd seen in years, Boss appeared nervous.

"See if she's there," Boss said.

He bit back a surprised response. He didn't expect Boss to make even that much of a concession. If Squishy wasn't on board the station, then they could return. The station might wonder what showed up on their sensors, but they wouldn't have a reason to pursue.

Maybe Boss mistrusted Turtle as much as he did. After all, there was nothing to stop the woman from giving them false information and letting them start a war she was too cowardly to start on her own.

"Kjersti," he said to his chief linguist, Kjersti Perkins. "Scan for me, will you?"

"Already on it, sir," she said. "We have multiple confirmations of Squishy's personal signature. She's on board. And I'll double-check, but I'm convinced we can pinpoint exactly where she is."

He felt his shoulders slump just a bit. He knew what Boss would say before she said it.

"We're not aborting," she said. "We're going to rescue Squishy and we're going to do it now."

"Well," he said, to make sure his crew knew that she wasn't giving an order. "We'll do it according to our plan."

Boss stood. He moved so that he was in front of her, so that she couldn't avoid him.

"I'd prefer it if you stayed here," he said.

"Not a chance," she said.

He had known she would say that, too, but he had to ask her.

"All right, then," he said. "Go join your team."

She grinned at him like a kid who had gotten a special toy. Then she winked at him and headed for the door.

He swallowed hard, hoping that wouldn't be the last time he saw her. Then he banished the thought.

He scanned the ships on the landing bays. There were three major bays and two emergency bays. Underneath one of the emergency bays, a ship he hadn't expected had docked on a special ring.

He cursed.

He wasn't that familiar with Empire design, but he knew what he saw here: a warship. And, judging by its size, an important one. This ship was bigger than the ship he'd encountered at Starbase Kappa.

"Wait," he said, hoping Boss was still there.

He looked. She had stopped right at the door. She walked back to him now, and he turned his attention away from her.

"Is that what I think it is?" he asked his crew.

"The large ship?" Anita asked. "It's some kind of battleship, maybe even a flagship. I've compared to our database. It's not in there."

"But it's Empire?" he asked.

"Oh, yeah," Anita said. "And it's suited for battle. It has fifteen different weapons systems that I can count. I have no idea how many are shielded from us."

"Not to mention a variety of missiles, fighters, transports, and God knows what kind of weaponry inside," Yash said from her position down front. She sounded annoyed. But then, she had sounded annoyed since Coop had agreed to this mission.

"It also seems to have a full crew," said Kravchenko from the first officer's perch.

And Coop's two ships were running on such skeletal crews that anything out of the ordinary would compromise the *Ivoire's* function. He couldn't engage in a major battle with this vessel, not because he couldn't out-shoot it, but because he didn't have the staff to maintain all of his systems.

Neither did the *Shadow.*

Plus with the kind of weaponry this imperial vessel had, it also had to have extremely fine-tuned sensors. It already knew the *Ivoire* and the *Shadow* were here.

"They're probably noticing us right now," Coop said. "We can leave before this gets messy."

Maybe this would convince Boss. A lot of people would die today if she didn't abandon this plan now.

"What's messy?" she asked, her voice small.

He felt frustration yet again at her lack of military savvy. "We were prepared for a well-guarded science station that has no exterior defensive capability. We weren't prepared to meet a battleship."

"Meaning?" she asked.

He took a deep breath to get his emotions in check. This was a mission. He had to treat it that way. She was.

"Meaning we take it out now, before you go in." He had warned her that he would be destroying the station. But she probably had hopes everyone could evacuate first.

She stiffened. She clearly wasn't prepared for a first strike, destroying hundreds of lives without a declaration of war.

"We'd take it out with the full crew on board?" she asked.

"Yes, ma'am," he said. If she wanted to play this like a mission, then he would treat it that way. Either she ordered the death of hundreds to rescue her friend or she backed out.

Now.

"Are there other options?" She seemed even paler.

He wished he had foreseen this. He wished he had prepared her for it, so they wouldn't be wasting precious time arguing about it now.

He said, "We try limited strikes, but I don't know what we're up against here. That might not be effective."

"Won't a full shot on the vessel destroy the landing bay?" she asked "Won't it hurt the station?"

"We're here to destroy the station," Coop said. "It either begins now, or we abort. Attacking that vessel is an act of war."

"So's attacking the station," she said, her voice surprisingly calm. "We're not going to abort. Do what you need to, Captain."

And she left the bridge.

Coop stared at the closed door for half a moment, then realized why he was surprised. He'd been having one conversation. She'd been having another.

He thought she cared about the blood that would be on her hands.

She just wanted to make sure the station would remain intact while the assault teams went in to rescue Squishy.

He whirled.

"All right," he said to his team. "Let's get to that ship before she gets to us."

24

THE SHOT WAS TRICKIER THAN HE EXPECTED because of the location of the military vessel. Boss had seen something Coop hadn't initially seen. The imperial battleship was too centrally located. An explosion at the location of that ship would have a strong impact on the structural integrity of the entire station.

Below decks, his fighter ships were gearing up to escort the transports to the station. The same things were happening on the *Shadow*. The launch of the assault teams would happen in less than three minutes.

"Can that ship fire its weapons from its location?" he asked Anita.

Yash responded. "Not without causing the station some damage. However, the station itself does have defensive capability."

"From everything I see," Anita said, "its defensive capability is no match for our shields."

Or their weaponry. But that part went without saying.

"So the ship will launch before firing," Coop said, maintaining his focus as best he could. He didn't want to think about Boss getting on one of those transports, then accompanying her team into the station itself.

"It's already gearing up," Anita said. "It should separate in less than a minute."

"The moment it detaches, hit it with all that we have," Coop said. "I don't want it to get a shot off, particularly against one of our fighters."

"Yes, sir," she said.

Yash didn't disagree, and she would have if she felt strongly enough. He probably should have made her first officer instead of Kravchenko because he trusted her more than anyone else on this ship. But he also needed Yash in engineering, and he knew she couldn't do both jobs.

In the situation they were in, he needed a good engineer more than he needed a first officer.

"The ship's shields are up, sir," Kravchenko said, as if she knew he was thinking about her.

"Is that going to be an issue?" he asked.

"No, sir. They're a little stronger than the ones Boss has on the *Two*, but not much."

He didn't consider the shields that Boss had on the *Two* worthy of the name, even though he didn't tell her that. He had asked Yash to reinforce them before Boss took that ship anywhere again.

If she got out of this, that is.

"The battleship's away, sir," Kravchenko said.

"Our transports?" he asked.

"Not quite out yet," Anita said.

"Warn them there will be debris, Kjersti," he said to Perkins. Then he nodded at Yash and said, "Fire!"

She did. She aimed more weaponry at that battleship than he expected, probably to make sure she got it in one shot.

The weapons streamed toward the ship almost instantaneously. The images on the screens blurred, leaving little afterimages in his eyes. Something moved in one of the station rings—more weaponry, he guessed, targeting the *Ivoire*—but just as he was about to give the order to destroy that as well, the battleship blew up.

It exploded into a million pieces, many of which were large enough to damage his fighters, which had launched just a moment ago. But the fighter pilots were nimble: they avoided everything.

The transports headed into that mess as well, flying like an entire squadron was behind them and space was littered with bombs before them. Maybe, technically, it was. Those pieces could damage anything.

"I saw something aim toward us on the station," he said, unable to call it up on the sensors.

"Me, too," Perkins said.

"I think they were aiming at us, but now they're trying to shoot some of those pieces away from the station," Kravchenko said. "The station either didn't have shields or couldn't put them up in time."

The damage to the station would be profound.

He almost asked the crew how far Boss had to go to get to Squishy, but he didn't. He looked it up for himself.

Boss had a good run ahead of her after landing. Longer than he had realized.

He cursed silently, then shook it off. He was doing all he could. He was here, wasn't he?

"The transports are landing," Anita said. "Assault teams already on the ground."

And so they were.

Parts of the station vibrated as pieces of the ship hit it. He could see atmosphere venting into space in other sections, and he prayed that the station had good environmental lock-down procedures.

The part of the station that Boss and the assault teams had entered seemed stable. No vibrations, no venting environment, nothing.

"We have reports of fighting in the station," Anita said. "We're making progress."

She'd reported previous battles for him, and knew he didn't want a casualty list until everything was finished.

"Time it," Coop said. "This entire mission shouldn't take longer than thirty."

And he knew that these thirty minutes would be the longest of his new life.

25

"THE EVAC NOTICE HAS STARTED STATION WIDE." This information came from Lynda Rooney on the *Shadow*. She and Coop had been monitoring the situation from their two ships as the transports remained on the research station.

The fighters circled, but so far, no one from the station had shot at them. The station's weapons had fired on the debris, and then stopped altogether, and Coop didn't know why.

He assumed it was because his people had shut down the weapons system and had taken control of the entire station, but he didn't know for certain yet. That wasn't their mission. Their mission was to get Squishy, guard the exits, start an evacuation, and made sure no scientist left with their research. No evacuee could take information chips or luggage of any kind. If anyone balked, orders were to shoot them. If anyone seemed shifty, orders were to shoot them.

If no one made it off the station before the assault teams, then the entire population of the station would be destroyed.

"You're listening to that notice?" Coop asked.

"I am too," Perkins said on his bridge.

"We have the notice, and we have movement inside. I'm told we have two minutes until launch." That from Lynda. "We also have casualties."

Apparently she had no qualms about hearing the list during the mission. He knew that there would be casualties among his people. He just didn't want any. He selfishly hoped that Boss wasn't among the dead.

"I know," he said, shutting off that discussion.

He watched the sensors and kept an eye on the screens. The fighters were moving back into position, readying for that moment that the transports lifted off.

His people's orders were to hit the evacuation alarm as they started to leave the station. So they were on the last part of this mission.

And so far, no other ships had arrived in the area. If there were other battleships in the region, they weren't close enough to come quickly.

They probably assumed this station was too far inside the secure area for some kind of attack.

Just like that commander had assumed no one had gotten into her sensor blanket around Starbase Kappa. Coop would have thought the Empire would learn that they should retire failed methods.

"Transports launched, sir," Kravchenko said.

He nodded. If they launched, then the assault teams—or what was left of them—had returned. He would find out soon enough what happened to everyone, who survived and who he lost.

He needed to focus on the rest of this mission.

"Have other ships launched?" he asked.

"Every transport the empire has on the station is launching now," Anita said. "They don't seem to have weapons."

"I see some life pods from areas without emergency bays or nearby ships," Yash said.

He knew better than to ask how many people remained on the station. He didn't want to know.

"The minute our transports are on board and the bays are closed, I want that station destroyed," Coop said.

"Yes, sir," Anita said.

"Lynda?" he said. "Got that?"

"Copy that, sir," she said sounding more cheerful than he would have liked. "You still want us to head back first?"

"Yes, I do," he said. "Fire and then activate your *anacapa*. Get the hell out of here."

Her pause was long enough for him to sense her disagreement. She had fought him hard on this part of the mission at the briefing. But, in the end, she had listened.

And he knew she would now.

"All of our transports are returning." Kravchenko looked a little relieved. He had forgotten that this was her first mission as first officer. She must have felt some pressure on that.

"They should dock shortly," Anita said.

"Good," he said.

He didn't ask about Boss. He didn't scan her transport.

He couldn't show favoritism, even when she wasn't part of his crew. He wouldn't allow that of himself, even though everyone on the crew would understand it.

He sat down in his chair and monitored the screens. He couldn't see the fighters or his transports. He saw the unwieldy ships the Empire used for transporting people and materiel. He saw some smaller ships as well, probably private ships, moving away from the station as fast as possible. He couldn't see the life pods, but then he hadn't magnified any imagery.

"Transports back," Yash said. "Bays closing."

"Lynda?" he asked.

"Our ships are back too," Lynda said. "You ready, Coop?"

"I am," he said. "Let's destroy this son of a bitch."

26

LYNDA FIRED FIRST, sending everything she had at that damn station. Then she activated her *anacapa* as per Coop's instructions and vanished so fast that he couldn't even tell her she had done a good job.

Her shots hit the station dead center. He had his crew fire as well, hitting the outer rims. He wanted nothing left of this place.

"Make sure it's destroyed," he said to Yash.

She nodded.

The crew fired more weaponry than needed. The station bloomed into light as shots hit targets dead on.

"It's coming apart," Kravchenko said.

"I want to see it disintegrate," he said. "Move back just a little."

The ship moved. He watched as every part of the station shattered. Debris headed like missiles toward his vessel.

"Coop, if we stay longer, we're in trouble," Yash said.

"Then get us out of here," he said as if she were the one delaying.

She hit the *anacapa* drive, and the *Ivoire* shuddered. Then its screens blackened for a moment.

His stomach clenched as he remembered this same feeling just before the *Ivoire* went into foldspace for two long and life-changing weeks. Then he looked at the screens.

He recognized the area of foldspace they were in. It was the same one they'd been in on the way out.

He wasn't sure what that meant—it didn't always happen that way—but it reassured him.

"I want a casualty report," he said, getting back to the business of command.

"We have none," Perkins said.

He frowned. "Someone reported casualties. Was that Lynda?"

"She said there were casualties, but none of them were ours," Kravchenko said. "Apparently there were a lot deaths on the station. Their security's armor couldn't handle our weaponry."

"So, we had no casualties?" Coop had been braced for loss. The fact that they had none made him giddy.

"Um," Anita said. "Not among the Fleet personnel."

His stomach turned. "But Boss's people?"

"No one that we brought," Anita said.

She raised her head. She was chewing on her lower lip.

"Boss is going to the infirmary, though," Anita said. "I think you might want to join her."

"She was injured?" he asked.

"No," Anita said. "But the rescue—let's just say that it was only partially successful."

"Oh." He ran a hand through his hair. Squishy. He hadn't really thought about what condition she would be in when she got here. At least they had gotten her off the station.

He looked at the sensors. They had gone dark again. The *Ivoire* was leaving foldspace. He waited until the familiar star map of the Nine Planets region of space appeared before he stood.

"Tell Boss I'm on my way," he said.

"She didn't ask for you, Coop," Yash said gently. "I just figure you should go."

He let out a small breath. "That bad?" he asked.

Yash nodded.

He closed his eyes. Always, the unexpected result. And Boss would tough her way through it. He understood that well.

He opened his eyes, nodded at Yash, and then left the bridge.

As he did so, he ran a hand against his forehead. At least Boss was back. At least his people had suffered no casualties.

But they had provoked the Empire.

And he had a hunch they had done so for all the wrong reasons.

27

GROUP COMMANDER ELISSA TREKOV stood in the Command Center, watching the information pour at her. Someone had managed to destroy all of the Empire's major research stations. This last station, the most important and the one they thought impregnable, had gone within the last six hours.

Around her, civilian employees with high security clearances sorted through the technical information pouring in from the surviving ships. So far, no one knew how many people had died on that station. What they did know was that some group had gone after the stealth-tech research in particular, although all of the general research had disappeared as well.

Soldiers in uniforms that no one recognized guarded the research station's doors as the evacuation notice blared, and prevented anyone from leaving with information, no matter how they carried it.

From the reports Elissa was getting, most of the scientists refused to leave without their research and did not manage to board ships before the station got destroyed.

The messages that had come through, some of which contained classified research information, were often heartbreaking, as the scientists realized they would not survive.

Those messages did not come through the communications systems of the station. Those systems had been among the first things destroyed.

From what Elissa could tell, the invaders—whoever they were—took over operations first, shut down command, disabled the shields, shut down the weaponry, and destroyed all of the communications systems except the internal station warning system.

The attack took less than thirty minutes, including an incursion to rescue a prisoner. The rescue had to be the main point of the attack, because those two ships could have come in and destroyed the station, then disappeared again without an evac and without running the risk of letting information out.

Elissa adjusted the sleeves of her uniform. It scratched against her wrists. The skin was still thin there, even though the repair on her hands had gone well.

Some of the other reconstruction done after she nearly died near the Room of Lost Souls hadn't gone as well. Her face looked mottled when she got angry, because the blood vessels under the skin didn't work evenly. She could have a dozen more procedures to fix the remaining issues—all cosmetic—and her friends had advised her to do so.

Her appearance had changed greatly since that encounter, and sometimes took people aback. She didn't look freakish. Her skin was obviously newer in some places, and her hair had gone completely white. She remained thin. The effect of all of that, plus the fact that she rarely smiled any longer, made her seem older than she was.

Her friends also told her she no longer had any softness about her. She might look like a hardass, but that didn't even begin to cover the way that she felt. She brooked no disagreement, and she expected everyone to do their jobs with no complaint.

She expected the most from herself. She was not going to lose a crew to her own mistakes ever again.

She did not consider what had just happened one of her mistakes. This was a sneak attack, designed, apparently, by the people who had attacked the other research stations.

A successful sneak attack, yes, but not one she could have foreseen.

After the destruction of the other science bases, her staff had re-viewed all new hires and found no one with the embarrassing gaps that had existed inside the resumes of those who had attacked the bases.

Most of those attackers had gotten away except for Rosealma Quin-tana, captured as she headed toward the rebels in the Nine Planets Alli-ance. Quintana was an interesting case, since she had once been a major researcher for the Empire, but had quit over a variety of issues. Even though some intelligence had shown her to be a terrorist, her research and discovery capability were so famous within the Empire itself that they trumped every political action she had taken.

And before she had destroyed one of the research stations, she had put herself back in the Empire's good graces by delivery a Dignity Vessel to the Empire. If anything, so many had argued, she was an undercover double-agent working for the Empire.

And those people had been wrong.

Evidence coming out of this latest explosion showed that Quintana had been a prisoner delivered to the research station just a few days be-fore for interrogation by scientists who knew her talents.

Elissa moved from desk to desk, gathering information. She had a staff to report to her, but she also knew that they would filter what they had learned.

And something about this attack disturbed her greatly—more than the loss of lives, more than the loss of the station itself. The methodology bothered her, and she couldn't quite put her finger on why.

The rescue of Quintana wasn't it entirely. Sacrificing so much to save one person made no military sense, unless she possessed incredible se-crets. However, Quintana had been in custody for days, so theoretically those secrets should have come out.

Although they might have been lost with the vessel that transport-ed her.

A full-sized warship, outfitted with the latest technology, including sensors so sensitive they should have known about the threat long be-fore it ever appeared.

Her people were scanning energy variations inside the region around the station. So far, they were finding nothing.

And that was it.

Her breath caught. She'd experienced this before.

She leaned toward one of the major technicians, a man named Northcutt.

"Confirm this for me," Elissa said. "We had an information shield around the entire region. An old, but highly advanced shield, composed of monitoring stations and ships."

"Yes, ma'am," Northcutt said. "We're constantly upgrading our technology there. If someone develops a new shield technology, we've compensated for it within hours of our discovery of it."

She nodded, not caring about that last as much as someone else would have expected.

"And there's no record of these ships arriving through that information shield? No record of their appearance at all?"

"No, ma'am. Not until we got word from the station before communications got shut down."

Her breath eased out. Only once before had the Empire experienced a ship arriving inside an information shield without leaving a trace. Just once.

And she had nearly died when it happened.

She had never seen the ship, and if her colleagues had had an image of that ship, it had gotten destroyed along with her entire command on that day at the Room of Lost Souls.

But she had seen the transport vessel. She had no visual record of the transport, just her memory of it.

"Do we have images of the transports that landed on the station?" she asked Northcutt.

"Yes, ma'am," Northcutt said. "And some not-real-clear imagery of the ships, taken by our evacuees as they left. The ships disappeared the moment they fired on the station, so those images aren't as good."

She'd seen the first few images. They'd been so poor that it looked like the two ships were part of the debris field.

"I want to see the transports," she said.

Those images were clear. They'd been sent from the research station the moment it believed it was under threat. Apparently the station hadn't noticed the two larger ships, or those ships had been cloaked at the moment the transports were launched.

The station did perceive the threat, however, and begged for help. Which she sent.

Only for the help to arrive in time to pick up survivors and begin mapping the debris field, searching for information and research and problems that might have developed because of the destroyed station.

"We have dozens of images of the transports," Northcutt said. "What angle do you want to view from?"

"I want to see what you have," she said. "And I want to see those things in motion as well. And if we have imagery of those soldiers, let me see that."

Northcutt created a large holographic screen in the center of the room. Three-dimensional images of the soldiers rose first, making Elissa's breath catch so hard that her chest actually hurt.

She saw those uniforms in her nightmares.

She could feel the color leaching from her face.

Then the transports appeared. Front, back, sides, heading toward the station, and docking. The movement smooth, the transports not cloaked like the one she had seen—as it left, of course.

This time, these soldiers didn't care if they were seen. She wasn't sure why, exactly.

"Son of a bitch," she said.

"What is it, ma'am?"

She couldn't blurt it out, not here. Not everyone had the right kind of clearance, even though this was a top-secret facility. Only a handful of people knew how the Room of Lost Souls got destroyed. And even fewer knew that a ship came in and obliterated an entire squadron with one shot.

This was a second attack by the exact same people. People whose technology was much greater than anything the Empire had, greater than anything on the Nine Planets, or at least that's what the Empire's intelligence told them.

Had the Nine Planets allied with an even greater power somewhere?

The ships might tell her. Two ships. Only two, and they had caused all this damage.

"Do we have better imagery of those ships?" she asked.

"Now we do," Northcutt said. "The images were pretty shadowy at first, but we've put them together and—"

"Just show me," Elissa said.

A three-dimensional ship floated above the workstation. A three-dimensional *familiar* ship.

"Holy shit," she said. "That's a Dignity Vessel."

"No," Northcutt said. "It can't be. It—"

"It is," said another researcher, a woman whose name Elissa had forgotten. "I've been comparing ship images to this one, to see if we knew who these attackers are. And Commander Trekov is right: that's a Dignity Vessel."

"We were attacked by two Dignity Vessels?" someone else muttered in disbelief. There was a low murmur throughout the room.

But Elissa felt no disbelief. She had known for a long time that factions now hiding in the Nine Planets Alliance had been taking the wrecks of Dignity Vessels and moving them elsewhere.

She had thought—because the intelligence community had thought—it was for the polymers the ships were designed out of and also for a way to reverse-engineer stealth tech. After all, Rosealma had given that Dignity Vessel to the Empire because—she said at the time— the vessel had active stealth tech, and she didn't want it in the hands of her former colleagues.

And then, years later, she destroyed stealth-tech research facilities.

Some scientists believed the ghostly death chamber on the Room of Lost Souls was nothing more than another malfunctioning stealth-tech field.

The soldiers that had attacked her four years ago had removed something from the Room, something they had then blown up, and it had destroyed six hundred lives.

One shot.

"Son of a bitch," she said again.

This wasn't a new, unknown threat. This was a known threat. The group that had fled to the Nine Planets and set up a research base was farther ahead in stealth-tech research than the Empire had believed.

That group had figured out how to make stealth tech functional, which was how these two Dignity Vessels slipped in and out of information shields.

And the group had also figured out how to turn stealth tech into a weapon.

How could they have gotten so far ahead?

And how could the Empire stop them?

THE STANDOFF
NOW

28

"CAPTAIN," PERKINS SAID, "we're getting a lot of chatter on back channels."

"Back channels?" he asked.

She nodded, studying the console in front of her. "The Empire ships had been using a dedicated channel to discuss matters, although never once did they truly discuss orders or anything. Now, there's chatter on a variety of channels, ones normally used by some of the planets on the outer rims. Only the voices, according to our systems, are some of the same voices we'd been recording from this array of ships."

Coop looked at the screens before him. He had them overlaid one on top of the other, some using heat signatures to identify the ships, some showing the ship outlines without the cloak, some showing the darkness of space as it appeared to the naked eye.

He still counted five warships, five battleships, and five support ships that might also double as battleships. The number had bothered him enough that he looked up standard imperial military practices. The standard armada had twenty-four ships.

Three of each type were missing. Or this was a non-standard formation.

Or something else was going on.

The Empire was a regulated, regimented society. He doubted that this was something else. He suspected that with a quick search of their systems, he would have found some of the non-standard formations.

He hadn't found any formation with fifteen vessels, especially when the Empire was trying for a show of strength.

What truly intrigued him was that this show of strength was, at the moment, happening while the ships were cloaked.

He kept feeling like there was a message here just for him.

"Captain?" Second Engineer Zaria Diaz spoke up. "I have that information you requested."

He frowned, thinking he had requested a lot of information in the last hour or so.

As he was about to ask her to clarify, however, she said, "That woman? You know, the voice we'd encountered before? Her name is Elissa Trekov. She's a Group Commander, which puts her in charge of this entire armada. I can't find the entire record of her command, because a lot of it is so classified that it would take a more sophisticated hack than I can do from here to discover what's happened to her, but there's some interesting stuff."

As Diaz spoke, Coop tapped one of the screens before him looking at the ranks in the Imperial Space Forces. A Group Commander was an extremely high rank. Only two ranked above her—the Flag Commander, and the person in charge of the entire Space Force, the Supreme Commander.

The name, Trekov, also set off something in his memory. He remembered Boss speaking the name, something about her first mission to Starbase Kappa being run by a Trekov. Only that Trekov had been the daughter of a major commander, but she wasn't military.

She had hooked Boss into a scheme to find her father in the Room, and that hadn't worked. Something had gone very wrong. Coop couldn't remember the details though. He'd only heard the story once, and that was a long time ago.

"This woman," Diaz was saying, "got promoted almost right after the incident at Starbase Kappa, but the reason for her promotion isn't listed."

That caught Coop's attention. "Is Starbase Kappa listed? It would be called The Room of Lost Souls."

"No, sir," Diaz said. "It's as if nothing happened there."

He raised his gaze to the actual windows and stared as if he could see through them to the border beyond.

He was right: Trekov had been at Starbase Kappa. She was the woman with whom he had spoken, and somehow she had managed to survive the *anacapa* explosion. She'd been close to it too. Every system on her ship should have shut down. Her environmental suits should have stopped working, and any ships in a large radius should have suffered the same fate.

Somehow she had managed to survive for hours in that situation, which took some ingenuity.

It would also have given her a strong motivation to find him.

And it would have given her enough information to know that the attack on the research station a month ago wasn't an anomaly.

Coop leaned back in his chair. Yes, that knowledge had enabled her to find him, probably more easily than anyone else could have, but it also gave him an edge.

Because she knew what he was capable of. He didn't have to demonstrate.

She knew he could destroy her armada with the *Ivoire* alone.

But she was career military. He had no idea if that made her cautious or reckless. If she was reckless, she was looking for payback.

If she was cautious, she would negotiate with him.

He stood.

She wasn't that cautious. She had been cautious before, and it had gotten her in trouble.

She had also been working with scientists.

She understood the value of that thing the Empire called stealth tech.

His ships had appeared and disappeared, seemingly traveling through a sensor blanket as if it didn't exist. She also knew that his team had gotten into a room on Starbase Kappa that her people hadn't been able to open despite trying, that they had taken something from that room, and that they had left quickly, destroying everything.

A very similar attack to the one on the science station, only that time, they had taken a person—Squishy. All of this was concerned with stealth tech.

And he hadn't identified himself in any of these encounters. For all she knew, he was flying a ship that Boss had rebuilt—a Fleet ship, yes, but something the Empire called a Dignity Vessel. Lynda was in a rebuild. It would stand to reason to this Trekov woman that Coop's ship was a rebuild as well.

"Oh my God," he said softly.

"What is it, Captain?" Anita asked.

He looked at her. Diaz was watching as well.

"They're not going to invade the Nine Planets Alliance—not here, anyway," he said. "They're going to raid the Lost Souls Corporation. They're going after Boss."

THE DIVE
NOW

29

IT SPEAKS TO THE DEPTH OF MY FEAR that only two people make the next attempt to enter the Boneyard—and those two people are me and Yash.

Any thought of actual diving is gone for the moment. We just want to get in and get out.

If we can't get out quickly—if it appears that we're stuck or lost in time or have become part of the Boneyard—Mikk has instructions to take the *Two* back to the Lost Souls Corporation. He also has instructions to tell everyone there that we are dead.

If we get stuck, I don't want anyone to get stuck coming after us.

Of course, I don't really want to get stuck with Yash either. The idea of spending a month with her in this skip, waiting to die, gives me shudders. I've brought all of my diving equipment, though, as well as extra food and water.

I have diving equipment for her as well. If we get stuck here, we're going to dive the nearby ships and see what we find. If we get stuck here, maybe Yash can find that place where the force field originates, and shut the damn thing off.

If we get stuck here.

Which I hope to God won't happen.

This skip is my favorite, but I never use it. I imagine using it. I *remember* using it. It's not our second skip. It's the third skip on the *Two*, the skip we never use.

I'm excessively cautious. Because the *Two* has a larger ship bay than *Nobody's Business*, I bring an extra skip, just in case something goes horribly, terribly wrong, and we need the skips plus the life pods.

Generally, if something went wrong on a dive, we would use the second skip. But Yash has installed an *anacapa* on that skip as well, because we need two functioning skips for diving emergencies. The medic has to be able to get to the diving crew quickly—and if the crew went into an area using an *anacapa*, then the rescue team needs an *anacapa* to get the crew out.

The third skip, the one we're using, is one I used way back when. Back when I didn't own the Lost Souls Corporation, back when all I had was my diving business. Back when putting a dive team together made my stomach twist and my heart pound, just because of the money involved.

I scrimped and saved to get this skip, and it was, when I bought it, the no-frills, bottom-of-the-line model. It doesn't even have an area to cook in. Whoever designed the thing believed that if the people using the skip wanted a meal, they had to make do with something cold that they had brought aboard themselves.

The interior is small, even by skip standards. The console is built off to one side, and the chairs, where any travelers can strap in, are on the other side. The rest of the interior is empty, except for the basics—water, bathroom facilities, some storage. This skip is designed for short trips, a small crew on a specific mission, and enough space to store whatever was retrieved (if anything).

Nothing fancy.

And I've made it even less fancy by not upgrading the equipment, cleaning it only after a trip (and not before) and keeping the original chairs, which are not only old, but filled with small tears. The straps are new—new*ish*, anyway—and solid enough to hold someone down should gravity fail and someone need to be held in place, but the chairs might not survive the strain.

The things I have kept up, though, are the controls, the engine, and the environmental systems.

The things that keep you alive.

Not that you can tell I've done any work by looking around.

Yash has to duck to enter, and she stops once she's inside. I can actually read her thoughts: *You've got to be kidding, right?* But to her credit, she doesn't say anything.

She just hauls her equipment inside, shoves it into the storage locker, and stops.

"One person console," she says, looking at the controls.

I nod. I have always liked to have only one pilot. If someone needs to save the day, they can unstrap themselves, move the dead, dying, or incapacitated pilot out of the way, and then get on with the business of flying the skip.

"I'm going to need access to those controls while we travel," she says, "and I haven't piloted anything this small in twenty years."

I shrug, and can't resist playing to her expectations. "Then we better hope the gravity continues to work, because we'll be standing side by side."

The one cool thing about this skip is that the pilot's chair becomes part of the floor. This is how the skip's console becomes a two-person console. The chair goes away, and we can both stand in front of that console.

I touch the button and the chair creaks and complains as it folds in on itself. Then it flattens into the floor, the colors blending so you can't even see that something is there.

I was told, when I bought this thing, that the color blending was a safety feature, although for the life of me I still can't figure out why it's important that no one knows the chair exists when it's flattened.

Yash gets that *You're kidding, right?* expression again. She sighs, moves to the console, and stares at it.

Simple, to the point, with nothing extra. Suddenly, I find myself worrying that it's too simple for what we're about to attempt.

"Can you do what you need to do?" I ask.

She activates the console, then runs her fingers above it, as if she's afraid that she'll activate the controls by touching them. Even this console is sophisticated enough to have a secondary activation before the controls work.

But I don't tell her that. I'd rather have her investigate her way.

She nods.

"It's going to be an adventure in flying," she says. "But I can do it."

"Okay then," I say. "Let's go."

30

PILOTING STANDING UP, on this skip, makes me feel decades younger. I haven't done this for a long time, but it feels like I left the skip just moments ago. I can still pilot this skip with my eyes closed, and have done so dozens of times a year because—I realize now—this skip features in some of my recurring dreams.

Not nightmares, just dreams of exploration. And in those dreams, I'm never piloting the *Two* or *Nobody's Business* or standing in the background on the *Ivoire*. I'm always on this skip, going somewhere, with two of my old teammates, Squishy and Karl, beside me.

It feels odd not to have them beside me now.

Right now, the woman beside me is tense and nervous.

"What exactly are you worried about?" I ask, my hands on the controls. Time to know now, rather than as we're heading to the Boneyard.

"I'm not real fond of your ancient relic here," Yash says.

"It's a good old ship," I say.

"Ironically, it's not that old," she says. "Not compared to the *Ivoire*."

Normally, I would smile at that, particularly if the comment came from Coop. He was starting to get to the point where he could joke.

But I don't know if Yash is serious or not, so I ignore her comment.

"It's either this or remove the *anacapa* from one of the other skips," I say.

"I know," she says. "And I'm ready."

Even though she's not. I decide not to challenge her. I have my doubts as to whether we'll get through that force field anyway, and if we don't, then we'll just turn around and go back.

We've already sent a probe to the force field—and the probe hadn't been destroyed or damaged when it wasn't able to go through. I expect the same thing to happen to the skip. Yash and I might be in for a few unpleasant moments, but we'll be able to handle them.

I power up the skip, activate the secondary controls on the console, then inform the *Two* that we're ready to go. I have cleared all of the windows, which on this skip is really impressive. Truth be told, that's one of the reasons I bought it.

The walls of the skip become clear. We can see outside as if we're standing on a platform in the middle of space. Or rather, at the moment, standing in the middle of the ship bay on the *Two.*

The other two skips rest on either side of this one, and ahead of us is the bay door. It's slowly rising, revealing darkness beyond.

My fingers are twitching. I want to get this skip out of here. I'm ready to leave, right now.

If I were wearing my suit, someone would be yelling into my comm about the gids. I grin at myself.

I'm thrilled to be on this mission, and I didn't realize it until right now.

Yash, on the other hand, isn't looking at the bay door rise. She's staring at the console as if she can will it to become something more sophisticated. Her hand trembles as it rests above the glowing imagery.

"You have a little time," I say. "You can put your arm down."

She lets out a small laugh, as if she too didn't realize what she's feeling.

"It's been a long time since I've been on a two-person mission," she says. "I never liked them."

"I love them," I say, "but not as much as I like traveling alone."

"You are much more courageous than I am, Boss," she says softly. "I prefer having the backing of the entire Fleet behind me. The fact that it's just the *Ivoire* now makes me feel unprotected and alone."

I doubt she would have admitted that to me in any other circumstance. I don't bother to correct her about being alone. I understand what she means. She doesn't count the Lost Souls because we're backward by her standards, and even if we weren't, we're not her people.

"Then this must be real awkward for you," I say gently.

"Oh, you have no idea," she says.

Actually, I probably do, but in reverse. I feel that way whenever the cockpit crowd grows past three or four. When I'm on the *Ivoire*, I feel the pressure of the hundreds of people on the ship with me. And when I'm at Lost Souls, where I now have so many employees that I don't know the number without looking and couldn't tell you their names if I tried, I get regular panic attacks.

"With luck, this'll be short," I say.

"With luck," she says, "it won't."

I grin at her. She grins back. Then we ease out of the bay, and into space.

31

The Boneyard looms before us like a gigantic planet. We can't see around it, over it, or under it. All we can see is a small bit of it, growing before us as we get closer.

The large old portholes on the skip are made of a different kind of material than the windows on the *Two*. Through these portholes, the force field looks like a thin shadow we have to cross.

"You see that?" I ask Yash.

"Yeah," she says. "I didn't expect the force field to be visible."

"Maybe as a warning?" I ask.

She shakes her head. "It shows up on sensors long before you can see it with the naked eye. It must be something in the composition of your ancient windows there."

This time, she says the word "ancient" with a bit of approval.

We're taking turns monitoring the sensors and looking at the Boneyard through the portholes. We started doing this without discussing it, but clearly we're both a bit nervous. We want to see what's ahead of us—visually, anyway—and we also want to know what, exactly, it is.

What we see—what *I* see—are ships. Ships and parts of ships that seem to extend forever. They are above us and below us and extending to each side of us. They disappear far into the distance in all directions. And they seem stationary, which takes some energy in and of itself to accomplish.

Some details are hard to see with that force field veil over everything. I can see shapes, but not outlines of doors or portholes. I see parts of ships, but I'm not processing what parts.

In fact, it's hard to focus on the individual ships at all. The Boneyard itself seems like an entity composed of ships. It's as if I want to concentrate on skin cells whenever I look at a human being. I sometimes see what the skin cells make, like an arm or a face, but I can't really see each cell clearly.

I keep losing the individual ships to the totality of the Boneyard.

My stomach clenches. The idea of diving ships here now seems impossible. Not because it would be hard—it probably wouldn't be. It would probably be a lot of fun.

But because there are so many ships.

This is the rest of my life, plus countless lives afterward. This is millions, maybe billions, of people hours, and I'm not sure what the point would be. One person can't dive the entire Boneyard. Nor can one team.

I swallow hard.

I guess I knew this on some level, but I didn't *understand* it until now. I want the person beside me to be Coop, not Yash. I want to pull him aside, somewhere private, and say quietly, *Your answers are probably here, but we might never find them—at least not in your lifetime. Whatever you need to know is probably buried in some ship we can't even see from this vantage point.*

Yash's hands are shaking. Something is going through her mind as well, but I'm not going to ask what it is. She's been through a lot, and this trip is making her nervous enough already.

She swallows hard, then says, head down, "I can send a modified signal to that force field, letting it know we're friendly. That's my first attempt. Do you still want to go in?"

Either she's feeling my sudden mood change or she's become even more hesitant. I'm betting on her hesitation, not my mood.

I'm not one to run from a challenge, particularly a challenge like this. We're about to enter a diving Mecca, filled with more questions than I'll ever find answers to.

In some ways, it's a personal heaven for me.

"Of course I want to go in," I say.

"Okay," she says, and taps the console. "Let's see what this does."

I know she has several other techniques planned to get us inside the Boneyard, so I don't expect this one to work.

So I'm as surprised as I can be when the force field clears right before us, creating a small hole in the shadow.

"Oh, my God," Yash says.

Exactly. Oh, my God, and any other expression of surprise you can think of.

My hands shake as I handle the controls.

As I send the skip inside.

32

AHEAD OF US, I SEND A PROBE. Decades of caution force me to take that step. I almost didn't do it, but in the end, I can't go into the Boneyard without taking the right precautions. I just can't.

I launch the probe on our trajectory. It moves much faster than we are.

"What the hell is that?" she asks, sounding tense.

"I have to send in a probe."

She swears in her language. "If this is a typical Fleet outpost, they'll destroy it and think we're hostile."

"Really?" I ask. "Because it has no weaponry at all. It's just a little informational gadget."

"The systems here should be automated," she says. "It's procedure."

As if it's procedure now, instead of five thousand years ago. I say nothing. She's probably right.

But if she's right, then even our skip, with its unfamiliar design, might be seen as hostile once it's inside, and then we'll get destroyed.

The probe goes inside, and I can't see it any more. I also don't see any obvious weapons' fire.

The hole in the force field remains. The hair rises on the back of my neck. Is this standard procedure for the Boneyard? Does something go in without follow-up from an active ship? Is that how the ships get inside?

Or did something else happen to the probe? Was it destroyed by some kind of weapon I'm not familiar with?

I slow the skip even more, planning to stop it if I can't figure out what happened to the probe.

Then telemetry starts appearing on a nearby screen. The probe is still working, still active, still unharmed.

I let out a breath I hadn't even realized I was holding.

The telemetry shows odd energy readings, some spikes, some readings I recognize from *anacapa* fields. It registers dozens of ships in proximity to it, and no active threats.

Yash looks at the readings as well. She glances at me, then shakes her head in silent acceptance.

I speed the skip back up. We're moving forward once again.

As we approach that hole in the force field, I realize just how large it is. Large enough for more than one Dignity Vessel to go through it. Large enough for a phalanx of Dignity Vessels in military formation to slide in. Large enough to dwarf us and make me feel even smaller than that probe.

I glance at Yash. She's staring at the looming hole before us, and I can read her expression. She knows, like I know, that this is the last moment in which we can back out.

Then the skip goes inside that hole. The force field thickness is five times the length of the skip. The hole seems to extend forever. We bump a bit as we hit some kind of energy wave, and that makes Yash look back at the equipment.

She touches her screen again. It looks, from here, like she's sending a confirm signal or modifying something on the skip itself.

I decide to focus on my piloting instead of on what she's doing. The Boneyard is distraction enough.

We finally leave the hole, and to my relief, it does not close up on us. At least, not immediately.

We have arrived in a small hole between four damaged Dignity Vessels. One has obvious weapons scoring on its underbelly. Another has a large hole leading through the ship to the bridge itself. A third is missing the engineering section, and the last looks just fine, from the outside anyway.

The ships are clearly inactive, and clearly empty.

"There are active *anacapa* drives in here," Yash says, her voice sounding rusty. "They're not malfunctioning. They're on the setting we call 'off' even though the drive really isn't off. It's more dormant than off."

I didn't need the full explanation. I've gotten it a dozen times. But I know why she's telling me this in such complete detail. She doesn't know what I know and what I don't. Hell, I don't know what I know and what I don't. So it's better to over explain. I'll never complain about that.

"Do you think some of these ships are just being stored?" I ask.

"I don't know," she says. "I doubt it. This is not the formation we use to store inactive but viable ships. I think they're all damaged somehow, but damaged in different ways. I'd like to go in farther and investigate the controls for the force field."

Suddenly she's courageous. I have to suppress a smile. She wouldn't think of it that way. She's forgotten why we're here, and how we conduct exploratory missions. How *I* conduct them.

She's acting like a first-time wreck diver overwhelmed with the sheer awesomeness before her. She wants to discover more and more and more. It's like a drug high, something that the diver can't get enough of.

And, like a drug high, it will kill if the diver isn't very, very careful.

"I know you would," I say, "but we're not going to deviate from our mission. We're going to download as much information as possible in the next ten minutes, and then we're going back to the *Two*."

"It won't hurt to—"

"It will," I say. "We'll make some kind of mistake. I know you want to understand what's going on here, and so do I, but if we do this wrong, we'll die in here. Right now, this is the only ship that we have that can even enter the Boneyard. No one can rescue us, Yash. Remember?"

She looks at me, shocked, then blinks as color fills her cheeks. She has forgotten. She's made a rookie mistake, and she's embarrassed by it.

"Of course you're right," she says in her most professional voice. "Let's get the information and then leave."

I nod—and we set to work.

33

AFTER TEN MINUTES IN THE BONEYARD, I ease the skip back along the exact same trajectory on which we entered. I don't turn the skip around. I just move the skip backward, not deviating in any way from the path we entered on.

"I'm not done," Yash says. "You should have told me you wanted to go."

"I did tell you." I've been through this kind of interaction with dozens of divers. If I weren't so tense, I would find this very amusing—the highly professional Yash getting lost in a dive. Or the beginnings of a dive, anyway. "We follow the rules."

"You're making the rules up as you go," she says.

"Actually, I'm not," I say. "These are the rules of any dive you would do with me. I've used these rules for years."

"And you've still lost divers," she snaps.

Her words, meant to push, do not hurt me at all. I have lost divers, and it's always painful. But I make sure I analyze the reasons why, and do my best not to make same mistake again.

"Yes, I have lost divers," I say, "but generally not because they've broken the rules. It's been because we encountered something we didn't expect and didn't know how to deal with, and not even the rules could save us."

I let those words hang. Or maybe Yash does, because she doesn't respond. She watches both the portholes and the console as we retrace our path.

Just as we're about to enter that hole in the force field, she asks, "You're not going to retrieve the probe?"

"No," I say. "I want to know if we can still receive its readings once the force field closes again."

"It may not close," she says. "Not unless I give it the signal."

"Then you'll give it the signal," I say. "Because we don't want to leave the Boneyard open to scavengers."

"They haven't shown up," she says.

"Not yet," I say. And maybe they won't appear while we're here, but I'm back in dive mode. I'm so cautious that it even annoys me. If I can think of something that will go wrong, I will do my best to protect against it.

Yash will come to her senses when we leave the Boneyard. Once she's away from the temptation. She will realize that cautious is best, and she'll be appalled at her behavior.

I know Coop would be reprimanding her right about now—if he wasn't caught up in the Boneyard's majesty too. And considering how he's acted when we've found abandoned Sector Bases, I think I'm lucky to have Yash at my side and not Coop. Coop is used to taking matters into his own hands, and that makes him hard to control.

Yash is used to following orders.

We back into that hole in the force field, and for some reason, this part makes me nervous. It takes me a second to figure out why: I'm afraid that the force field will close before we leave.

I resist the urge to change our speed while we're inside. Any deviation might cause more problems. We might be seen as a threat if we hurry out, especially if this is as automated as Yash thinks it is.

Finally we emerge into our part of space. I'm just a little dizzy. We're done moving and I feel nothing but relief.

On a subconscious level, I find the Boneyard terrifying. Or maybe the level isn't that subconscious. Maybe I'm being my old cautious self because I know so many different ways to die in that Boneyard.

And I also know that all of those ways I can think of are probably only a fraction of the ways to die in there. They're the ones I can predict, I can understand, I can guess at.

I have no idea what else lurks in there.

But, silly me, I do plan to find out.

34

YASH WAS RIGHT: the only way to close the force field was to send a signal. She's encouraged by this. She believes it means the Fleet hasn't changed much since she was with it.

I think if the Fleet still exists, it has changed a lot. I see no evidence that the Fleet exists now. I only see evidence that the Fleet existed a long time ago, and abandoned a lot of places all over several sectors.

The Boneyard itself might be an abandoned place.

That's what Coop initially assumed, and I'm still working on that premise. The fact that Yash has made some kind of contact with Fleet technology—technology that's not broken or antiquated, but somewhat unfamiliar to her—makes her believe that the Fleet still exists.

All of this makes me realize that the belief has always been just beneath the surface for her, and she's a lot less sensible about her loss than I thought she was.

I store that information for later, in case it becomes important.

I was right about one thing: Yash is appalled at her behavior inside the Boneyard. I try to tell her that such behavior is normal on a first dive, but she doesn't think we've dived. We didn't don suits and head out into a wrecked ship. We were just inside a graveyard of wrecked ships. I try to tell her that's part of what diving is, but she's having none of it.

She thinks she's failed somehow.

Considering the fact that it was her technical knowledge that got us into the Boneyard in the first place, I see no failure anywhere. I can't tell her that either. I realize, after a few fruitless conversations with her, that she is going to flagellate herself for a while, and that's her way of dealing with the lost millennia and the death of everything she knows.

She had that reinforced inside the Boneyard, whether she realizes it or not.

I'm not going to be the one to help her realize what's going on.

I have too much to do.

I have data to analyze. And unlike my usual dives, I'm not going to do so with the entire group watching.

I want Yash to examine the data her way, and I want time alone with the rest of it.

I quarantine the information we've gotten from the dive, and make sure that—at the moment—only Yash and I can examine it. I know Mikk wants to see it as well, but I'm not going to let him. I need to think about all of this unfiltered.

For that reason, I use the non-networked system inside my quarters to go over everything we've seen. Ever since my first dive, I've had a completely different computer set up in my quarters than anywhere else.

I initially established this because I am such a loner; I didn't trust my very first diving crew, and I didn't want them to know anything about the dive.

I soon learned that that was bad policy. I needed more minds than mine on everything. Even then, though, I wanted to protect some information, often because I never wanted the locations of our wreck dives on any public network—or any chance of them finding their way to a public network.

A lot of times, I left the wrecks where they were, a tribute to their history, not so they could be used for scrap or confiscated by the Empire or even allowed to become a tourist wreck dive, which I do recognize as ironic, because I used to make a living taking tourists on wreck dives.

But preservation is one of my loves, history is one of my loves, and I'm careful not to betray either.

Except when militarily necessary.

I smile grimly and get to work.

My quarters are larger than I like. They have two rooms, both larger than any other cabin on this ship. If the bed weren't built in, I would place it in the front area so that no one could see me working. Unfortunately, the bed, like so much of the furniture, came already attached.

My main desk is as far from the door as possible. I work with my back to the wall and my screens facing that wall. That way, no one can enter and take images of what I'm doing for later consumption.

Not that anyone enters these quarters except me. Coop tried joining me once and learned why that was a bad idea. If we wanted time alone, we took it in whatever cabin I assigned him for the trip.

These quarters have a tiny private galley kitchen, which I use on days like this. I'm focused on information, research, and discovery, not on socializing and eating. I know that drives my crew nuts, but I don't care. I'm busy; they should find a way to be busy as well.

Yash and I gathered a lot of information in our ten minutes inside the Boneyard. But that's not what I'm looking at first. First, I'm examining the telemetry from the probe.

It sent nearly an hour's worth of material before its feed shut down. For all I know, it's still trying to send information.

But, as I expected, the moment the force field closed, the probe's telemetry feed stopped. Our designs are no match for that Fleet force field.

Yash has assigned some of the engineers that she brought with her to modify a probe to see if they can get it to send information through the force field. I insisted that if they develop something like that, they also make sure that we can shut it off from *outside* the force field. I'm still concerned that others—particularly those scavengers—will figure out a way inside.

I've spent most of the day examining the telemetry from the probe and looking at what Yash and I discovered. I also have a third computer system, untethered to the one I'm using for the downloads and telemetry, matching information from all of the devices we used, so that I'm not doing the yeoman's work of information sorting.

Because there's really too much information to deal with.

I have discovered a few things, things that have made me pause with each revelation, and forced me to reconsider plans.

First, the Boneyard's sheer size is daunting. It makes what sounded like a simple mission into a very difficult one. Some modification of the force field keeps the ships in position. Or, as Yash suggested, some device got placed in all of the ships and partial ships that locks them in place.

I put her on investigating this, since I don't even know what to look for.

My brain is still processing the vast number ships, all Fleet built. If this Boneyard is the only such thing of its kind, *and* the Fleet still exists, that means the Fleet has lost several ships per year, and then placed them (or parts of them) in the Boneyard.

But Coop once told me that the size of the Fleet varies. Some generations go through a ship-building mania, and they add a lot of new ships to the Fleet. Those ships aren't as heavily peopled—at least at first—and they move along with the rest, or remain at one of the Sector bases until needed.

So if the Fleet still exists and it is composed of 1,000 ships, then it lost and recovered a lot of ships. Not every ship that gets damaged can be salvaged, and I'm sure that some get completely destroyed.

Not to mention the Dignity Vessel wrecks that we've found so far. They never got rounded up and put into the Boneyard. Coop tells several stories of ships he knows about that got lost in foldspace—or at least, that he believes got lost in foldspace—not to mention the ships that never returned from some mission.

I would assume that any ship that gets put into the Boneyard has been found by the Fleet.

But the location of this Boneyard, plus the design of the force field and some of the ships, tells me it was placed here after Coop disappeared from the Fleet. So of course he wouldn't have known about the Boneyard before he left.

Still, the place's sheer size is disturbing and doesn't make a lot of sense to me. Mathematical or otherwise. I did have our scanners do a cursory search for Fleet-only materials, and they reported back that everything they could scan—which was an interesting phrase in and of itself—showed only Fleet-based ships.

I had also asked that the scanners do a count of all the ships in the Boneyard, but they didn't have enough time or enough information. The parts of ships—especially three-quarter ships—confused the computers. They didn't know if those were a full ship, a partial ship, or something to be ignored.

We'll have to design a program to figure out exactly what we've stumbled upon.

Just that thought alone got me up and out of my chair, pacing. The number of ships overwhelms me, particularly when I want to dive them all. I won't be able to.

I knew that, but I didn't really *know* it. For some reason, the number—even though it is an estimate—makes the Boneyard even more real to me.

It is now a thing, not an idea, something with recognizable limits and measures, even if those limits and measures are huge. I can wrap my brain around all of this, and make plans, when I couldn't do so before.

Before we got here for our second visit, all I knew was that the Boneyard was large and it probably had a lot of Fleet ships inside it. Maybe it had other ships from other places, maybe not.

There is no way that it could be the remains of one battle, like Coop initially thought. I'm not even sure it could be the remains of one large war.

I let that sink into my imagination for a moment, and then I continue.

I have much too much to think about: not just the information the sensors provided, not just the number of ships, not just what we're facing, but also I must plan. I have a mission to accomplish—theoretically—and now it's my job to figure out if that mission is even possible.

Because there's one problem that I have yet to discuss with Yash.

We both knew that the thing which generated the force field was in what we think is the very center of the Boneyard. But we thought we'd be able to get to that center using an *anacapa* drive.

We still might be able to, after some futzing and some reworking or maybe even using one of the ships from the Boneyard itself.

But that's the *only* way to get there.

Besides, that's much too much work for this trip, if we combine it with liberating a few of the ships.

Frankly, we need more ships more than we need to understand what's going on with the Boneyard. At least in the short term. And I'm not sure how to convince Yash of that.

She wants to know what happened five thousand or so years in the past, and I'm worried about the next five months ahead of us.

This wouldn't be such a big concern, except for one thing: I need her beside me to explore that Boneyard. I need her concentration and her expertise, and I'm not sure I have either.

I need a plan, and I need to develop it before I talk to her.

Because, in that conversation, I'm going to have to convince her that I'm right, that I'm worth listening to, and I'm worth following.

And I'm not sure I can do that, all on my own.

35

I SPEND TWO DAYS GATHERING FACTS and putting together a presentation just for Yash. My hands are shaking as I wait for her in the conference room. She can make or break this entire mission.

She can convince the Fleet members on the *Two* that the mission isn't worth doing. She can also take over this ship with very little effort, although my people will defend me as best they can.

They're divers, though, and scholars, and pilots. Not fighters. She has fighters—and I can't believe I'm thinking this.

Only I know that I can't get it out of my brain.

Two reasons:

I've angered partners before, and had them do something horrible and unexpected.

And, now that I've realized that Yash isn't totally focused on remaining in this future, I have rethought her volatility level. She could go off the deep end if I push her too hard away from discovering what she needs to know about her family and friends.

I consider Coop a very sane man, considering all he's been through. I also know (now, anyway) that captains in the Fleet don't get to that position by being weak-minded or overly emotional people. He thinks things through, he doesn't panic, and he makes sound decisions. It's in his character, it's part of his job description, and it's what he needs to do for his people.

And he still goes a little crazy once in a while over the changes he's been through since the *Ivoire* arrived here.

Yash doesn't have that personality or that level of stability as part of her job description. That I attributed her with more calmness with Coop has to do with the way she presented herself to me, not with the actual truth of her position.

I've reassessed, and now I know that she could go just a little crazy right here, right now, on this mission. Normally, I wouldn't blame her. I probably would be a lot harder to handle in her circumstance.

But I need her to listen to me or I need to sideline her or, if she gets too intractable, I need to abort this mission.

And I have to do it without angering everyone else from the Fleet.

I'm trying not to pace. Pacing makes my nervousness really hard to miss. Shaking, though, is something I can easily hide. I can press my hands against the tabletop, or fold them in my lap. Yash won't know.

Yash enters. She has deep circles under her eyes, and she looks thinner, even though I know that's not possible, not in this short a time. But she's tired and stressed, and I'm not even sure she's entirely here. I think her attention is elsewhere, and I think that just because of the look in her eyes.

"We don't have time for a sit-down," she says.

"We need it," I say, keeping my voice calm. It is the only calm thing about me.

"We need to follow this information, figure out—"

"We need to agree," I say.

She blinks, then puts her hand on the back of a nearby chair, and leans toward me. Now I've got her full attention.

"*We* need to agree," she says, in a tone filled with sarcasm. "You mean I have to agree with you."

Yes, that's what I mean, but that's not what I'm going to say. At least, not quite that directly.

I say, "I've been going over the information we got in the Boneyard and—"

"So have I," she says, "and it's pretty clear to me that you need me on all trips into that Boneyard."

She's afraid I don't want her to travel inside? I almost smile. That's the reaction of an addicted diver, someone for whom the search, the hunt, is more important than anything else.

"I do need you," I say, "but that's not the point I was going to make. If you sit down, we can finish this discussion."

Like adults, I want to add, but I don't.

Her eyes narrow and her lips thin, but she sits down heavily, reluctantly, like a teenager making silent protest. The chair creaks from the violence of her movement.

I ignore that.

I've thought about how to approach this almost as long as I've been thinking about the information we got from our trip.

"Our mission—"

"Your mission," she says, and I sigh. Audibly. With full exasperation.

"*Our* mission," I say, "is to bring back ships so that we can study them, so that we can find out information—"

"And so you can fight your stupid Empire."

She has gone full teenager on me. If I weren't so tense, I might find it amusing.

"So that I can fight 'my stupid' Empire," I say, nodding toward her.

That shuts her up.

"You want to find out about the Fleet," I say.

"Get to it," she snaps. "What do you want?"

"I want to plan the dives my way."

"And you're afraid I won't let you," she says.

"Yes," I say.

"Because why? We all know that you're in charge of this ship."

"Because," I say, "if I were in your shoes, I would be fighting me all the way."

She inhales slightly. I have surprised her.

"What are you talking about?" she asks.

"The Boneyard is too big to handle with one skip and a limited crew," I say. "I want to change the point of the dive. It'll enable us to fulfill *my* mission, but not yours, not yet. I have ideas on how to do yours as well."

"Mine?" she asks. "Technically, mine is the same as yours."

"Technically, maybe. You're doing what Coop asked," I say. "But we both know that realistically, following the short-term mission makes you mad. It's hard, and it's not what you personally need, which makes it hard, or should I say hard*er*, to work for me."

I deliberately use the word "for" instead of "with." I'm not sure she'll catch that, but if she does, she'll get what I mean even more.

"What are you proposing?" she asks.

"That we dive the closest prospects. Three ships, which is all we have pilots for. We make sure—well, *you* make sure—their *anacapa* drives are viable. Then we send them back to Lost Souls. We follow, with as much data as we can gather, and figure out a couple of things. First, we figure out how to enable an *anacapa* drive that you or your team has built to enter that Boneyard. Second, we figure out where exactly that force field generator is, and third—"

"I already figured that out," she says. "There's an actual substation of some kind. I told you that."

"I saw it," I say. "And it looks like it is the generator, but you also told me that you don't know if it's an actual generator or an amplifier."

"I told you that before we went in," she says.

"Has something changed your mind?" I ask.

Her cheeks pinken. "Not yet."

I nod, careful not to say that simply proves my point.

"What I'm looking at here," I say, "is—"

"Your own concerns, just like I said," she snaps.

"Is," I repeat, "how to best to use our limited resources with limited risk. Diving is all about risk, Yash, and we don't know a lot of things, like what's really holding those ships in place, where they come from, if anyone monitors this place, and what its real purpose is."

"We'd know that if we went to that center substation," she says.

"You *think*," I say. "You *hope*. You don't *know*."

My gaze meets hers. She looks away. After a moment, she nods. "I hope."

"We dive this, we come back in a week or two with the ships we need, and then you can hand-pick your team from the *Ivoire* to dive this Boneyard properly. We go into that substation prepared. In fact, we might have to dive this with the ships we bring back. They'll be part of the Boneyard, after all."

That makes her turn toward me. "You want to get the ships, take them back, get them working, and then bring them here as a kind of spy ship?"

"I guess you can put it that way," I say. "We're not of the Fleet, and we'll be using one of their ships, so yeah. A spy ship works."

Her gaze goes down, toward the table, and a small furrow appears on her forehead. She's clearly thinking about this. This part of the plan has surprised her.

"And we bring back engineers," she says.

"And whomever else you believe needs to come with us," I say. "By then, we will have gathered enough information about the Boneyard, about the force field, and about the layout to bring the right people."

She grunts, then leans back. Her hands thread behind her head. She looks up at the ceiling. I suddenly realize she's been as nervous about this meeting as I have.

Had she planned to take over the mission?

I don't know and I'm not going to ask. I don't want to derail whatever she's thinking of. Because I did get her moving in a new direction, and I want her to continue doing so.

"I don't like going in with one ancient skip," she says after a moment, still looking at the ceiling.

"Neither do I," I say. I want to tell her my plan to remove the *anacapa* from one of the other skips, but I'll let her speak first. I owe her that much.

"I can easily remove the *anacapa* drives from the two other skips," she says. "That way all of our skips can get inside the Boneyard without being boomeranged back, or whatever happened to us."

"All?" I ask, in spite of myself. I had only planned to redesign one.

"We need two rotating skips and a medical vessel, right?"

Ideally, she is right. But I had never planned to rotate the skips I had, not with the skip she calls "ancient." I had planned to use that only in an emergency, which I guess this is.

"Can you see any reason to leave an *anacapa* on board one of the skips?" she asks. "Because at the moment, I can't."

She's still thinking of the Boneyard and the dives, not of the whole mission.

"If something happens to the *Two*," I say, "we need an escape vessel, even if it's one of the skips heading back to Lost Souls with a request for help."

She grunts again, then sits up, her hands falling to her sides. She swivels so that she's looking at me directly. Intensely. It makes me a bit nervous.

"You don't think conventionally," she says. "But you have a tactical brain. I wouldn't have expected it."

"Thank you," I say. "I think."

"We'll do it your way," she says as if she were the person in charge of the mission, and I was a junior officer suggesting a new path. "In the end, it may take less time than mine."

And that's the moment I know with certainty that she was planning to take over the entire mission, to guide us deep into the Boneyard with no backup at all. If Yash had been in charge of this trip, it would have ended in disaster, no doubt about it.

Now there's less chance of a disaster, although the chance remains.

I'm not going to ask her what her plan is/was. I don't dare. If she explains it, she might get reattached to it.

"How long will it take you to remove the *anacapa* from one of the skips?" I ask.

"Two days, tops," she says. "We'll have to scrub it, make sure none of the *anacapa*'s energy signature remains. That'll be the hard part."

It certainly is the part I don't understand. But I don't ask her to explain what she'll do. That's not important to me. What's important is that she'll do it, that this mission will go forward the way I want it to, without trouble from my crew.

"Let me know when it's done," I say. "I'll use the time to examine our data and figure out which ships appear to be the most intact."

"You realize we might not find an intact *anacapa* on any of these ships," she says. "Then we'll have to piggyback."

"Or something," I say. I'm not making contingencies about that damn drive with anything or with any of my people. "We'll figure it out if we have to."

Or we'll go back to the Lost Souls and report my mission as a failure. Either way, it won't be an entire loss, because we will have gathered a lot more intel about the Boneyard itself.

I'm not going to make any assumptions, though. I'm going to plan this dive as if it were any other dive, filled with danger, excitement, and the unknown.

My spirits lift. I had no idea how nervous I had been about this meeting, but now that it's gone well, I'm relieved.

We can start diving proper.

I can start diving.

And that thrills me, more than I can say.

THE STANDOFF
NOW

36

ELISSA STOOD ON THE OBSERVATION DECK of the flagship *Ewing Trekov*, named for her great-great-grandfather. She thought it an unfortunate coincidence that the command ship for this operation was the *Ewing Trekov*. Not only did she dislike the ship's name and its implications, she also thought it an outdated monstrosity.

But it was the only ship available. The other flagships were on maneuvers elsewhere in the Empire and couldn't get to the border region quickly enough. The moment Elissa let General Command know she had identified the perpetrators of the attacks on the research stations, General Command demanded immediate action.

They wanted to punish the perpetrators, of course. They wanted to let the Nine Planets know that they could not house terrorists. And they wanted that stealth tech, even if it meant stealing the Dignity Vessels.

It hadn't taken Elissa long to come up with a plan that the General Command had approved.

Before she arrived here, she wasn't sure if her plan would work. But now that she saw the two working Dignity Vessels and the junk vessels pretending to be some sort of defense force, she knew her plan would succeed.

She just wished she were doing more than observing from a distance. That's what she hated about promotion. It took her out of the middle of the fighting and put her in charge of the battle.

She liked planning a campaign. She liked the entire thought process that went into it—figuring out what ship would be needed where, planning for contingencies, picking out her dream commanders, and then dealing with the actual ones. But she liked fighting just as much. She loved being in the fray, thinking on the fly, surviving the moment.

Even after the attack she had barely survived on the lost, lamented *Discovery,* she still loved being in the fray. She had almost died in space. As deeply as it had terrified her that day, she would face it all again if she had to.

It was probably some kind of adrenalin addiction. Or maybe it was just part of being a commander. Her personality was suited to this in all of its ups and downs. Even some of the Flag commanders didn't quite believe she wanted to return to the field. They had tested and retested her since she survived that attack at the Room of Lost Souls.

Each psychological test cleared her for duty. In space. In a ship. Commanding a crew. Fighting an enemy if she had to.

She wasn't lying or being tough. She preferred being here.

Except for the waiting part.

She glanced at the time.

She needed to get back to this ship's bridge. She was using it as a command center. The operation would start in just a few minutes.

She needed to oversee it, even if there wasn't much she could do from here.

She'd already studied the border of the Nine Planets Alliance. The Nine Planets agreed about a lot of things, but the one thing they couldn't agree upon was how to defend this border.

Which meant they didn't have an adequate information shield covering every meter of it. Nine of her ships had already slipped through the border. They would launch a surprise attack on the Lost Souls Corporation.

She had some data on the Corporation, although not as much as she would like. Some of the conspirators who helped Rosealma Quintana blow up various research stations had been caught, and had given their interrogators information on the layout, the defense systems, and the way the corporation was run.

The information contradicted somewhat, and it also was woefully incomplete. The conspirators didn't know much about a defense system besides a ship they called the *Ivoire*, which was one of the ships on the border now. One of the Dignity Vessels.

And the conspirators also didn't know much about the inner workings of Lost Souls. Most of the conspirators claimed they didn't know much about stealth tech, although that proved mostly untrue. However, what they did know was about as detailed as what the researchers in the Empire knew.

She had been continually told that Rosealma Quintana knew more, but so far as Elissa could tell, no one had managed to interrogate Quintana properly. And now Quintana was no longer in Empire custody.

So Elissa was going in with less information than she usually had. But judging by the ships on that border, there wasn't a lot of firepower at the Lost Souls Corporation.

Besides, she had enough of the layout to know how to deploy her soldiers on a quick strike. They were going in, killing whomever got in their way, and taking the research. At the same time, she would have other strike teams invading the Dignity Vessels still docked at the station. Those strike teams would capture the vessels and—if the vessels worked—would bring them back to the Empire.

While the main force was occupied here on the border, she would take what the Empire needed. Then let the Nine Planets fight the Empire.

Let them try.

She glanced at the time and smiled to herself.

She had just enough time to get to the bridge to monitor everything.

She took one last look at the observation deck. She wished she could see those ships on the border. She wished she could see that betraying bastard when he realized he was defending the wrong location.

She wished she could know when she hurt him as much as he had hurt her.

THE DIVE
NOW

37

THE BONEYARD CLOSES AROUND US. I ease the skip inside the opening in the force field, my stomach twisting. On this newer skip, more problems register. The sensors are better, and more attuned to differing energy patterns. The sensors are finding a lot of them.

It has taken Yash five days to strip this skip of its *anacapa* drive and to scrub all of the *anacapa* signatures out of it. She thinks we have a clean skip, but she's not sure.

For that reason, she's come with us. Again.

I understand the reason for her on this trip, but honestly, I would have preferred one or two of her engineering staff, someone new, someone a little more trained in the art of diving, someone a tad more willing to listen to me.

I've brought the entire main dive team on this mission, partly because I'm worried about Yash. I've also added one more diver, this one from the original *Ivoire* crew.

Gustav Denby is one of the youngest full crew members on the *Ivoire*. He had just received his commission before the ship got trapped in foldspace. He had only served on the ship for a few days before leaving the Fleet forever.

His lack of service on the *Ivoire* made him a great candidate for me. Even though he's loyal to Coop and the Fleet, he's also pliable. His training hasn't hardened into rigid ways of doing things.

Of all of the Fleet members I've trained as divers, only Denby is able to follow my instructions without a momentary hesitation. I recognize that hesitation for what it is: it's that second when the brain registers a complaint—*That's not how we do things!*—and then dismisses it. Denby doesn't complain, not even with that short delay.

I like that about him.

I don't expect him to join us on the dive. He'll remain in the skip with Yash and Nyssa. I don't want Nyssa anywhere near the inside of a Dignity Vessel unless there's an emergency. I need her for her calm and her medical skills.

The people who will dive this first ship will be me, Orlando, and Elaine. And we'll go by the book. Well, my book, anyway.

I have warned them all about this. I've also told them that Nyssa will be in charge while we're gone. I've pulled Nyssa aside and let her know that if Yash gives orders in routine matters, she's to be ignored. Only when she deals with *anacapa* drives or Fleet technology should Nyssa listen, and even then, she should remember that I will be looking over her shoulder.

If I can.

What makes me nervous about this dive (more nervous than I usually am) is that we don't know a lot of things about the Boneyard. Yash, her engineering team, and I have studied the energy readings inside the Boneyard itself, and we can't identify everything. We're not exactly sure what we're looking at.

Yash had a small group try to recreate those readings to see if they would have an impact on our diving suits, and the result was the one we wanted. She believes that the dive will be safe. But she's not going to guarantee anything. She's not willing to admit everything will work out just fine. She's not even willing to give me a percentage.

Which, I have to admit, makes me secretly glad. I have accused Yash of diving addiction, but I have it much worse and in a completely different way. I have learned to curb some of the addition with structure, but that structure only exists so that I can continue to dive. I have knocked some sense into myself over the years.

The skip makes it all the way into the Boneyard, and I let out a small sigh of relief. Yash, sitting next to me at the skip's controls, also lets out a small sigh. Out of the corner of my eye, I can see the rest of the team relax slightly.

We all knew the first test was just getting into the Boneyard. We've passed that.

Now we have a dozen or more other tests. Some I won't even register. Yash will see a lot of them. She's reconfigured the console to have what she calls a science station. I refer to it as the engineering array—or I started to, after I'd initially called it the *anacapa* controls. Yash corrected me quickly.

Now that there no longer is an *anacapa* drive on this skip, it has no need for controls. But Yash did configure everything to monitor all of this strange energy more completely.

I'm glad she's doing that, because I can feel the ships yanking my attention away from this skip and her crew.

We've chosen three ships to dive over the next few days. The first thing we will check for, once we get inside, is a working *anacapa* drive. If the ship lacks that, then we move to another ship.

But we're not even going to see the first ship's drive today. We might not even get inside the first ship. Our primary mission today—and maybe for several days following this—is to test the Boneyard herself.

My biggest worry is one that I haven't confessed to anyone: since the Boneyard rejects vehicles with an unrecognizable *anacapa* signal, will it reject people with unrecognizable uniforms? Will it examine our tech somehow and deem us unfit for the Boneyard proper?

All I have told the dive team is this: we will proceed according to our slowest protocols. We don't know what we're facing, so we'll take readings on everything, even the slightest thing.

We've brought backup environmental suits, extra dive suits, and more oxygen than we need. We have some standard environmental suits from the *Ivoire*, which I don't want to dive in, but we will use them if we have to. We also have a few of my oldest dive suits, the kind that have no tech that the Fleet recognizes, just in case we need that.

And Nyssa has more medical supplies than I've ever brought on a skip before. I'm very worried about what will happen outside of this ship.

Mikk saw it before we left. He's been with me for so many years that he knows all the signs of my worries. He even asked if he should go along. Yash keeps insisting that everyone without the genetic marker will be fine, but I'm not taking her word for it. I'm not assuming anything on this trip. I'm going to make sure it all runs as smoothly as it can, and as by the book as possible.

Of course, the book is *my* book, but still.

The first ship we've chosen is a Dignity Vessel that appears intact. Yash assures me that this ship dates from the same period in Fleet history as the *Ivoire*. She's been clear about what she means by the same period. She believes they were built within 200 years of each other.

She won't know how similar the ships are until she actually goes inside this one—which won't be today.

Right now, we're calling this Ship One. I hope, if we decide the ship's worth our time, that we'll find out its name. I'm also hoping that it comes from a few years *after* the *Ivoire* disappeared, so Yash doesn't know the ship's immediate history.

I'm fully aware that not every danger to our mission is the physical kind. I'm worried that too much information too soon might actually harm the performance of my Fleet colleagues.

Yash's reaction to the Boneyard itself reminds me just how fragile these people actually are.

First, I run the skip the length of the ship. We scan it, looking for a compromised hull or other damage that would make the ship unusable in its current condition.

I'm doing that scanning as well as piloting the skip. Yash is monitoring the energy readings. Orlando shifts in his chair. I know he wants to be involved, but I'm not going to let him.

Right now, Yash and I will control the information the divers receive. If we decide to abort, I don't want that decision to become an argument.

My divers aren't military. They don't follow orders as well as Yash would like, or even as well as I would like sometimes.

Mostly, though, I prefer the way they all think for themselves.

It only takes a few moments to run my scan. The information I get matches the information we got the first time we were in the Boneyard. This ship seems to be intact.

"*Anacapa* readings?" I ask Yash.

"Oh, yeah, more than I can count," she says. She sounds tense.

"I meant from Ship One," I say calmly.

She glances at me, and then grins. She's excited, and this time, it has raised her mood.

"Sorry," she says. "I'm looking at all of this, and it's—well, we'll talk later. But as for Ship One, I have no idea. I can't isolate anything in here."

"At least we haven't been knocked out of the Boneyard," I say. "That's a start."

Or, at least, it's a start for the skip. We haven't tried to go into the Boneyard with just a thin layer of nanofiber between our skin and whatever the hell those readings are.

I move the skip near the center of Ship One. Theoretically, we're above the bridge. We might be able to get some readings from it, if we do things right.

We debated about whether or not we would release a probe and have it attach to Ship One. After a lot of discussion, we decided against it. Even though it's my standard procedure to send in as many probes as possible, Yash convinced me that doing so here might trigger the wrong reaction.

She's worried that a still-active ship on low power might consider the probe to be a weapon. The probe will be giving off an energy signal after all, and it will be sending telemetry back to the skip. That might be enough to wake up a sleeping giant, and convince it—and maybe other still-functioning ships inside the Boneyard—that the Boneyard is under attack.

I've never dived anything that might attack me back, so I take her advice very seriously. I've dived wrecks in the past, not ships that might be stored for reasons other than damage. And we don't know why some of these seemingly intact ships are here.

"Is it going to be possible to keep the skip steady?" I ask Yash.

We were worried that whatever it is holding the ships in place might interfere with the skip's controls or make our normal maneuvering impossible.

"Looks like it," she says, without glancing up. "I'm still worried about this line you're going to attach."

That's where we fought. I always attach the skip to whatever wreck I'm going to dive by a strong line. I've had divers get wreck-blindness, divers nearly die, divers who pushed off wrong and nearly toppled head-over-heels into space when the gravity in their boots did not save them.

The only thing that saved all of those divers was the line. It was something the diver could feel, something that gave the diver hope, something for the diver to cling to that wasn't part of the wreck so that the diver felt safe.

Even if that feeling of safety was a false sense of security. Sometimes that was all it took to save a life.

"Yeah, I'm worried about it too," I say, "but I'm even more worried about not having it."

Those three sentences we uttered encompassed hours of arguing and planning. We aren't going to change our plans now, unless we see something outside this skip that gives us a compelling reason to do so.

"Should we suit up?" Denby asks, and Orlando touches his arm. Wrong question. Denby should wait for orders. But he's new, and he's as eager as a diver can be.

Orlando actually has a small smile on his face as he glances over at me. He can remember his first dives as well—if you call what he did back on Vaycehn diving.

"We're going to send that line over first," I say.

And we're going to give Ship One a chance to react to it. If the reaction is violent, I want my divers in their chairs and able to hang on while Yash and I try to get us the hell out of here.

"You ready?" I ask Yash.

"As ready as I'll ever be," she says, managing to convey her disapproval with her tone.

I send the line to the spot near one of the outside entrances. We chose that spot before we ever left *The Two*.

The line wobbles as it goes, which I've never seen it do before, and then it scrapes against Ship One. For a moment, I don't think the line will hold. Then it grapples on, about two meters to the left of the spot we had chosen.

I glance at Yash. She looks back, her mouth a thin line.

If anything is going to happen with that line, it'll happen now.

I watch Ship One. Nothing changes. Its exterior doesn't flare, it doesn't shake off the line or the grapple. The power levels around the ship don't change at all.

The skip has gone through a slight change—the normal change when we extend a line. It yanks a little, stabilizes some, moves a bit to the left. I've taught Yash how to maintain the skip when the line's extended, because there are some tricks to keeping the line taut and the skip stable.

"See anything?" I ask her.

"Not yet," she says.

"All right," I say. "Then we're good to go."

38

Orlando and I suit up. We're going first. If everything checks out, then Elaine and Denby will go next.

It sounds so simple, but there are a lot of ifs between my trip and Elaine's trip. I'm still not sure what we're getting into.

The suits we use now are so different from the suits I originally used diving that it almost feels like I'm not suited at all. These suits, designed with the help of the Fleet's teams, are made of a nanofiber so thin that it almost feels like they don't exist.

I have clothes thicker than these suits.

But not stronger. These suits can go through anything—fire, water, complete vacuum—and not get a tear or a split. If anything even thinks of rupturing, the suit repairs immediately.

There is a second layer beneath the suit's top layer, but I can't feel it. I've only seen that second layer in the lab. Beneath that layer or near it or around it, are all of the environmental functions, including the oxygen. I used to strap oxygen containers onto my hip, so I find this part of the suit both fascinating and frightening.

I know, just from looking at the containers, how much oxygen I have left. The suit tells me its levels, and sometimes I worry that the damn thing lies.

It also itches, at least on my face. Everyone tells me that the reaction is purely mine. I don't like the helmet, not that it's a helmet, not really. It's more of a hood that attaches to the skin, covers everything, and provides protection.

The engineers gave me a choice on the diving suits; I could have a helmet, whatever you wanted to call it, that hid my face from anyone looking at me—which is what Coop prefers for any environmental suit—or I could have a clear helmet. I opted for clear.

I need to see my companion's expression at all times, and he needs to see mine.

I tug on the gloves last, and they adhere to the rest of the suit. It seals up, and then informs me with a little running commentary along the bottom of my vision that the suit is safe for vacuum now.

I still double-check. I've always double-checked safety protocols and I'm not going to stop now, just because I'm wearing something that's more sophisticated than what I wore before.

Everything on the suit checks out.

I glance at Orlando.

He looks even smaller in this suit. He's become more athletic over the years, but he still strikes me as the bookish man I first met. He has a talent for exploration, though, and a fearlessness that I appreciate.

Mikk argued for Elaine on this first dive, but I need Elaine's caution on her dive with Denby. I need Orlando's willingness to try anything, reach for anything, in this first part of the dive.

Orlando grins at me.

"You guys are already using too much oxygen," Nyssa says. "Boss, you'll have the gids if you're not careful."

I smile just a little. That's how a dive should begin, with someone warning me that I'm too excited about it.

"Thirty minutes." I'm speaking more to Yash than anyone else. "I need someone to mark the fifteen minutes even though it shows up in our suits. I want to make sure our clocks remain synchronized."

Malfunctioning *anacapas* often distort time, so this is a simple precaution, one that we can deal with immediately if we have to. Neither Orlando nor I want to get stuck like I've seen others do.

Yash, of course, assures me that this won't happen, but I don't believe assurances, particularly in a place like this.

"The thirty minutes starts the moment we leave the airlock," I say. "And it's hard and fast, no matter how much we plead for an extra minute. Got that?"

That last is more for Denby, since he might have to be part of the team who pulls us in if we don't want to return. Or can't return.

Still, it's Elaine who nods. Yash frowns and looks away.

I step into the airlock. Orlando's right behind me. The doors close behind us. The airlock vents its environment, and then the doors open ahead of us, leading into the Boneyard itself.

My breath catches, and before I can even acknowledge it, Nyssa is in my comm.

"Watch the gids, Boss," she says again.

"Yeah," I say, probably too curtly. I respond so that she knows the comm is working, but that's the only reason.

My heart is pounding, and I'm thrilled beyond words. Of course, I'm breathing irregularly. She would be, too.

The Boneyard stretches before us. Most places that I've dived have a single wreck against the backdrop of space. I'm very conscious of the starlight and the shape of distant galaxies.

But here, all I see are ships. Ship after ship after ship. They're not in formation, so it doesn't look like they're about to attack us.

They almost look fake. They're at odd angles, as if some unseen hand holds them there.

Orlando looks at me, as if he expects me to say something.

Then I grin at him like a maniac, reach out, grab the line, and step into the Boneyard.

The line feels solid beneath my gloved hand. I attach to the line—procedure—and slide forward, almost expecting to be buffeted by all those different energy patterns.

But the line holds solidly. It does bounce a little as Orlando grabs on, but that's it.

Then it's just the two of us, in the silence. I'm braced, hoping that no one from the skip speaks to us. I love the majesty of this, the sense that I'm stepping into a graveyard of ships.

It almost feels like a dream to me, something I have only imagined and never seen.

In the corner of my eye, the timer runs down, and it looks normal to me. It's been five minutes, the timer tells me, and I hope that it's accurate.

I don't want to check with the skip. This moment is private. This moment is *mine*.

I glance over my shoulder to see if Orlando is following me.

He is. He looks as stunned as I feel. He's gazing upward, looking at the bottoms of the ships we're moving between.

Then I look down, see even more ships. They seem to go on forever, even though I know they don't.

I decide in this moment that I love this place.

Then I worry that my love for the Boneyard is just another form of the gids. Or something even more treacherous. Something like the strange reaction my mother had inside the Room of Lost Souls.

Beautiful, she muttered. *Oh, so beautiful.*

I glance at Orlando. His gaze meets mine and he winks.

Eight minutes. If we're not careful, we won't get a chance to look at the ship at all.

I move faster, thinking maybe I should contact the skip. But I don't want to talk to anyone, and no one has talked to me.

They're not supposed to. Not yet. If they don't synchronize with me at fifteen minutes, I'll start to worry.

Ship One looms ahead of us, its sides gleaming in the strange light of the Boneyard. The ship shouldn't be clean—should it? It shouldn't gleam—should it?

I hope I remember to ask Yash when we get back.

I have to remind myself to take regular breaths. I count them, trying to keep them even.

But Nyssa hasn't said anything about the gids again, so I assume I'm doing fine.

Or maybe she can't hear me, speak to me.

I refuse to let that thought lodge in my mind.

I reach the ship at eleven minutes. That gives us eight to play with, and we'll need all of it.

Orlando comes up beside me. Together we each put one gloved hand against the outside of the ship. Our gloves have all sorts of sensors in them, and just this simple touch will give us readings.

It'll give Yash more information than she can probably sift through on this trip.

The sides of the ship look smooth and unharmed. From this angle, there's no way to tell why the ship's here.

I look over at the door. I can see its outline. There is a small square shape near it, like Yash hoped. She believes that's an override, which someone with the proper codes can use to get into the ship.

The key is the proper codes. Will ancient codes work? Are Yash's codes new enough to get us inside that ship? Or will we trigger something?

There's no way to know without trying.

"Fifteen minutes." Yash's voice makes me jump.

Orlando looks over his shoulder as if he expects to see her directly behind him.

I glance at the display from my suit's internal clock. Yep, she's right. Fifteen minutes.

"Acknowledged," I say and, on the same channel, Orlando echoes me.

Then we move sideways, gripping the side of the ship with our boots. There are built-in handholds, things I never found on the exterior of the Dignity Vessels I dived. They existed, but I never saw them. You have to know about them, know how to reach them, know what they are.

Orlando reaches the door first, and I feel disappointment. I wanted to be the first one there.

He places a gloved hand against it, then looks at me.

"We have to go back," he says.

For a moment, I fear that he's seen something. Then I glance at the clock display.

Eighteen minutes. It took us eleven to arrive. We can only be gone thirty. My rules.

I need to follow my own damn rules.

I nod, and reach for the line. He follows. We're going to have to go back faster than we arrived.

I want to linger.

I want to see the ship itself, open that door, head inside.

I want to continue diving—and I will. I know I will. Each trip will grow longer and longer. That's what I do, how I plan things. But this first one has to be short.

Just like the first one with Denby and Elaine will be short.

Already I'm thinking about my next dive, and I wrench my attention back to this moment.

To the skip, bobbing in the Boneyard as if it were part of the ship graveyard. To the ships beyond it, the edges of the Boneyard itself, flickering just a little.

I don't know what that flicker is, so I focus on it, wishing I can reach out and touch it. Still, I make sure that my suit records it. We need all the information we can get.

We get back to the skip with thirty seconds to spare. We stumble into the airlock, lean against each other.

I'm tired. I don't look at how much oxygen I have left. I suspect I used more than I should have.

It was spectacular out there.

It *is* spectacular out there.

I love it here.

And at moments like this, I could stay forever.

39

WE ARRIVE AT THE *Two* HOURS AFTER WE LEFT, but it feels like days. I dock the skip inside, and the team staggers out, exhausted, elated, not thinking clearly. We've done something fascinating, something wonderful, and we survived it.

We're a mess, even Yash.

Maybe especially Yash. I can sense just how much she wants to go inside the Boneyard, how much she wants to touch that ship herself. She's barely holding herself in check because she knows the plan. She doesn't get to go in unless we need her. Unless we find what we're looking for.

A working ship, an active *anacapa* drive, *something* that'll make this ship useful for the Lost Souls.

I head to my cabin, after giving orders for everyone to eat something solid and get a few hours rest. We're in no hurry here, and I want to prove that with my behavior.

I'm also unwilling to wait too long for the next dive. I try to space them out by twelve hours minimum, even though I usually prefer twenty-four. If there's some problem in the telemetry, however, I want to know tonight so that we can plan the future dives even better.

My cabin always looks dishearteningly normal after a dive. All that excitement makes the everyday seem flat and uncomfortable. I still have a lot of adrenalin, even though I know it will fade as soon as I step into my post-dive routine.

Which always starts in the shower.

I crawl inside mine—an expensive water-based shower, one of the few luxuries I've permitted myself on the *Two*—and let the hot, recycled stream flow over me, reminding me that I am both alive and not in the vacuum of space.

I try to pretend that I don't already miss it.

With just a bit of envy, I watched Elaine and Denby repeat the dive that Orlando and I did. They moved slower—which I expected due to Elaine's caution and Denby's newness. I gave them permission to use an extra three minutes so that they could get to the door; I wanted Denby to look at it and get a reading from it.

He's had more experience with the exterior of all Dignity Vessels than I have.

They came back, later than I would have liked, but in one piece, which also reassured me.

But when we retracted the line, it wobbled like it had done before. I thought that odd, and would have said something to Yash if she hadn't looked so puzzled. We'll discuss it at our meeting.

After I get out of the shower, I manage to eat something, but I suspect sleep is beyond me. Still, I rest—what good is a leader if she doesn't follow the instructions she gives her team for their health?—and to my surprise, I do doze off.

The sleep isn't deep, and it's filled with a review of the dive. I wake up, wondering not what my gloves downloaded or what my suit recorded inside the Boneyard, but what it recorded about me.

Nyssa didn't remind me about the gids once we were outside the skip, and she should have. I felt like I had them, and I also felt like I used a lot of oxygen.

I go to my computer and check my own bio readings. Then I compare them to the readings from my previous first dives on exciting missions, years ago. Aside from some age-related differences (my body mass is slightly higher, for example), the readings should be the same because I react the same way no matter what project I'm diving—at least on the first dive.

And they're not.

My heart rate actually slowed down as I stepped out of the skip and into the Boneyard. My oxygen consumption returned to something approximating normal.

Which is odd, considering I still *felt* like I had the gids.

I flag this and plan to mention it to Nyssa. I'm the only diver we have with information on dives like this that goes back years. Orlando and Elaine dove lots of strange situations, but rarely dangerous wrecks in space.

I wish we had more information. There's something here that's bothering me, something I haven't consciously recognized.

But what I have learned is that my subconscious often offers up answers long before my conscious brain is aware of the question.

I dress, eat a little something else, then gather all the materials that I need for this meeting.

Then I leave, feeling a bit more apprehensive than I expected.

40

THE DIVE TEAM AND MIKK wait for me in the conference room. Mikk is great at interpreting data, plus I want him to run the dives when I can't. *If* I can't. I'm not sure he can run the dives either, given what's going on with those energy fields, but I need the security of some kind of backup.

He sits in the far corner of the room, apparently trying to be invisible. It appears to be working; Yash doesn't seem to notice him at all. She sits at the head of the conference table, not because she's taking over control, but because she's still filtering through information.

I hand my personal readings to Nyssa. I know she doesn't have the past history.

"Compare these for me, would you?" I ask. "See what you can find."

She nods, looking a bit confused.

In fact, my words stop everyone and make them glance at me. I realize I haven't spoken a greeting, but neither have they. We all look a bit tired and withdrawn, instead of adrenaline-filled and excited like we had been a few hours before.

If I hadn't seen this after every single major dive of my career, I would have been worried. I'm rather surprised Yash isn't, until I realize that she glanced up for only an instant.

She's deep inside the screens again.

"Yash," I say. "You have something?"

"When it fits into the review," she says, not looking up.

Normally, if this were an isolated dive team without the Fleet back-up, I would pick on Yash, force her to focus on the discussion, and get her under my complete command/control.

But I don't need to do that here. She's not going to dive for days, maybe a week or more, and I have plenty of time to rope her in.

Instead, we review. We talk about timing, and how the technical aspects of the dive went. We focus on Denby quite a bit because he's new, and he needs to know exactly how he did—good and bad.

Mostly, I see good. I have no qualms about keeping him on my dive team. I've seen excellent divers who start out with a terrible first dive. Most divers improve after their first dive, and Denby's was nearly spotless. I try not to have high hopes for him.

It's hard.

About thirty minutes in, we finish. That's when I turn my attention back to Yash.

"So," I say, moving my hand toward her so that she can see it next to the screens, "what has your attention?"

"That line," she says, and it takes me a moment to follow. She means the line attaching the skip to Ship One, rather than some line in the conversation.

"It bothered me too," I say. "It shouldn't have wobbled."

"It didn't wobble," she says, and that has my full attention.

"It *looked* like it wobbled," I say.

"But it was steady when I put my hand on it," Elaine said. "So the wobble was long gone after you guys went through your dive."

It was steady when I put my gloved hand on it as well, even though I didn't say that. Instead, I look at Orlando. He is the only other one with enough experience to know when a line feels off.

"Felt fine to me too, but I know what Boss is saying." His hair needs a comb, and he has deep circles under his eyes. The adrenaline rush always leaves him drained. Once, after a long series of dives, I worried that he was sick. Instead, it was just the way his body handled the stress. "I remember that when I reached for it, I worried that it wasn't secure."

"Because your eyes told you otherwise?" Denby asks. He sounds nervous. Maybe his default tone is nervousness, because he's not acting nervous.

"Did yours?" Orlando asks him.

Denby opens his mouth, then closes it tightly, and shrugs. "I don't have enough experience to trust any of my senses out there," he says.

"You need to," Mikk says from the far side of the table. Three heads turn toward him. Yash still acts like no one else is in the room. Everyone else seems to have just remembered Mikk is there. "Sometimes your senses are all you have out there."

"I'm still learning," Denby says, but in a tone I recognize. It's an *agree-with-the-leader* tone, not a tone actually filled with agreement.

"Clearly," Mikk says, and leans back. He's watching Yash too.

"The line *did* wobble," Yash says. She raises her head and looks at me. She seems to know what I'm about to say because she adds, "When I said earlier that it didn't wobble, I meant that it didn't wobble because something from the outside impacted it, like a wave in an ocean or a breeze in the air. It wobbled because of the way it was released."

I frown. I don't want to have communication issues here. I want to understand everything she means, which means I have to focus.

"What happened is that we sent a command through the equipment from the controls inside the skip. That command went through the skip's internal equipment to the equipment controlling the line. That equipment operated just fine *until* the little hatch opened and the line started to leave the ship. Then something had an impact, not on the line, but on the commands coming from the skip."

"We were hacked?" Orlando asks.

"No," she says. "Those energy signatures that we see, they have an impact on some things. Not on the line, because it's a physical object. It doesn't have any engine of its own, no nanotechnology, nothing that makes it anything other than a line. But the equipment that sent it out has its own energy readings, and that equipment also interacts with the skip."

"And," I say, "apparently it interacts with the energy signatures inside the Boneyard."

"'Interact' is too strong a word," Yash says. "I am more willing to say that the energy signatures had some kind of microscopic impact on the equipment, enough to send the line out at two different speeds and with a slight error in its target."

We're all leaning toward her. She doesn't even notice.

"What's fascinating to me," she says, "is that it started out on the correct course at the right speed, but the second that hatch opened, the speed and trajectory changed ever so slightly. It created the wobble."

"It also wobbled on the way back," I say.

"Because it was being pulled by the same equipment," Yash says. "And the same interaction occurred as it was being withdrawn."

I let out a small sigh. I glance at Nyssa. She raises her eyebrows at me. I should confess right now that there's something odd in my readings, but I'm not going to. I don't want to have my own rules bench me.

What I do say is this:

"We need to make sure there's nothing odd about the readings from our suits. And we should check the voice prints to see if our voices were distorted, or if there was a millisecond of difference between the moment Yash told me that fifteen minutes were up and the moment I received the message."

"You're thinking this has a physical impact on us?" Elaine asks.

I shrug. "Not on us, necessarily, but on our equipment, and that includes our suits. We have to be able to trust the readings."

"That's what I'm thinking," Yash says.

"Then we'll need to study this before we send anyone out again," Mikk says.

The voice of reason. The reason I've brought him here. He's not addicted to the dive, so his stomach doesn't clench at the very thought of delaying.

But the rest of us look stricken.

"Can't we keep going?" Denby asks. "There's so much to learn."

Like Yash, he feels the press of time—*all* of time: now, his future, and five-thousand lost years.

"We've just gotten started," Orlando says. "I'm not behind waiting."

"It's not a vote," I say. Because if it were, waiting would lose. Everyone wants to keep going, to go through the risk, the adventure. "We do this as safely as we can."

"We *are*," Orlando says.

I smile at him. I understand how he feels. "I know," I say. "We're going to continue doing that."

I turn to Yash, who isn't as focused on the screens before her as she was. She's clearly listening to this conversation with half an ear.

"How long will it take you to figure out if these energy signatures pose some kind of threat?" I ask.

"I don't know," she says. "You might be asking the impossible."

She heard the scientific question—*when can you explain the phenomenon?*—when I was asking a practical question—*how soon before your best guess allows us to dive safely again?*

So I ask that question.

"Oh," she says. "I'm going to need to check the readings on all systems. Maybe we can calibrate something."

She glances at Mikk whose expression doesn't change. It's as if she's asking him for permission to do this right.

"I can't promise complete safety," she says to him.

"I'm not asking for complete safety," I say, directing her attention back to me. "I'm asking for an assurance that we're not diving into a disaster."

"You know I can't give that," Yash says.

"But you can tell me if we can make tweaks that will let us trust our equipment."

"Not with certainty," Yash says.

"We're in space," I say. "It comes with a guaranteed amount of risk. I want to know if, all things being equal, we can dive the Boneyard with the same level of safety we dive the area around Lost Souls."

"No, of course not," Yash says. "Expecting that—"

"We have a good bunch of engineers here," Denby says, ignoring his superior officer. I mentally cheer him for that. "I think we can figure out some things in a few days."

"That's not your call, Denby," Yash says.

"Actually," I say, "here, it is. He's part of the dive team. He knows what we need and what we don't."

"He's already said he's in a hurry," Yash says.

"We all are," I say. "Which is why I'm putting Mikk in charge of the scientific side of this dive. He'll be the one to determine when we can dive again."

I do this in part to keep me out of it. I also do it because this meeting has convinced me of something I'm not telling anyone—at least not yet.

I'm convinced that those who lack the genetic marker cannot dive the Boneyard. And that includes Mikk.

"He doesn't know anything about science," Yash blurts.

Mikk grins, then he shrugs. He's playing the ignorant, which used to irritate me. I finally figured out how smart he is, and I've trusted that ever since.

But he's got Yash fooled.

"Oh," he says calmly. "I know enough to help with this dive."

"I beg to differ," Yash says.

"It won't make any difference. Mikk will clear us for the next trip." Then I give him a stern look. "I want to dive this within the week."

"I hope to get you there within a day," he says.

I smile at him. I miss him on this dive. It'll be nice to have him as part of it, however small.

"Good," I say, and work hard not to add, *The sooner the better.* Because I don't want him to know how addicted to this dive I've become. I'll deal with that myself.

Even though I can feel those ships out there, their history locked inside them, knowledge I have no idea even exists waiting for me to discover it.

I make myself look away from him. I make eye contact with every member of the team, and then I say—as much to myself as to them, "Let's get some rest. This might be the last chance we have to prepare for a difficult week. Let's take advantage of it."

They nod, and leave one by one.

Mikk waits until they go.

"This is no different from any other dive," he says, and in that sentence, I know he's seen right through me.

"Oh, Mikk," I say. "We can say that all we want. But we both know that's not true. There's so much—"

"And it's been here for a long time. It'll wait."

"I suppose it will," I say. "But I don't want to."

"I know," he says. "I also know that's why you brought me in. To make sure you follow the rules and stay hooked to the line."

"You know me too well," I say.

He grins. "Thank God," he says.

THE THIRD SKIRMISH
NOW

41

COOP STOOD NEAR HIS CAPTAIN'S CHAIR, trying to ignore the odd feeling in his stomach. His bridge crew was working quickly, seeing if they could find confirmation of his assumption that the imperial ships planned an attack on Lost Souls.

He had a secondary realization, one that worried him deeply. His rescue fantasy—the idea that Boss would come to the border with dozens of Fleet ships—had become a nightmare. Because he'd been thinking about it and he realized that if she returned soon, she would return to Lost Souls.

She would arrive at Lost Souls at the same moment the Empire's ships attacked. They'd think the Fleet vessels had a full crew and active weapons systems.

The Empire's ships would go after the Fleet ships first, and would destroy all of them.

"More chatter, sir," Perkins said. "A lot is happening through their comm system, not all of it verbal."

He forced himself to concentrate on what was happening now, not what he imagined might happen. Even without Boss there, the arrival of imperial ships at Lost Souls could be a complete disaster.

Everything Boss had worked for—everything he had worked for in the past few years—would get destroyed.

Coop frowned at the three-dimensional screen in front of him, wishing he had studied Empire tactics more.

He had gotten lax in his years here. He had ignored most of his training, concentrating not on how to work with the existing cultures, but on how to find the Fleet.

Maybe his decision had been a mistake.

If he had followed his training, he would know whether or not this kind of behavior—a splitting of an armada—was a common tactic for an imperial sneak attack.

"Anita," he said, "Lost Souls monitors the area around it, right?"

"They do," she said, "but for ships off course, someone who doesn't belong, stuff like that."

He cursed silently. He had always monitored the surrounding area when the *Ivoire* was docked at Lost Souls—he always monitored the surrounding area, period. And he knew that Lynda did so as well.

But neither of them were at Lost Souls.

He said to Anita, "Contact Lost Souls. Make them expand their sensor range as far out as it goes. And make sure they're monitoring for cloaked Empire ships."

"That'll scare the hell out of them," Anita said.

"It should," Kravchenko muttered.

Coop nodded. He couldn't agree more. He had tried to get Boss to think about defending her borders, but she believed she would know if Empire ships invaded the Nine Planets. Her replacement, Ilona Blake, was even more lax.

"Coop," Anita said, "they're reporting nine ships, all cloaked, not far from the Lost Souls. The ships'll probably arrive within the hour."

He straightened. The tactic was smart if this Trekov woman believed that the Lost Souls only had two Fleet ships. Keep the big ships busy on the border, and invade the Lost Souls, steal what it had, or destroy its research facility in retaliation for all the facilities Boss, Squishy—and Coop—had blown up.

"Mavis," Coop said to Kravchenko, "we still have some former tactical people on Lost Souls, right? Retired?"

He had to ask because he knew a number of his people had given up the search for the Fleet, started a new life either in the Nine Planets or on Lost Souls. But he hadn't kept track—he couldn't keep track; it broke his heart—of where they ended up.

"At least a dozen," Kravchenko said.

"Get them into what passes for command at Lost Souls. I want them to fire whatever weapons we have there, not the stuff Boss cribbed from the Empire, but ours."

"I don't know how quickly we can get them into position, sir," Kravchenko said.

He shrugged. "The Empire ships believe we don't know about them. We probably have thirty minutes. Get someone in command as fast as you can, someone who knows what they're doing."

"All right, sir," she said.

"I'm going to give the word from here," he said. "And our folks need to be in charge of the defense of Lost Souls. I don't want the amateurs there in charge. If Ilona Blake has a problem, have her contact me, but tell her to be damn quick about it. Because she's about to get blown off the grid."

"Got it, sir," Kravchenko said. "I'll be as plainspoken as I can."

He smiled again. He'd had her do a lot of the interaction between Lost Souls and the *Ivoire* in the past. He hadn't much liked Blake when he first met her, and he liked her less now, even though he knew why Boss had put her in charge. Blake was exceedingly competent. She just had her own agenda, and her agenda was never the same as his.

Except right now.

"No problems from Blake, sir," Kravchenko said. "She asked what she can do to help."

Yep, competent.

"Make sure whoever is in their command center does *exactly* what I say," he said. "And give me visuals from Lost Souls, would you? I want to see what they see."

The images from Lost Souls bounced up on his screen almost immediately. The imperial ships were still fifty minutes out, and still cloaked. The cloak made them appear gray on the Lost Souls feed.

"We got our people in the command center yet?" he asked.

"Coming now, sir," Anita said.

"Let me know when they're in place." He turned to Perkins. "How's the chatter?"

"If they're monitoring the internal activity at Lost Souls," Perkins said, "I can't tell. Chatter remains heightened, but no different than it was when we started."

"So they're not monitoring our communications," he said, more to himself than to the others.

"I think they've been trying, sir," Perkins said. "But I've been scrambling everything with Lost Souls, and then scrubbing it. I've also been keeping up our communications on normal lines with the Nine Planets vessels."

He noted that she used the word "vessels" too. No one on the *Ivoire* wanted to give that decrepit group the title "ships."

"Good job, Kjersti," he said.

"We're ready," Kravchenko said. "And we have some good people on weapons. They shouldn't have retired, sir."

"Well, they're not retired now," he said. "Put me through."

"You'll be talking to Jason Xilvii," Kravchenko said.

Coop remember Xilvii. He'd been a junior officer, working weapons and tactical five years before. Coop had been keeping his eye on him before they came here, thinking Xilvii would work his way up the ranks fairly quickly.

Instead, Xilvii had left the *Ivoire*, deciding it was easier to acknowledge just how much his life had changed. He'd actually told Coop he believed there was no future on the *Ivoire*—for anyone, not just for him.

Coop hadn't known how to respond.

"Captain?" Xilvii appeared in a small square on Coop's screen. Xilvii looked older than Coop remembered (didn't they all?), his face thinner and lined, with a sad downturn to his eyes. "We have a situation."

"We do," Coop said. "Does the Lost Souls have enough weaponry to take out these imperial ships if we want to?"

"I'm more worried about our so-called shields," Xilvii said. "They won't hold."

"It's not going to come to that," Coop said. "Can you—easily—take out those ships, considering we have the advantage of surprise?"

"Yeah," Xilvii said. "If they're not firing on us at the same time. And we'll only get one try at this."

"Then we'll do it in one try," Coop said. It was probably better to be surgical anyway. He had a backup plan, but if executed wrong, it would have terrible implications for Lost Souls.

"Just give me the word," Xilvii said.

"Monitor those ships," Coop said. "If they notice what you're doing, if they power up, then you fire immediately. Otherwise, fire everything you've got in five minutes."

"Got it, sir." Xilvii said. "Thank you, sir."

Coop monitored everything from his station. He didn't see any other Fleet vessels near the Lost Souls except the ones that had been there before he left.

Boss wasn't back yet.

He hoped she wouldn't arrive in the next ten minutes, because that would throw everything off.

42

ALL TWENTY PEOPLE ON THE BRIDGE of the *Ewing Trekov* were busy at their stations.

Commander Willem Sherwin immediately vacated his captain's chair as Elissa Trekov entered the bridge. He was a slender man whose close-cropped hair had gone gray. It only made him look older than he was.

She waved him back into his spot and took a secondary command chair near the back.

It wouldn't fool anyone. They all knew that she was the one who was truly in charge.

"Status?" she asked.

"We're forty-eight minutes out from their research facility," Sherwin said. He sounded both formal and nervous.

She understood the formal. She hated the nervous, although she accepted it. It was the price she paid for her hardassed reputation.

She had made it to the bridge just in time, then. The attack would begin within fifteen minutes.

"Commander?" one of the line officers said.

"Yes?" Sherwin said.

"I'm sorry, sir, I meant Commander Trekov." The officer, a woman, sounded even more nervous than Sherwin had. "A man from one of the ships on the border says he wants to speak to you."

"Commander Sherwin is in charge," Trekov said, hating to explain how command worked sometimes. These junior officers sometimes got confused when the enemy asked for the person in charge.

"No, sir, ma'am, I'm sorry," the officer looked quickly at Sherwin, then at Trekov. "He specifically asked for Commander Trekov."

"What?" Sherwin asked. "Are you certain?"

Trekov felt cold. She let out a small breath.

"Yes, sir," the officer said. "He asked for Commander Trekov, said they'd met before…?"

"They're monitoring our communications," Trekov said to Sherwin. Her tone was crisp, but she was certain he heard the accusation in it. He should have been using protected channels. "There's no other way any-one would know that I'm here."

"Unless it's a guess." Sherwin said. "If they knew how our systems worked, then—"

"Forgive me, sir," the officer said. "It's no guess. He said he knew that Commander Trekov was here, and she needed to talk to him within two minutes or they would relive their first encounter."

Relive their first encounter. Trekov ran one hand over the new skin on the back of her other hand, then realized what she was doing. Son of a bitch. If this man was the person she thought he was…

"Put him through. I want a visual."

She wasn't going to talk to this man in private.

"We can't get a visual, ma'am."

"Then on speaker," Trekov said.

The officer nodded as the channel opened.

"This is Group Commander Elissa Trekov. Identify yourself."

"*Group* Commander." The man spoke with wry amusement. "And here I thought you were just a lowly soldier when we first met. Surely, you weren't a Group Commander then."

The voice made her throat go dry. She remembered every inflec-tion, every nuance. The strange accent seemed fainter now, but it was still there.

She made herself take a deep breath before she answered him. She didn't want to sound nervous or unsettled when she spoke to him.

"It would help if you identified yourself," she said, and was relieved to hear that she sounded like her usual commanding self. "Maybe then I could place you."

"Ah, commander," he said. "You haven't forgotten me. No one forgets the person who nearly kills you."

She felt the color drain from her face. Everyone on the bridge looked at her. The junior officers looked startled. Sherwin's expression held compassion and worry at the same time. Those farther up in the ranks knew how close she had come to dying and some of what had happened.

"I'm quite impressed you survived," the man was saying. "That was not luck. That took skill. Let me salute you."

"You still haven't identified yourself," she said.

"So," he said, with that wry tone, "a lot of people have tried to kill you, then?"

She wasn't going to dignify that with an answer. She waited in silence.

"We met at the Room of Lost Souls," he said.

"And I seem to recall you didn't identify yourself then either," she said. It was him. The betraying bastard. She had known it, but she had hoped, somewhere deep down, that she was facing someone else.

She hadn't realized until now how much he frightened her.

And how badly she wanted to kill him right now.

"All this concern with names and identities is simply wasting time," he said. "Because my people have orders to destroy the nine ships you've sent into Nine Planets in less than three minutes unless I tell them otherwise."

Sherwin's gaze met hers. Now he had gone pale. The bridge remained silent—well disciplined to the last.

"What do you want?" she asked.

"I want you to leave and tell the Empire to leave the Nine Planets alone. In fact, I want you to guarantee that the Empire will never encroach on Nine Planets' space."

"And in return?" she asked.

244

"We won't destroy every last one of you."

He's bluffing, Sherwin mouthed.

She shook her head. The betraying bastard wasn't bluffing. But she couldn't do what he asked. Even if she had the authority, she wouldn't.

"You have the ability to negotiate for the Nine Planets?" she asked.

"Of course I do," the betraying bastard said. "I'm the one with weapons trained on your ships."

"I need more time," she said. "I have to contact my commander. I am not authorized to speak for the Empire for anything past this matter, and even then, they'd have to know who they're dealing with."

"Ah, names again," he said. "For a woman who is amazing in a crisis, you're quite focused on protocol, Commander Trekov. You have less than a minute."

"You're a soldier," she said, remembering the man from nearly four years ago. She'd recognized him from his bearing even then. "I know that the Nine Planets have no formal military. I know you can't be representing them. So tell me who you are, and I will work with you."

He sighed audibly. Then he said, "Maybe the next time I give you a warning, you'll heed it."

And then he severed the connection.

"Check our ships," she said to Sherwin. "*Now.*"

He whipped toward his command post as everyone on the bridge bent over their consoles.

"Get that man back," Trekov said. She figured if he was talking, he wasn't doing something untoward. "And tell me what those ships on the border are doing."

"Ma'am," one of the junior officers spoke. Dammit, she should have bothered with names. This one was a middle-aged man whom she knew she had met before.

She didn't like his tone.

"What, Officer?"

"Um, our ships, ma'am. The ones we sent to the Nine Planets? To the research facility? They're gone."

"Gone?" she asked. "What do you mean 'gone'?"

"I'm sorry, ma'am," he said, his voice shaking. "They've been destroyed."

43

COOP WATCHED THE SCREEN BEFORE HIM as nine imperial ships exploded. They didn't explode into bits. They lit up and then essentially evaporated.

He nearly let out an unprofessional whoop of triumph. But he managed to contain it just in time.

Jason Xilvii didn't screw around. Coop had said he wanted those ships destroyed, and Xilvii made sure the ships were destroyed, with no opportunity for retaliation.

Apparently, Lost Souls had more firepower than Coop had thought.

"Get Xilvii for me," Coop told Kravchenko.

Kravchenko had a small smile on her face. Most of the bridge crew were smiling. Either they were relieved or felt as giddy as he did. Coop did his best to keep that feeling of victory under control.

Xilvii's face, cheeks flushed, eyes bright, appeared on the screen in miniature.

"Excellent work," Coop said. "You seeing any other potential problems?"

Xilvii tilted his head just a little. "Not yet, sir."

That was the answer Coop wanted. "Keep an eye out. Set up a team to defend Lost Souls. We don't know if this ended everything or if this is just the first round in a long series of battles. I'm putting you in charge of defense until I return."

"Yes, sir," Xilvii said. "Thank you, sir."

Coop wasn't certain if he could do that in Boss's absence, but he just had. Let Ilona Blake contact him if she had a problem with it. He had just saved her life and her station, after all.

He signed off with Xilvii.

"Captain," Anita said, "the imperial ships have uncloaked. They're powering up weapons."

"Oh, for God's sake," he said. Sometimes he hated dealing with established militaries. They had protocol, and certain leaders followed it to the letter, even when doing so was damn dumb. "Get me Trekov, and this time, let me see her."

When she appeared on the screen, she wasn't the woman he remembered. Or rather, she was an older, scarred version of the woman he remembered.

Had he done this to her? Her mottled skin, her flat expression. The bone structure was the same, but her face had suffered damage that hadn't healed well. He knew that this culture had the ability to enhance appearances, so he figured she had probably opted against some of the cosmetic fixes, maybe to remind herself of what had happened.

"Group Commander Trekov," he said before she could speak. "I am Captain Jonathon Cooper of the *Ivoire*. You have invaded the sovereign space of the Nine Planets, and did not heed my warnings. Because of that, we destroyed your ships. Now, take the remainder of your ships away from our border, and let the Enterran Empire know that it cannot invade the Nine Planets again."

"You're in no place to negotiate, Captain Cooper," she said. "The defensive systems of the Lost Souls Corporation may have had enough firepower to stop our ships, but your little armada there with its joke ships does not. You started a war with the empire at our first encounter four years ago, and we mean to continue that war. So consider this my warning: vacate the border or suffer the consequences."

Coop sighed silently. He shook his head ever so slightly. "You're amazingly intransigent, Commander. We have just destroyed nine of your ships. I am sending you a star map with new borders defined in red.

We're claiming additional territory in Empire space. I am now declaring that to be the border between the Nine Planets and the Empire. This puts your ships in Nine Planets' territory. Since you're in our territory, we will destroy you."

"I've looked at your weapons systems, Captain," she said. "You do not have the firepower that your space station had. I do not accept your terms."

This time, he let her see how disgusted he was. "Have you truly forgotten our first encounter, Commander? I have a weapon that will take out your entire fleet. I did so with one shot four years ago. I can do so now. And if you fire upon the *Ivoire*, my colleague, Captain Lynda Rooney of the *Shadow*, will destroy you before you can order a second shot."

Trekov's skin had turned a sickly gray.

Coop had finally gotten to her, so he pressed on.

"Tell the Empire that our terms are simple: we have now moved the border to the coordinates I have just sent you. Any Empire ship that crosses that border will be destroyed. You are in our territory, and I am warning you. You have fifteen minutes before we destroy your entire fleet."

She severed the connection.

Coop looked at Kravchenko. "Think she believes me this time?"

Kravchenko grinned. "I think she might, but you put her in a terrible position. What's this about moving the border?"

Coop shrugged. "It seems like a good idea. The new coordinates are farther away from any inhabited areas and easier for the Nine Planets to defend. I had to give her something to let her salvage what she can of her reputation. She couldn't just turn tail."

"This isn't salvaging anything," Anita said. "You're forcing her to give up territory."

"And if she remembers what happened before, that's not much. We just destroyed nine of her ships, for God's sake," Coop said. "You'd think she'd realize the position she's in. She should take my deal and run with it."

"What if it isn't her choice?" Kravchenko asked.

"Then Kjersti will see some activity on back channels," Coop said.

"I already am," Perkins said.

"Let's hope her commanders listen to her," Coop said. "Or this time, she won't survive."

THE DIVE
NOW

44

MIKK WANTED US DIVING WITHIN A DAY. Yash thought it would take us a week. Somehow we have split the difference. We're back in the skip three days later. I'd like to say we're less nervous, more certain of ourselves, but I believe it's the other way around.

Yash's team has tweaked our suits to register things in real time and Boneyard time. All that study determined that by the time the dive was over, we had deviated .25 seconds from real time. Over a long dive, that time differential might add up—or it might stay the same.

We won't be able to get more information without diving the Boneyard, and for once, Yash is more cautious than I am. She wants to dive without going near Ship One. I believe that if we're going to dive in the Boneyard, we dive the ship. We may as well know the worst-case scenario.

That time differential is worst-case scenario for me in one way. *Something* is malfunctioning in that Boneyard, and given its impact on time, I'm going to guess that the something is an *anacapa*. I don't know if the *anacapa* is inside Ship One, or if the *anacapa* is part of the Boneyard itself.

Or maybe things operate like they did in the Room of Lost Souls or on Vaycehn. Maybe the impact of the *anacapa's* malfunction has had an impact far away from where the actual *anacapa* is.

No matter what's causing it, our dive teams are now limited to the *Ivoire's* crew and a handful of my people who have the marker. No one else, including some of our most experienced divers, can go anywhere near that Boneyard.

I am not losing anyone to that kind of carelessness ever again.

Yash has brought some of her engineering team. She's staying on the skip and so is the team. But she wants more than one eye on everything that we send back in real time, and she wants some help, in case she needs to do two things at once.

Nyssa certainly can't help her. Nyssa's great with the medical stuff, but knows nothing about the *anacapa*.

She did compare my physical reactions inside the Boneyard to previous reactions on dives, and says there is a difference—I wasn't imagining it. But, she also says that right now the difference isn't dangerous. Or at least, that's what she believes.

Still, she's put a chip just under my skin. She's done the same for every other member of the dive team, and she's going to look at what we record on that, and compare it to the suit's information.

That's the best she can do.

With the other three members of the dive team on board, we're pushing the skip to its weight and passenger capacity. Yash and I believe it's necessary this one time.

We've made it inside the Boneyard. As we head toward the same spot we worked from before, the engineers from the *Ivoire* crowd the windows. The engineers haven't seen the Boneyard from the inside.

I have to give them credit; they're professionals. They don't say much. But they do move slightly, point, elbow each other. One woman whose name I haven't bothered to remember stands slightly to the side, her fist pushed against her mouth as if she's physically holding back tears.

I can't pay attention to the *Ivoire* crowd, even though they press too close to me. I hate having so many people on the skip, on a dive. I made Yash promise she'd be responsible for them, but that's not quite enough for me emotionally. I need to block out their presence, their heightened tension, their worries.

I have to focus, or I can't dive.

And on this dive, the entire dive team is going.

That's the decision I made before we left. I've thought long and hard about the best way to do this dive. We could follow the procedures I had in place before—we could go for the scheduled forty minutes the rules require—but that might not get us inside the ship.

I want us inside the ship for a variety of reasons. The first reason is that I'm curious. We all are. But mostly I want to be inside that ship to check readings. We know how the time differential works outside the ship. If it changes at all *inside* that ship, then I don't want us in there—or in there for very long.

I'm still trying to figure out how the differential is happening. Technically, those of us with the marker, and that includes Denby, shouldn't be subject to problems with the *anacapa*.

I asked Yash about this, and she gave me a haunted look. She said, "If your assumption were really true, then we wouldn't have had so much trouble in foldspace."

I'm not sure she's right about that either, but what her comment made me remember is this: At its core, no one understands the *anacapa*, the energy it produces, or where, exactly, it sends people.

I'd like to think I'm more cautious than I am. I'd like to think that I wouldn't mess with this stuff if I didn't understand it.

But the truth of the matter is that I began playing with *anacapa*s long before I knew what they were, and I've continued as I've realized that no one else understands them either.

If I were truly smart, I'd take this crew away from the Boneyard, lie to Coop, and tell him the place is undiveable.

But I'm not going to.

Because I'm hooked.

45

I GET THE SKIP TO THE EXACT POINT we'd been to before. Being around all of these silent Dignity Vessels startles me all over again. I both love and fear it here.

This time, Yash believes she's compensated for the wobble, so we all watch carefully as I send out the line.

The line wobbles again, like it did on the last dive, but it hooks right near the door that we're targeting on Ship One. Yash did compensate, then, and that makes me feel just a little less tense.

The team finishes putting on our diving suits. We normally change right in the skip, but with so many civilians, we decided—independently of each other—to get half dressed before we left.

All we have to do before our Boneyard dive is put on gloves and helmet-hoods and seal the suits. I press mine, listening to the seals lock in place—a sound added to the suit to ease the worries of the wearer. Then I feel a coolness as the suit's environment activates.

Finally, the suit makes its little self-satisfied announcement that it's ready to go.

I can do without an announcement, and someday I will tell our new suit designers to take that part out of my suit, in the very least. Other people can have it, but I'm not going to.

I turn toward the remaining members of my dive team to see how their suit assembly's going. Orlando waits by the airlock, suit in place.

Elaine pulls on her gloves, checking their tightness. Denby tugs on the center of his suit, loosening it just a little.

Nyssa has moved beside me. She'll monitor the dive beside Yash. The rest of the crowd hovers in the back, trying to pretend they're not interested or excited about anything that's happening before them.

Yash nods at me. I sweep my gloved hands over the controls, a formal maneuver—at least for me—that helps me relinquish the skip. I'm more nervous than I want to be for this dive, so a bit of formality actually makes me feel better.

Then the four of us go to the airlock. We'd decided on an order before we left. I'm leading so that I set the pace, but Denby follows me. He's going to get us inside that ship—at least I hope he will. Then Elaine follows, and Orlando brings up the rear.

I have given us one hour to open that door and get back to the skip.

We crowd into the airlock and head out. As my hands grip the line, I take a deep breath. I can feel my heart rate increase. I have butterflies in my stomach, but I can't tell if they're caused by nerves, excitement, or both.

Again, I look at the ships around me. For a brief moment, I turn down the communications link so I don't hear any white noise at all. I turn on the exterior headset and listen to the sounds of the Boneyard.

I hear looping harmonies, soaring chords, and multiple voices. In the past, I'd retrained my hearing so that I recognized those sounds as the sound of malfunctioning tech, not as music. But out here it sounds like music again, primarily because of the sheer preponderance of it. I can't even catch a thread of notes—there are too many. It's like walking into a space port and trying to catch not only each voice in a crowd of thousands, but each word spoken.

Haunting and beautiful, like the Boneyard itself.

I have to force myself to shut down the exterior sound and turn the comm back on. Through it, I hear Yash, "What the hell was that?"

"The sound of the Boneyard," I say, a bit startled that she could hear it. "You might want to get the skip's audio system to record that."

"I never even thought of doing that," she mutters. "And how come you shut off your comm?"

"Accident," I lie.

Orlando leans his head out from his position at the end of the line. He doesn't buy that excuse for a moment. He grins at me, then nods me forward.

I slowed us just a bit, so now I move more quickly, getting to the door within nine minutes instead of the eleven of the first dive.

Denby arrives beside me. He's got firm instructions. He waits beside the door's hidden exterior control panel. He'll jump in, if the door doesn't open right away.

I use the sensors in my gloves' fingertips to find the door's latch. Yash assures me that this model Dignity Vessel still has a latch that can be accessed from the exterior. Too many incidents, apparently, of repair crews getting stranded or other problems getting into this part of the ship. Later, redundant entries were built in, but for now, this ship has an old-fashioned finger trigger that can be activated by someone on the outside.

That someone, though, won't get through the airlock without help from a control panel, a password, or permission from someone on the inside.

And, of course, our scans show that there is no one on the inside.

The latch feels rough against the tip of my glove. The suit itself warns that I might snag it if I'm not careful.

I pull my hand back, turn on my headlamp, and peer at the latch. It looks broken, but I'm not certain. I've only seen the specs Yash brought with us, and none of them are from actual ships, only from ship designs.

I send the image back to her.

"Broken," she says.

I nod, even though she can't see me. By now, Orlando has reached me. He runs his hand along the edge as well, looking for backup. Elaine is on Denby's far side, preparing to help him with the control mechanism.

"You're on," I say to Denby.

He doesn't have to be told twice. He pulls open the control panel with an ease that surprises me. The panel itself looks dead, but Yash assures me that there's a touch-backup here, one that works without any kind of power running through the ship. Apparently, most Dignity Vessels have that sort of reinforcement. The key is finding it.

As he works the panel, I frown. The key isn't just finding the reinforcement; the key is working on a ship that is new enough to have its redundant systems work. The first Dignity Vessel I ever found had been empty and floating in our space for five thousand years. It had centuries' worth of damage, maybe millennia's worth. I don't know exactly, because I lost that ship to the Empire.

The others we've captured all have serious aging issues.

The only ship I've ever seen that seems—is?—relatively new is the *Ivoire* herself. Because she is, in her own lifespan, maybe fifty years old.

I place my gloved hand flat on the side of Ship One, like I had done with the *Ivoire* when I first found her. I want to make sure I get all kinds of readings here, from composition to age to rate of decay.

The look of this ship bothers me, and I can't quite express why.

"She doesn't open automatically," Denby says. "And she's rejecting my personal code."

He doesn't sound discouraged. That's something I love about the *Ivoire* crew. If they have an emotional reaction to setbacks, they generally don't show it.

"I'm going to try a system backup code now," he says.

The system backup codes are given only to ship leaders throughout the Fleet. Occasionally, those codes get revamped, generally when the areas that use the code are considered too far away to ever need the old code again. For a few years, there's code overlap, and then the new code takes its place.

The one thing Yash doesn't know, the one thing she never asked Coop, is whether or not the older codes remain in the system, so that someone sent via *anacapa* drive to old (or new) places has the ability to get into a ship if need be.

I want to hold my breath as Denby works. I do bite my lower lip. But I also concentrate on inhaling and exhaling—slowly, so I don't get the gids.

"Got it," he says.

I look at the door, expecting it to slide open the way that the *Ivoire's* door does. But it doesn't. It jerks just a centimeter or so, then stops.

I let out a small breath when the door jerks again, then slowly slides to the left. Halfway across, it sticks.

We all stare at it for a moment, as if we can't believe what we've just seen.

Then I reach in and shove on the door, trying to loosen it again.

"You want me to try the code again?" Denby asks.

"I want you to find what has it jammed," Orlando says, and there's no way to know if he's joking. I suspect he's not.

Normally, I would give him a harsh look, but Denby is so straight-laced that he doesn't seem to notice. He's still looking at me.

"Don't bother," I say. "We can fit through this."

I run my gloved hand along the edge of the door to make sure there are no other sharp edges. I'm not feeling any, and the gloves haven't warned me of any.

I turn, peer inside the airlock, with my headlamp on.

The airlock's interior door is open.

My breath catches. For a moment, I wonder what kind of crisis caused that door to stay open—did someone die in the airlock?—and then I realize that the ship was deliberately stored that way.

The door itself is a barrier. Two doors and an airlock might've proven too difficult for anyone to get through, especially if they needed to quickly.

Of course, I'm assuming, guessing, which is something I always do on dives. Something not entirely necessary here.

"Yash," I say through the comm. "Is it Fleet policy to leave airlock interior doors open on decommissioned ships?"

"Decommissioned?" Orlando asks. I know he understands the term. But I seem to have confused him.

Good thing I hadn't addressed the question to him.

"Of course," Yash says. "But the other part of a decommissioning procedure is to take all of the valuable and proprietary tech out of the bridge and engineering."

She sounds disappointed, and I have to admit, her statement disappoints me too.

Then I realize she's also assuming. She's assuming that the Fleet did a standard decommission on this ship. What if they had a different policy for Fleet ships in the Boneyard?

I don't ask her that. We'd be guessing and wasting time.

Instead, I cling to the side of the door and look at my team.

"You guys ready to go inside?" I ask.

Elaine grins like a crazy woman. "Are you kidding me? Of course."

Orlando's smiling too.

But Denby remains by the control panel. He's not looking happy. "Maybe I should stay here."

In his tone, I hear the same fear I've heard from Yash, from all the other *Ivoire* crew members. A fear of what they'll discover, of what their discoveries will confirm.

"We'll need you inside," I say.

I hope. I have no idea if we'll make it to the bridge in the forty minutes left in our dive—thirty, if you count how long it will take us to return to the skip.

"But, if something goes wrong with the door...." he says, and deliberately lets his voice trail off.

"If something goes wrong with the door," I say, "then someone from the skip will come over and deal with it."

Or not. Depending on how long we've been inside, and what actually did go wrong.

If everyone inside the skip has reason to believe we're dead, no one will come after us.

But I don't think that's what Denby's thinking of at the moment. I think he's just realized he's about to go into a dark and empty space ship, with only a thin suit between him and disaster.

I think he's just realized that something could go horribly wrong in there—and that something isn't just a discovery of some awful past. It might also be something he can't get out of.

Every diver encounters this moment early in his diving career. What he does at that moment determines if he will remain a diver or if he will give it up at the first opportunity.

I can cajole Denby through a handful of dives. But I can't convince him to make diving his life's work—even with the Boneyard all around us.

He gives me a funny smile, relieved and sheepish and terrified all at the same time.

"Do we go in with same order as we took the line?" he asks.

"Yeah," I say.

Which means that I get to go first.

46

I SLIP INSIDE THE AIRLOCK. It's dark, spacious, and somewhat familiar. It looks like the *Ivoire's* airlock if the doors were open, the gravity off, and the ship sideways. My headlamp makes one small yellow circle in the darkness. I turn on my glove lights as well. I'm the first one inside; I have to make it as light for my companions as possible without blinding them.

I use the interior door as the next handhold. I've also turned on the marking function inside my gloves. It's an old habit of mine, but a good one: I make sure we all use the same handholds, the same stops, the same path, by marking each.

That way, only one of us damages something inadvertently. The others know where to avoid it. Or, conversely, we all know where the safe handholds are, and we can proceed accordingly from one dive to the next.

Ahead, I can see vague outlines in the intact corridor. We're at a side door, not the door into one of the cargo bays like I had initially thought on our first dive.

Yash had shown me a map of all the entrances on the *Ivoire* and similar ships. She knew, from the location of this one, that it was more of a maintenance door than one the crew generally used. She prepared me for the corridor, and showed me a map so I had it in my memory, as well as one in my suit's memory, so that I can compare.

I'm glad she's done so. It makes the dive easier, if a bit less dramatic.

The others crowd into the airlock. I move into the corridor.

The suit records my time on this mission at twenty-one minutes.

"Yash, you able to hear me?" I ask.

It takes a moment before she responds, just long enough for my heart to stutter with worry.

"What time does your suit's internal clock show?" she asks.

"Twenty-two minutes, ten seconds," I say. I can see Orlando nodding near me.

"I had twenty-two nine," she says. "Is that enough of a discrepancy to abort?"

Probably. I don't know. I don't care. It's fascinating in here.

"Not yet," I say. "Keep pinging us."

"Will do," she says. "With that second loss, you need to come back a little early."

I understand what she means. She wants us to return on time, and to plan for losing precious minutes inside this ship.

It's probably sensible, and I can't ignore every sensible suggestion someone makes. The me who runs dives from the skip would get irritated at me the diver in charge if I did that.

"Got it." I beckon the others. I don't know how far we'll get inside the ship. If Yash's map is accurate, then we're a long distance from the bridge, but not that far from engineering. The *anacapa* drive is somewhere in between.

As Denby comes out of the airlock, he glances at the ship's door.

"It's still open," he reports as he reaches my side. I guess he believes I'm worried. I'm not. I've been in much worse situations. We have a lot of oxygen, a backup ship, and probably two dozen other ways out.

Elaine says nothing as she joins us. She carefully puts her hands where mine have been. She has only a general light on around her suit, making sure that we can see her, but not something that will distract us from what we're doing.

"This is frighteningly familiar," Orlando says as he reaches the group. "It seems we've been here before."

Denby looks at him in shock, but I don't.

"The practice dives," Elaine whispers to Denby to clarify.

We did a few in some of the half-restored Dignity Vessels at Lost
Souls. We shut off the environmental systems and practiced wreck-diving techniques. It felt fake to me, but apparently not to Orlando and
some of the others.

Although Denby hadn't noticed the comparisons.

Of course, Denby lived on the *Ivoire*, so a Dignity Vessel probably
always feels familiar to him.

"Where to?" Denby asks me. He hasn't forgotten that I asked him to
lead us once we were inside.

I check my suit's timer. Twenty-five minutes. We only have five more
before I have to order us to retrace our steps.

"I think we need to see the *anacapa* first," I say. Besides, the closer we
get to it, the more we'll know about whether or not it's malfunctioning.

"We won't get there in five minutes," he says.

"Well, let's get part of the way there," I say, gently reminding him that
we're mapping—or at least confirming the Dignity Vessel map—with
each trip.

He nods and moves forward, hands shaking a little as he follows protocol, going from one good handhold to another.

As we go deeper inside, I can see some things are different from a
working Dignity Vessel like the *Ivoire*. The corridor has no decorations,
but I don't know if that's normal for a decommissioned ship or if the lack
of power has something to do with it or if some ships never have corridor decorations. Some of the back corridors on the *Ivoire* now depict
images of the long-lost Fleet life. Others display very abstract art. I believe both are ways to cope with the changes, but Coop tells me that the
ship's crew has always divided itself into realistic, representational, and
abstract factions.

Some of the corridor's doors stand open, others remain closed, and I can't
see any pattern in it. I'll check with Yash when we return. She might know.

I don't think it worth asking Denby. I don't want to distract him.

"Thirty minutes," Elaine says, and she sounds disappointed.

I know I am.

"We have to turn around," I say, and then I wait for Denby to do so.

He pauses just ahead of me, his entire body pointed forward as if begging to continue. Then his shoulders go up and down in a silent sigh.

He pushes off and moves ahead of me, again following the protocol we established. I'm going to bring up the rear on the return.

Orlando leads us out, and we move twice as fast as we did upon arrival.

Denby, to his credit, doesn't ask if we can spend the time we saved inside the ship. He knows better.

We reach the airlock, and I feel my stomach clench.

There's no way to know if that exterior door remained open—at least not from where we are. And I'm not going to ask Yash to check.

Orlando ducks inside the airlock first.

"We're clear," he says, and I exhale.

I hear Elaine let out a grunt of approval. Denby puts a hand against his forehead, as if the relief is almost too much for him.

After we're done with the initial stages of the Boneyard, he won't be back. He's done diving.

I don't know if it's the ship that has upset him, or if it reminds him of those days trapped in foldspace, or if he's just not wreck-diving material. I won't ask either.

But I ratchet down my expectations of him just a little bit.

I'm the last into the airlock. I glance over my shoulder at the ship's darkened interior.

I feel a little bit of giddiness—*we're going to figure you out*, I promise Ship One—and then I slip into the strange lights of the Boneyard, and grab the line that will guide me back to the skip.

47

YASH AND I DECIDE WE NEED to evaluate this dive together before we bring in the rest of the dive team. It's unusual, I know, but that time differential isn't something we want everyone else to argue about.

We meet in the conference room with the door sealed. I have brought in dinner. Even though I've eaten and rested, I know that Yash and her engineers have spent the last few hours examining that time differential. I suspect she hasn't eaten.

As I watch her tear into the stew and bread that I've brought, I know that I'm right.

I eat slowly, savoring the rich broth and the spices and the warmth, knowing that I need to maintain my strength, which means I have to watch everything from my food intake to my sleep. The more the better on dives, because you never know what might go wrong.

Yash eats for a few minutes before she shoves a tablet at me. It's covered with all kinds of equations and squiggles and graphs that I suppose I could understand if I took it into my cabin, plugged it into my computer, and asked tons of questions as I went through it line by line.

I hate doing stuff like that, so I just glance at it.

"What am I looking at?" I ask.

"A mess," she says, her mouth partially full. "But a fascinating mess."

I raise my eyebrows. I didn't expect the word "fascinating."

"I didn't think to examine the sound of the Boneyard," she says as she pulls off a hunk of bread. She holds it in one hand while she talks, clearly waiting to take a bite when she's finished with some important sentence. "Thank you for that."

"You're welcome," I say. "I was just curious."

"That's how science begins." She smiles. The hunk of bread has vanished in the short few seconds it took me to answer her. She rips off another and dunks it in the stew, holding the bread there this time so it won't drip on her. "The exterior of that ship—the Boneyard itself—is amazing."

"I know," I say.

"No, you don't," she says. "But I'm getting ahead of myself."

She takes a bite from the second hunk of bread and sets it on the edge of her stew plate. I take this moment to eat some of my bread.

She leans back, hands moving as if she can't contain her enthusiasm.

"I checked all of the times—the ones on your suit, the ones inside you and the others, the ones we have here, and there is a time differential."

"Crap," I say.

She holds up a finger. "Let me finish. The differential exists inside the Boneyard itself, and it changes according to where you guys are on that line."

"What?" I ask.

"It stops inside Ship One, and inside the skip. That's what this is." She taps the tablet, which is upside down from her perspective, and she enlarges one of the graphs. "You're the red, Orlando is the blue, Elaine is the green, and Denby is the yellow. This is the skip, here's the line, then these are the times. You can see how each line is different depending on where you guys are along the line we strung between the two ships. You see…"

I shake my head just a little, frowning. "I'm not going to look at charts and stuff. Just give me the short version right now."

"There are all kinds of energy waves in that Boneyard," she says. "Most are *anacapa*, but others are *anacapa* waves times ten million, things we have never seen before—not my culture or yours."

"Okay." I'm a bit stunned. I really did think—like Coop—that the Boneyard was built by the Fleet. "Is it something the Fleet could have developed?"

"You're too far ahead of our analysis," Yash says.

"Meaning you know the answer and you're going to build to it, or you don't know the answer and need more research?"

"We need more research," she says. "But here's what you're going through. When one of those energy waves hits you, it changes your measurement of time—or at least the measurement in your suit."

I push my plate away, feeling a little cold. "What do you mean, my suit? Does that mean my internal chip is fine?"

"Yes," she says. "It keeps time consistent with the time on the skip."

"So the suit is untrustworthy," I say. "Did you check its overall integrity?"

"I'll get to that," she says.

I let out a sigh. I hate it when people do that. I really only need a bit of information: Can we do the next dive? How safe will it be?

But I trust Yash enough to give her a few more minutes before I hit her with those questions.

She continues, "There was no *anacapa* reading from inside Ship One. Or outside of it either, that we can tell anyway, given all of the interference. Ship One's *anacapa* is either completely shut down or it doesn't exist anymore."

I let out a small sigh. We're going to have to dive her to see which of those is true. "And that's good news?"

"It is," she says, "in that Ship One seems to be intact and her shielding seems to protect her from all those energy waves in the Boneyard proper."

"You checked the readings I got on my glove?" I ask. "I mean, did anybody add shielding to Ship One's exterior?"

"The shielding is just like the *Ivoire's*. Ship One is much older—not in design, but in actual time passed—but she seems relatively similar otherwise."

That's exactly what my eyes already told me. It's nice to get the confirmation.

"And the skip is protecting us when we're in the Boneyard," I say.

"Yes," she says.

"So," I say. "Tell me about the suits."

She sighs. "You should say, 'Tell me about the Boneyard.'"

"I would've, but I didn't think you could," I said.

"I can't exactly," she says. "Just the information you four got on your three dives will take my team weeks to process."

"We don't—"

She holds up her hand to stop me from saying any more. "I know we don't have weeks, at least on this dive, and if we fulfill Coop's mission."

The "if" catches me.

"But you like risks," she says.

"Risks?" I ask.

She pulls off another hunk of bread. She looks at it like it has the answers. Then she sighs.

"Here's what I know," she says. "I know that all of that energy, all of the things happening in the Boneyard, have an impact on the suits. I know that the impact varies from whatever point you're at inside the Boneyard, and whatever's happening with the energy at that moment. I have no idea if that energy will compromise a suit's integrity."

"Over time?" I ask.

She makes a small sound, almost of disgust. "That's even harder to answer. Let me try it this way. Clearly some of those waves have an impact on the suit's function, at least in its clock, and I suspect, although at the moment I cannot prove, in the suit's entire system. So, 'over time' isn't a great phrase. I would say that at one second, your suit could be working fine and at another, you could have catastrophic suit failure. It'll seem like one second to the next for you, but that suit might experience a century in that second."

She takes a bite of the bread, chewing, allowing me to take in that comment. I'm going to wait for the rest of it before I say anything.

"Or, those energy waves might not be having an impact on time inside the suit, just on the suit's entire function. So it might be happening in real time, but the suit ceases working for a moment. When we're dealing in tenths of a second, you might not even notice, but if something were to change for the worst—a minute, two, three—you will notice. You'll die out there."

I almost say *That's always a risk*, but I don't want to sound flip. Besides, I'm not feeling flip.

"So," I say, "let me be clear. You saw an impact on the suits, other than inside their clocks."

"Yes," she says, "enough to worry me, but not enough to prove anything. I can tell you that the integrity of those suits won't survive more than a handful of visits to the Boneyard. You'll have to switch suits."

I frown, thinking. We all brought backup suits, and then there are others that some of the people on the *Two* have that we can borrow. But it's not ideal.

"We're not going to be able to get a lot of ships on this trip, are we?" I ask.

"It depends on how you want to run things," she says. "I think we can send someone back with one of the skips and have them return in one of the *Ivoire's* transports with some suits."

I nod. I'll think about that later.

"Are we guaranteeing a catastrophic suit failure by continuing to dive?" I ask.

"Eventually, yes," Yash says. "Can I tell you whether it will happen to your suit or Denby's? I have no idea. Can I tell you if it will happen while we're here on these dives? No, I can't. I may have enough data, but I haven't processed it, and I'm not sure I entirely understand it."

"You want to get to that control station in the Boneyard," I say.

"It would help," she says. "But I'm not willing to do it right now, given what we know and the equipment we have. I'd rather try with the *Ivoire*."

Or one of the ships we're diving for.

I nod. Then I grab some bread for myself, more to give myself something to do than because I'm hungry.

"Well," I say, "let's go take a vote."

"What?" Yash's shock comes through that one word.

I grin at her. "This isn't a military vessel," I remind her. "My divers are volunteers. They know they're risking their lives, but now we have evidence of the kinds of risks they're facing. They need to know, and they need to make the best choice for themselves."

"I think it's too late for that," she says. "We have a mission—"

"And I don't want a terrified or reluctant diver on it," I say. "*I'm* going to go. But the other three get to make their own decisions."

She shakes her head. "Just when I think I am beginning to understand you," she says, "I realize I'm entirely wrong."

"It's just a different way of doing things," I say, "and it works for me."

What I don't tell her is this: I don't want to be the person who orders someone to their death. I've had too many people die on dives with me. Their ghosts still haunt me. I don't want a fresh set of ghosts, reminding me how terrified they were, and how I forced them to do something they didn't want to do.

Yash might understand. I'm sure a lot of commanders in the Fleet understand.

But she would do it anyway, and I will not.

Not ever.

48

My team comes through, even Denby. Maybe I should say especially Denby. I gave them the choice about whether or not they want to continue the dives, given the threat to the suits and the horrible way we might die out here, and they opt to continue.

I'd like to say I didn't doubt it for a second, but that would be a lie. I did doubt it, and not just Denby, whom I knew might just follow orders. But for everyone. When you rip your own suit, that's one thing. The suit might reseal itself, it might save you. There are a million ways to die while diving, but most of them—I'd say 80% of them—are user inflicted. You know if you behave properly, you have a better chance of getting out.

But a collapse of suit integrity at the wrong moment through no fault of your own, that is probably something you will not survive. It makes even the toughest of us rethink what we're about to do.

We all rethought, and yet here we are, floating outside the door to Ship One's *anacapa* room. This is our third dive since my conversation with Yash. We've explored a goodly portion of the engineering side of the ship, and each time we return to the *Two* we check our suit integrity.

Elaine, our cautious one, has opted for a new suit on this dive. Mine might be ragged—that's Yash's term—but I want to wear it this one last time. The others have less damage to their suits, even though I believe that Nyssa will order everyone to use new suits sometime soon.

It took half a dive to open the *anacapa* room. We didn't have the codes. Yash talked with other Fleet crew members to see if they could remember old codes or the patterns for new ones.

We finally got the door open on the last dive.

On this dive, we have made it to the *anacapa* room in record time. This is the heart of our dive. If the *anacapa* doesn't work, then we're going to have to start all over again with a new ship. I'm not sure I'm willing to do that, with the suit problems and the things that we don't understand in the Boneyard. And if I'm not willing, I'm certainly not going to expect my team to dive it.

Coop will simply have to wait for his fleet of Dignity Vessels. Even though I don't want to be the one to tell him that.

We don't have to tell him yet. We crowd near the door and coordinate our clocks. We have decided to use two hours on this dive. We're fifty-three minutes in.

I go in first, because if there's any obvious danger here, I want to be the one who discovers it. I still have vivid memories of what a destroyed *anacapa* did to one of my crew members years ago. If anyone ends up trapped and mummified, it will be me. Not because I'm heroic, but because I'm not. I don't think I can live through that again.

This *anacapa* room is small compared to others I've seen, and a bit more centrally located. It has thick black walls covered with the nano-material I first encountered on Vaycehn. I know where the drive should be, and the area, which has all kinds of controls I just barely understand, looks intact.

I signal Denby with my right hand, then hover near the controls. We actually debated turning on the gravity and the environment—from what we can tell, it works just fine—but we decided against it. We're not doing anything to this ship until we know that it suits our needs.

Denby pulls his way forward, moving as fast as he can toward me. I hope Nyssa is monitoring him for the gids. He seems almost too eager. He has brought a hook with him this time, and he grapples onto one of the side columns so that he can remain in place without holding something.

He bends over and begins to power up the console.

Orlando and Elaine guard the outside of the room. Not that I believe anything will hurt us; mostly I'm worried that there's some kind of fail-safe and the door will close. Denby and I will be trapped inside, which is not something I want to experience.

The console turns a light blue. Yellow symbols appear. I can read some of them, including the ancient word for *danger*. I glance at him. Denby grins at me.

"So far so good," he says.

He taps one side of the console, and beside me a compartment opens. It contains one of the larger *anacapa* drives I've seen.

"A little newer than ours," Denby says. "I'm guessing not much."

I know he means in design, not in age. In age, this thing is thousands of years old. My shoulders ache, and I realize they've risen upward, a sign of nerves. Old *anacapa* drives malfunction.

This is the test, for all of us.

"Can you start it?" I ask.

"It looks like it's completely intact, and the console is working," Denby says.

"So that's a yes," I say.

"No," he says, "that's an I'm-going-to-do-my-best."

I nod. I understand that. One of my divers would be less specific, but Denby's training makes him about as accurate as a human being can get.

I make myself breathe evenly—once in and once out. *So there, Nyssa,* I think, just in case she's worried about us.

"Okay," I say.

He touches the console. The *anacapa* glows orange for just a moment, then fades to silver. I can hear the normal thrum that I associate with the *Ivoire's anacapa*, but none of the harmonies I've heard with malfunctioning ones.

"It's working," he says. "I'm going to run a diagnostic, but I think it's a go."

A go. In more ways than one. We have a ship to take back to Lost Souls. I take in a shallow, shuddery breath.

Holy crap, I think but don't say. *This is going to work. This is really going to work.*

49

I DOUBLE-CHECK THE TIME. We have fifty minutes left on this dive. "How long does it take to get the *anacapa* powered up?"

Denby grins at me. "It's not like other drives, Boss," he says, and somehow he doesn't sound patronizing. "It's ready now."

"Can you program coordinates into it and get us out of the Boneyard?"

"I can send us back to the Lost Souls if we want to go," he says.

I trust him and I don't trust him. That's probably not accurate. I trust what he's telling me; I just don't believe it could be that easy. But I'm paying attention. He's here for his expertise, after all.

I think about what he says, then I realize what bothers me about it. Yash would end up in charge of the *Two*. And she's arrogant enough to believe she can lead another dive, get more ships out of the Boneyard.

With the suit issues, the weird energy signatures, and the Boneyard itself, I'm not willing to take that risk. In fact, it's less the weird energy signatures that bother me than it is the Boneyard.

I have the odd sense that it's alive, watching us, waiting. I've felt like that since it expelled us earlier in the mission. I don't want to rile up whatever is here, if anything is here.

"We're not going to Lost Souls yet," I say. "We're heading to the *Two*."

He moves just a bit, as if I surprised him.

"You're going to need me in engineering, right?" I ask.

"Just in case something goes wrong," he says, as if I can make one of the Dignity Vessels work. But better me than Orlando or Elaine. Yash would have to talk them through everything. I can guess at some of it and probably not do any damage.

"You want Elaine or Orlando with you?" I ask.

"No," he says a little too fast, which gives me an adrenalin spike. He's worried about something. I am not going to ask, though.

"What's bothering you?" I ask.

"Boy," he says, "there are a million ways to answer that question."

"About being alone," I say.

"Nothing," he says, which makes me wonder if I guessed wrong. I'm not going to push further, however. If he thinks it important, he'll tell me.

As I pull my way out of the *anacapa* room, I hit the comm. "Yash, you listening to all of this?"

"I am," she says after a delay that's about five seconds longer than I want.

"I hope you've already removed the line," I say.

"I was waiting for confirmation from you."

I curse silently. Sometimes the military aspect of Yash irritates the hell out of me. I would have preferred more initiative, even if she got it all wrong.

"Do it now, then get the hell out of here," I say. "I want the skip out of the Boneyard before we move the ship."

"That means you'll be in the ship longer than the agreed-upon two hours."

She's exacting to the very end.

"Yes, it does," I say. I don't want to point out to her that if something goes wrong, it doesn't matter how long we're in the ship. "Get out of here."

"You don't have to tell me twice," she says and signs off.

I'm glad she's off the comm, because I wanted to tell her that she's right: I don't have to tell her twice. I have to tell her at least three times.

I keep my mouth closed, and ease out of the room. Elaine and Orlando wait. Orlando's closer to the door than I like.

"You want me to come with you?" he asks.

I'm in new territory here. I have no idea what I want or need. I'm not sure where the potential problems are, here or in engineering. I shrug.

"We're going to need one person here at the door," I say to him and Elaine, "the other with me in engineering. You guys figure it out."

"I'll come with you, Boss," Elaine says. "I've been working with some of the Dignity Vessels at home. I might be useful."

I look at her in surprise. I hadn't known that. If I had, I might have made other choices earlier in this mission. Maybe the military way of doing things isn't so bad after all. At least you know what everyone's doing most of the time.

"You're right," I say. "You might be useful. Come with me."

We make our way through the wide corridor, using the handholds we'd set when we first dived Ship One. As soon as we get to engineering, I'll tell Denby to get us out of the Boneyard.

I hope that gives Yash enough time to get the skip out.

At least she'll have it away from Ship One. That might be enough. With all of the various weird energy signatures in the Boneyard, I'm not sure if adding one more from Ship One's *anacapa* drive will have an impact.

Or maybe I should say have a negative impact.

I'm pretty sure there will be an impact. I just don't know what the impact will be.

50

THE ENGINEERING SECTION ON DIGNITY VESSELS isn't one room or even a manageable area. It's large enough to be a ship in and of itself. In fact, I would wager all of the *Two* would fit inside of the engineering section of Ship One, and leave room for at least three more *Two*-sized ships.

Denby tells me that the rows and rows of equipment, the consoles, banks, closed off areas, are all normal on certain types of Dignity Vessels. He says this is a different class than the *Ivoire*, but from the same period, which is why he can get so much done here. He also says that everything inside this section is intact.

Which is why I'm so grateful that I'm familiar with this kind of ship. Otherwise I would have no idea where the control panels are, the ones that can override the bridge, if need be, or act as a secondary bridge when the main bridge is out of order.

Or shut down.

That control panel is three banks in, hidden in the middle of what looks like very mundane equipment consoles. The design is purposeful. Anyone who tries to take over the ship from engineering would need to know where the consoles are, which isn't something the average spacefaring person could easily figure out.

I pull myself there, and power up the console with the touch of a hand. Yash had assured me that the entire vessel would power up for me because of the marker, but I hadn't believed her until now. I'm relieved to see the blue lights becoming yellow, even if I'm suddenly annoyed at myself for failing to learn the old language.

None of the words on this panel look familiar.

I do recognize the configuration, though. I've watched Yash work the same configuration on the *Ivoire*, and I helped navigate the *Shadow* on her maiden voyage. I really didn't fly her at all, but I pretended I did, just because I wanted her to be my ship from the very beginning.

"Hey, Denby," I say, "I'm ready, but I hope to hell you can do most everything from there."

"Me too," he says, and he sounds extremely serious. What I would have given for a touch of wit at that moment.

Then Yash comes through the comm. "The skip is almost out of the force field. I'll make sure it closes behind us."

"Thanks," I say. I guess we're ready. I let out a small breath. My heart is pounding hard. I suspect I'll hear about that from Nyssa later.

"Coordinates are in, Boss," Denby says to me. I guess he wants me to give the go-ahead.

"Then let's go," I say.

He doesn't have to tell me it's done. I can feel it as the ship makes that stutter I've become so familiar with on the *Ivoire*. My heart stutters too, both in surprise and wonder, and just a little fear. We're using an ancient vessel and attempting to move it out of a place we don't entirely understand, using a drive we're not certain about.

I can't see any of the screens—I haven't powered them up—so I have no idea if we're looking at a new and different star map. Then the ship stutters again.

"We're out, Boss," Denby says.

My knees wobble. I am much more relieved than I expected. "I guess we can turn on the environmental controls, then," I say.

I reach for them, then slid sideways. The entire ship vibrates and something flashes on my console, something I can't read.

"What the hell?" I ask.

"The Boneyard is firing on you!" Yash says.

281

It takes a moment for that to compute. The Boneyard itself?

I slam my hand on the console, trying to get the screens up. Elaine pulls herself closer to the controls.

"Do you know where the shields are?" I ask.

"Yes," she says, sounding calmer than I feel. "I'm turning on the gravity too."

"How's the *anacapa*?" I ask Denby.

"No trouble yet, but that shot was frighteningly close."

"Screens up," Elaine says.

"Can't tell," Yash says through my suit's comm. "I'm coming to you."

"No," I say. I don't want to wait for the skip. The ship vibrates again.

"Boss," Denby says, "they're aiming for the *anacapa*."

I curse. This is what happened to Coop, to the *Ivoire*. A shot on the *anacapa*.

"Put in the coordinates for Lost Souls," I say to him. Then I contact Yash. I hate being blind, and the screens aren't coming up. "Are you being fired on, Yash?"

"Not yet," she says. "Although a few shots have hit the *Two*. They have their shields up. Do you want them to fire back?"

"No," I say. "Dock with them. We're getting out of here. We'll meet you at Lost Souls."

"Boss, I'm not sure if that's a good—"

I cut her off. "Let's go, Denby. Right now."

THE THIRD SKIRMISH
NOW

51

"Get me Flag Commander Janik," Trekov said to Sherwin.

Sherwin pointedly looked around the bridge. The crew did their work, but stiffly, as if they weren't certain what would happen. Sherwin was clearly scared. He had become scared when this Captain Cooper made his threat to do the same thing he had done at the Room of Lost Souls. So Sherwin did know the details after all. Trekov hadn't been certain.

"I need him *now*," she said, since it looked like Sherwin froze. She didn't blame him. Group Commanders usually didn't go to Flag Commanders in the middle of a battle.

"I'll—um—put him through to the conference—"

"In here, Sherwin, and the entire damn fleet can listen in. You now know this man Cooper doesn't bluff, and I've been through what he's thrown at us before. I survived—barely. He says he has more this time, and I believe him. So get me the goddamn Flag Commander and tell him we're fucking short on time."

"Yes, ma'am," Sherwin said.

She paced the back of the bridge. Damn this Cooper. He had given her no choice. Nine ships gone, which she couldn't think about. She had known going into the Nine Planets' territory was a risk—they all had—but she had expected the loss of only a few ships, and a fight for the remainder.

She hadn't expected to lose them all in one big attack—before the ships should have shown up on any sensors at all.

She had no idea how the Nine Planets had gotten so far ahead in technology. It was as if they had taken a quantum jump—going from ocean-faring vessels to star drives in ten short years.

"Commander Trekov," Sherwin said. "I have Flag Commander Janik."

Flag Commander Janik appeared on the big screen in the center of the bridge. He was wearing full dress uniform and looked a bit red-faced. She wondered if he had come from dinner.

"Commander Janik," she said. "We're in a terrible situation here."

She briefed him on the Lost Souls disaster, and then explained Cooper's ultimatum.

"Commander," she said, "I've encountered this Captain Cooper before. He's the man who masterminded the attack on the Room of Lost Souls, resulting in the loss of a fleet of ships and six hundred lives. He does not bluff, and we're running out of time, sir."

"Get more time," Janik said. "We'll send in reinforcements."

"I tried to stall before, sir," Trekov said. "He doesn't stall. He has no qualms about taking hundreds of lives. I am suggesting a tactical retreat for now. We regroup and figure out how to retaliate in the future."

"I thought this was a retaliation for all those attacks on our facilities," Janik said.

"It is, sir, but—"

"You said we have superior firepower, and you see no superior firepower on his end," Janik said.

"That's what our sensors say, sir," she said, feeling like a goddamn cadet. "But I read no weapons on his ship four years ago, and he destroyed us as if we were made of paper. If I had the authority to order the changed borders, I would, sir, but I don't."

'You're recommending a retreat without a shot fired?" Janik asked.

"Beg pardon, sir, but shots were fired. We lost nine ships already. We have fifteen remaining. I don't think that's enough, sir."

"Against two rebuilt Dignity Vessels and sixteen tugboats? Commander, have you lost your mind?" Janik asked.

She stiffened. He was the one who had seen the carnage from the Room of Lost Souls. If anyone knew what this Captain Cooper could do, it was Janik. He should have been on her side.

"No, sir, I have not lost my mind," she said. "I just have experience with this weapon and—"

"He knows it, doesn't he," Janik said.

"Knows what, sir?" she asked.

"That you're the commander he met before," Janik said.

"Yes, sir, but I don't see how that's relevant."

Janik grinned. The grin was almost feral. "Commander, it's basic strategy. He defeated you once with a lucky shot against some kind of ancient technology. He's bluffing, and he knows that you're the only person who'll believe that bluff. He expects you to retreat. I'm ordering you to attack. He's not prepared for it, and he won't survive it."

"Sir," she said. "I—"

"I'm *ordering* you, Commander," Janik said. "And when you get back, we will have a long talk about your work in the field. Understood?"

Her cheeks heated. He was going to take her command from her, and he had said so in front of the entire armada. They wouldn't listen to her now, even if she could countermand his orders.

"Understood, sir," she said. "We'll carry out your orders on one condition."

"You're in no position to make conditions, Commander."

"Still, sir," she said. "I want it on the record at General Command that you are denying my field experience with this captain and this weapon. This attack is *your* idea, not mine, and if it goes awry, I am not taking the blame for it, sir. Do *you* understand?"

"I don't think it's anything we need to worry about, Commander," Janik said patronizingly, "so long as you do what I say."

Then he severed the connection.

She took a deep breath and looked at the bridge. They looked back at her, all of them, trying to hide their emotions. She saw everything from fear to anger to confusion.

"We're going to attack that little ragtag force," she said. "We go in traditional formation."

She gave the rest of the orders so that the armada heard.

Then she looked at Sherwin, and gave him the signal to momentarily cut off communications with the rest of the armada.

"I want you to set a backup course as far away from this location into the Empire as we can get," she said. "I want that course to be ready at the touch of a finger. Have the star drive ready to go as far as it can as fast as it can."

"We're not going to join the attack?" Sherwin asked.

"Oh, we'll join," she said, "and we'll lead from behind like traditional formation dictates. But if I give the word to ignite that star drive, you do it, understand?"

"Why ma'am?" he asked.

Everyone was suddenly discounting her. Maybe she should have spoken to Janik alone.

"Because," she said, "I've experienced that weapon Captain Cooper was describing, and there's no beating it. We are not going to die today, do you understand me, Commander?"

"Respectfully, ma'am, shouldn't we give the same order to the other ships in the armada?"

She blinked at him, knowing that the ships in the front of the formation would have no chance at all. But better for the crews to believe they had a chance than not.

She punched some information into her console. "That's the signature of the weapon. If our ships see anything like this coming their way, they have my permission to retreat as fast as their damn vessel will take them. Please let them know."

"Thank you, ma'am," Sherwin said. He sounded relieved. He hadn't been disrespecting her. He had been as frightened of the weapon as she was, and he wanted to make sure everyone else survived.

They wouldn't. It was going to be a bloodbath.

The only difference was that this time, it wasn't going to be her fault.

52

Coop shouldn't have felt compassion, but he did. His entire bridge crew had listened to the exchange between Commander Trekov and her superior officer, Flag Commander Janik. Trekov had believed she was on a secure channel, and she had sounded both sensible and realistic.

Her commander was an ass.

Her commander should have known what happened at Starbase Kappa. He should have respected the woman's opinion. Coop had half a mind to butt into the conversation, but he didn't.

Although he did wonder this: if he hadn't insisted on that moved border, would Trekov have retreated? She was in charge of this operation, after all. Would she have had more leeway? Would she have been able to move back, to retreat, without major repercussions for her?

Probably not. She would have had to have that talk with her commander no matter what happened. But giving her the opportunity to retreat would have caused Coop more problems.

It would simply have forestalled the inevitable. The Empire would have come back, with more reinforcements, and they might have brought enough numbers—or enough waves—to make it through any *anacapa*-like attacks that Coop could pull off.

"Captain," Kravchenko said, "they're powering up weapons."

He toyed with contacting Trekov one last time, then changed his mind. Trekov had done all she could.

Now it was time for him to do what he needed to.

"Tell Lynda to prepare the *anacapa* weapon like we had discussed," he said. "Then have all of the Nine Planets' ships retreat as fast as they can."

That should scare Trekov. Maybe she thought he wouldn't make the attack because the Nine Planets' ships wouldn't survive it. Well, this was the first volley.

"They're already on the way, sir," Kravchenko said. "And Captain Rooney wants to know if she has the privilege of firing first."

"Tell her we're doing it together on my mark," Coop said. "We each take a side of this armada. Then we activate our *anacapas* and go back to Lost Souls as fast as we can. Got that?"

"Yes, sir," Kravchenko said.

"We're ready, Captain," Anita said.

"All right then," Coop said. "Let's teach these people a lesson they're never going to forget."

53

THE JUNK SHIPS RETREATED, AND ELISSA'S STOMACH TWISTED.

"You need to fire on those Dignity Vessels now," she said to Sherwin. "Before they can do anything to us."

He gave the command, and the front part of the armada fired, blue weapons' light flaring across the blackness of space.

Elissa saw that out of the corner of her eye. She wasn't focused on the actual fight. She was watching for the switch in energy signature.

"Their shields are stronger than anything we've seen, sir," one of the officers said.

"Fire again," Sherwin said.

Then the energy signature appeared on Elissa's screen. She involuntarily clenched her right fist.

"Now," she said, and her voice squeaked. She cleared her throat, so that she could be heard. She wasn't going to let her own fears get in the way of saving these lives. "Now, Sherwin! Get us the hell out of here *now*."

He gave her a frightened glance, then repeated her order, not just to his crew, but to the entire armada.

She felt the ship shift, then the screens went dark as the star drive kicked in.

She hoped to hell this weapon couldn't follow them now. She hoped to hell she had spoken fast enough. She hoped to hell the rest of the armada got out as well.

THE DIVE
NOW

54

THE SHIP VIBRATES A THIRD TIME. Everything shudders. I'm beginning to wonder the wisdom of my plan.

"Denby?" I say.

"I'm firing up the drive now, Boss," he says.

I grab the console. The ship stutters. The stutter feels odd, bigger than usual. Usually it feels like we've all tripped over a rug simultaneously, but this time—this time it feels like we nearly fell.

I hope to God I'm imagining this.

"Anyone have visuals?" I ask.

"I just have coordinates," Denby says. "We're in foldspace."

I don't ask him if it feels like we've been in foldspace too long, because it certainly does to me. Elaine looks at me from across the engineering section. I can't see her face well from this distance, but her posture looks fearful.

Then the ship stutters again, and this time it feels normal. Or maybe it just feels that way because I want it to.

"The coordinates say we're at Lost Souls," Denby says.

Unknown vessel, the words—in Standard—blare through the engineering section. *This is the Lost Souls Research Corporation. You are violating our space. Identify yourself.*

I hit the comm on the console but nothing happens. "Elaine, can you let them know it's us?"

"I can't get this part of the console working," she says from her location.

Unknown vessel. This is the Lost Souls Research Corporation. You are violating our space. If you do not identify yourself, we will be forced to destroy you.

What the hell? I haven't authorized that message. I never want to tell anyone they'd be destroyed.

Are we in the future, then? Lost Souls exists. We're in the right part of space. I can't get the console to work, and then I realize just how panicked I am.

I use the comm in my suit.

"Lost Souls, this is Boss. We've brought a Dignity Vessel from the Boneyard. Sorry you didn't get warning." *We didn't either,* I think but don't add. "The *Two* is on the way. Don't shoot at us."

"Boss?" the voice belongs to Ilona Blake. "Really? It's you?"

"Yes, Ilona," I say. "What the hell is going on? How long have we been gone?"

"Two weeks," she says.

"Oh thank god," Elaine says behind me. Apparently she was as terrified as I was about getting trapped in foldspace or ending up in a weird future.

"Then why the hell are you trying to shoot us out of space?" I ask.

"Long story," Ilona says. "We're newly tough."

She sounds proud of that, whatever it means.

"You're only bringing one ship back?" she asks. "We were hoping for more."

As if I didn't know that. "Only one, Ilona. We'll end up with more."

I hope. If the Boneyard lets us.

If we can get back in.

So many ifs.

"We'll need help docking this thing. We're essentially flying it blind."

"We'll send a skip," Ilona says.

"Make sure the team is suited up," I say. "Not everything works on this vessel."

"Copy that," she says. "And welcome home."

Welcome home indeed. I grip the console in front of me. I've never been so relieved to be back at Lost Souls in my life.

I usually like the risks, but this one was a bit too dicey for me. Or maybe I'm too aware of what can go wrong.

"Is Coop back?" I ask.

"He got here just ahead of you," Ilona says. "He'll be coming over to your ship."

Coop, diving after all. I haven't been able to stop him, even though I wanted to.

Then I grin. I can't wait to see him.

I am so happy to be home.

THE AFTERMATH
NOW

55

THE *EWING TREKOV* ARRIVED WELL INSIDE the new border that Captain Cooper had mandated for the Empire and the Nine Planets. Elissa couldn't help herself. She let out a sigh of relief, and hoped it wasn't audible.

Several of the bridge crew—on one of the best ships in the Empire, a post that took a lot of discipline—bowed their heads for just a moment. She didn't know if they were reacting to the retreat, or to the loss.

She had a hunch it was both. These people were trained to fight.

"Four other ships have joined us," Sherwin said softly.

Four.

She had gone in twenty-four strong and had emerged with five ships. Against a space station, two Dignity Vessels, and a bunch of things that didn't even deserve the name "ship."

Her right fist was still clenched. She unclenched it, finger by finger.

"What's happened to the rest of the armada?" she asked, as if she didn't know.

"We don't have information from them directly, ma'am. But they're clearly without power. They're drifting."

If these five ships got back soon—if others joined them—the loss of life might not be total.

"Contact Flag Commander Janik and ask for rescue ships. We need people on site as fast as we can." She stood. She knew how to do this. "Most of the crews on those ships are alive at the moment. They have a maximum of two hours. We have to mount the largest rescue operation we possibly can."

Sherwin nodded. "Do you want to triage, ma'am?"

In other words, did she want to decide who to save and who to let die? Of course not. But she had no choice. She was still in charge of this goddamn mission.

"Yes, I'll triage," she said. She knew what had happened to her fleet four years ago. The ships farther away from the explosion would have more survivors. "Let me see where the charge hit."

"There were two, Ma'am," one of the officers said.

Two. She'd been hit with one. Now she was less certain that anyone would survive. But she had to act like everyone would.

"All right," she said. "As we head back, I want to see how that energy signature waved outward. We start with the ships that got hit with the smallest amount of energy and move inward."

That command was met with silence. She looked up. The crew watched her, expressions grim. Then Sherwin nodded.

"I wish Flag Commander Janik had listened to you, ma'am," he said, then turned and began issuing orders.

He wasn't the only one. Elissa was certain that an entire armada of ships wished Janik had listened to her.

But he hadn't.

And now she had to clean up the mess.

56

Coop cradled Boss in his arms on the large couch inside his quarters on the *Ivoire*. He wasn't quite willing to call an end to his mission yet. He and the *Shadow* would take turns patrolling the area around Lost Souls for the next week or more, as the Lost Souls defensive system powered up.

Five imperial ships had escaped his attack at the border. One of those ships was the flag ship, commanded by Group Commander Elissa Trekov. He suspected she would find herself in power after this—after all, she had been right and her boss hadn't. Even if she didn't rise any farther in the ranks, she would be the person everyone went to for information on this Captain Jonathon Cooper, even though she knew little about him.

That was just the way such structured military societies worked.

Not that Coop cared at the moment. At the moment, he enjoyed the feel of Boss against him. She was as tired as he was, but she wanted to find out what had happened on the border, just like he wanted to find out what had happened at the Boneyard.

The ship she had brought back was in fantastic condition. It just needed help getting its systems up. He suspected—from the short look he'd taken when he'd come on board—that it would take very little work to make that ship as functional as the *Ivoire*.

He was going to have to train new crews. He had already spoken with Lynda Rooney about setting up some kind of academy, like the one the Fleet used to run on the *Brazza*. It would take years to build up the right kind of crew, but he knew they would need every second of those years.

Just like they would need another group—an older group—who could man the ships in the interim.

He and Boss had just finished dinner. He had told her what happened on the border, and here at Lost Souls. She was stunned, not at the attack, but at his belief about the outcome: He suspected the Empire would leave them alone for a while.

"Large governments like that," he said, "generally go after easier prey if they want to expand their borders. We just made the Nine Planets tough to conquer. The Empire will look at its other borders before it looks at us."

"While it develops weapons to defeat us," Boss said.

"It'll be hard for them to do so," Coop said, "particularly as we get more ships from the Boneyard."

The look on her face at that moment discouraged him. She believed it hard to get ships out of the Boneyard. She was probably right.

But he didn't care. What pleased him the most was the fact that the Boneyard had an active defense system. Such systems didn't last throughout five millennia. Bits and pieces lasted, but not an organized system that kicked out unfamiliar *anacapa* drives and tried to destroy ships stolen from inside the Boneyard itself.

In fact, that news filled him with great joy. Someone—something— ran the Boneyard. And, he suspected, that someone, that some*thing*, was the Fleet.

He didn't tell Boss this right now. Right now, she needed rest. He did too. And she hadn't taken too kindly to his joke as he boarded the new ship.

This is your idea of a rescue flotilla? he asked.

He'd thought it was witty. She thought it insensitive.

Maybe it was. He still wished she had brought back a dozen ships and those ships could patrol the new border. But that wouldn't happen, not for a while.

"You're not going to dive the Boneyard with me," Boss said, as if she could hear his mind turning.

He smiled, his chin resting on top of her head. She had anticipated the next phase of this conversation.

"I don't want to explore ships," he said. "I want to find out what the station in the center is, and what it can tell us."

"We're not going back until we know what all the energy patterns are, Coop," Boss said.

"I think—"

"I know what you think," she said. "You can argue with me, you can try to manipulate me to your opinion. But I run the dives, remember? And right now, the Boneyard is too much of an unknown."

"I agree," he said.

She sat up and looked at him. She had deep circles under her eyes. "You do?"

"I do," he said. "We need to figure some things out, and make careful plans. We're not in a hurry right now."

"We're not?" she asked.

He shrugged. "You watch. We won't need to worry about the Empire for a long time."

She smiled, but he could sense her disbelief. "I hope you're right."

"I know I'm right," he said. "You'll see."

She laid her head back down and snuggled up against him. "If you had asked me how this was going to go two weeks ago, I wouldn't have come up with where we are now."

That had been his entire life for the past five years. But he didn't remind her of that. He didn't want to talk about the strange and almost unfamiliar feeling of hope her experience at the Boneyard had given him.

Even if the Fleet didn't run the Boneyard, somewhere in those ships was the answer of what had happened to the Fleet. Maybe enough of an answer that he could find them.

He pulled her close, and marveled at himself. He was making plans for two different futures: one in which he rejoined the Fleet and one in which he recreated it.

He wasn't sure which future was his. At the moment, they both were. And he liked that.

He rested his cheek against her hair and closed his eyes, realizing that for the first time in five years, he felt he had a future. One of his own making. One he could believe in.

One in which he belonged.

ABOUT THE AUTHOR

INTERNATIONAL BESTSELLING WRITER Kristine Kathryn Rusch has won two Hugo awards, a World Fantasy Award, and six *Asimov's* Readers Choice Awards. For more information about her work, please go to kristinekathrynrusch.com. For more information about the Diving universe, to which this story belongs, go to divingintothewreck.com.

Also by
Kristine Kathryn Rusch

Alien Influences
The End of The World (novella)
The Retrieval Artist Series

The Diving Universe:

NOVELLAS

Diving into the Wreck
The Room of Lost Souls
Becalmed
Becoming One with the Ghosts
Stealth
Strangers at the Room of Lost Souls
The Spires of Denon

NOVELS

Diving into the Wreck
City of Ruins
Boneyards
The Diving Omnibus, Volume One
Skirmishes (September 2013)

18969225R00187

Made in the USA
Charleston, SC
30 April 2013